THEN
SHE'S
GONE

BOOKS BY WILLOW ROSE

DETECTIVE BILLIE ANN WILDE SERIES

Don't Let Her Go

THEN SHE'S GONE

WILLOW ROSE

bookouture

Published by Bookouture in 2024

An imprint of Storyfire Ltd.
Carmelite House
50 Victoria Embankment
London EC4Y 0DZ

www.bookouture.com

ISBN: 978-1-83525-264-2
eBook ISBN: 978-1-83525-263-5

ONE

November

Cocoa Beach, Florida

Jonathan, an eight-year-old boy with a mop of curly brown hair, stepped onto the beach and felt the sand between his toes for the first time. He looked around with wonder, taking in the sun glinting off of the waves, the sand stretching endlessly across the distant shoreline. He felt a smile tugging at the corners of his mouth, and before he knew it, he was squealing with delight.

His mom had been right, he thought to himself. This was it, he was finally here. This was what he had been waiting for. He felt himself slowly relax as he let the ocean breeze wash over him.

Jonathan's wonder was only heightened when he saw the seagulls soaring and diving around him, the salty smell of the ocean in the air, and the sound of the waves crashing against the shore. He had never seen so much beauty in one place, and he wanted to make sure he never forgot it.

He closed his eyes and inhaled deeply, the sun's warmth on

his face, and a feeling of peace washing over him. Jonathan had barely slept all night in anticipation. When they had arrived at the hotel in Cocoa Beach, the night before, it had been dark. He had been able to hear the ocean, the waves crashing the shore, but not see it till now. And what a sight it was. His momma hadn't been lying to him. It was spectacular.

Jonathan stood at the edge of the beach, staring in awe at the endless expanse of bright blue water before him. The sun shone down from a cloudless sky, and the wind gently blew his hair back from his face. He shifted his gaze to the white sand beneath his feet, feeling the grittiness between his toes as he took a few tentative steps forward.

As though pulled by an invisible string, Jonathan started running toward the shoreline, faster and faster until he was nothing more than a blur.

"Jonathan!" His mom shouted after him as he got closer to the ocean, the hypnotic call of the sea too strong to resist.

He laughed and grinned back at her, feeling an inexplicable sense of freedom as his tiny feet left tracks in the sand. His mother shouted after him to be careful of the rip currents, to stay close to the shore, but he ignored her, lost in a world of his own creation. He reached out and tried to scoop up a handful of the blue water, allowing its coolness to calm him as he splashed it in his face, laughing. Then he dove in. Headfirst he let it cover his small, chubby body, pretending to be a dolphin or even a mermaid. He played in the water for a long time, before he finally noticed it.

What is that?

A few feet away, Jonathan spotted something—a suitcase tucked away near the dunes of the beach. He felt like it was calling for him, and he cautiously approached it, apprehension rising within him as he considered what could possibly be inside. Could it be a hidden pirate treasure? Could it be gold coins enough for him to bathe in like he had seen in cartoons?

Maybe it was enough money for him to be able to buy his momma a brand-new house by the ocean? The temptation was too strong. He had to know.

The latch seemed locked in place, and fear suddenly paralyzed Jonathan as he tried to reach out for it. What if it was something dangerous? What if he got in trouble for opening it? Finally gathering all of his courage, he flipped open the latch with trembling hands.

What Jonathan saw made him scream in terror; instead of finding some hidden treasure within the suitcase, he found himself faced with something far darker. Before he had time to process what had happened, his mother's voice was calling his name, and her footsteps were already racing toward him.

But it felt like they were too late.

TWO

Melbourne Airport, Florida

Lisa Baxter, a savvy businesswoman with a sharp eye for detail and a penchant for order, dreaded the prospect of air travel. The mere mention of it sent shudders down her spine. She hated the airport. The long lines, the lack of privacy, the constant hustle and bustle of people of all walks of life merging and mingling—it was overwhelming. She hated being wedged in a tiny seat between strangers who felt entitled to take up more room than their own, and she couldn't stand the unfamiliar, unpredictable movements of the airplane as it bumped through the sky.

But most of all, she dreaded the people. They always seemed far too loud, far too intrusive, and far too eager to strike up a conversation. Even when Lisa was content to sit in silence, they seemed to sense her unease and take it as an invitation to talk. She wished more than anything that she could just disappear into her own mind and forget about the rest of the world.

The airport was an overwhelming mixture of noise, bright lights, and distracted travelers. Lisa made her way through the bustling crowd, searching for an out-of-the-way spot to sit down and collect her thoughts. Everywhere she looked there were blinking screens, loudspeakers making announcements, and people hauling suitcases behind them. The air was filled with the scent of disinfectant as the hum of fluorescent lighting buzzed overhead. Despite the soothing familiarity of it all, Lisa couldn't shake the fear that flew in with her ticket—a fear of what had happened in the sky before and what might happen again, when she had been on a plane to Denver and they'd had to do an emergency landing. She hadn't flown since then. She didn't trust in the airlines or the airplanes or even the pilots.

As she stood in line for check-in, her gaze landed on something strange—a duffel bag lying forgotten near her feet. It seemed oddly out of place where it was, and Lisa felt her heart begin to pound as she studied it warily. Who owned it? Why was no one standing near it?

She stared at it for a long time, while waiting in the line.

Nobody stepped forward to claim the duffel bag, and Lisa tiptoed nervously toward it. She bent over cautiously, half expecting something hazardous to jump out at her.

"Excuse me, officer," Lisa called out. "There's some abandoned luggage over there. I'm not sure who it belongs to."

The security officer approached her, one hand already resting on the gun at his hip. She showed him the bag. He gave the duffel bag a wary once-over, assessing it for any signs of danger.

And then his face dropped as he spotted something. A dark red mark on the zip on one side. It looked wet. Drenched in something. He looked up and locked eyes with her as they both realized what it was. Blood.

THREE

BILLIE ANN

"I want the house."

I couldn't believe what I was hearing as I looked up at Joe. "Excuse me?"

He nodded, his lips tight. "You heard me."

I narrowed my eyes. Did I just hear him right? "What do you mean you want the house? Where will I live with the kids?"

Joe and I were having another heated argument, the likes of which we had been having almost every day since we had started to discuss the logistics of our divorce. He had agreed to move out and had gotten a condo downtown, not far from our family home. Meanwhile I had been staying with the children in the house. We were sitting in the living room, me on the worn leather sofa we'd chosen together when we moved in, and he in the armchair that had originally been his father's, but had quickly become his own favorite. The room was bathed in a soft light, and the air was thick with a tense silence.

I was the first to break it.

"What do you mean you want the house?" I repeated, incredulously, barely recognizing my own voice.

Joe didn't flinch. "I want the house," he replied, his voice resolute. "What's so hard to understand about that?"

He leaned forward, resting his elbows on his knees. "I love this house. It was my dream home when we bought it. I've always wanted a canal front house, and you know it. I want to get a boat and have it back there. I want to go fishing from time to time."

My heart raced. This was not the Joe I knew. There was something different in his voice, something determined. His eyes were locked on mine, searching and pleading. I felt a sickening wave of panic wash over me and the room began to spin. I know I was the one who ended our marriage, but did that mean he got the house in the divorce?

"Joe, I—"

He cut me off. "I don't want to fight anymore. I just want the house." His voice was soft but unrelenting.

I felt my throat close up with emotion. I was also sick of the fighting. This was one thing we could agree on. We had both changed in the last year and the house was no longer ours. It was our past, a reminder of what had been and could never be again. I looked away, unable to bear the intensity of his gaze any longer. I was exhausted, sleep-deprived after having searched for a woman, Joanne Edwards, who disappeared two weeks ago. I hadn't been able to sleep as thoughts of what might have happened to her kept lingering in my mind. I really didn't need this right now.

Silence hung heavy in the air once again. I took a deep breath, gathering my courage, and met his eyes once more.

"I'm not giving you the house."

I looked down at the papers in front of me unable to understand how we had come to this. For some reason we both believed we could do it without any lawyers, but now I was having my doubts.

"But I want it."

"I don't even understand. Where is this coming from? You haven't said anything about the house before?" I asked.

"Just because I haven't talked about it doesn't mean it hasn't been on my mind. I've been thinking about it for a while, actually," Joe replied. "The kids and I need this stability. You can find another place to live, maybe even a better one. And it would work better for you during cases. But I want to raise them in this house."

My heart felt like it was being squeezed. This was not what I had expected. I never imagined he'd want to stay here; I thought I'd end up living with the kids full-time. My work was busy, and yes there were times when I had to put it first, but I was perfectly capable of looking after the kids and giving them the security they needed. They weren't little anymore, after all.

"Joe, I don't think—"

"Think about it," he interrupted. "You'll get a good settlement, I promise. The kids will be taken care of, everything will be okay."

I looked at him, feeling a mix of anger and hurt. "You can't just demand the house like that. We've both put in equal amounts of work and money into it."

"But I'm the one who loves it."

I shook my head. Was this coming from a place of anger? Dealing with the news that I was gay had been hard for Joe, and I understood that, but I had hoped he'd be able to hold on to our friendship. Perhaps I'd been naïve.

Joe's eyes narrowed, "I don't think you understand. I'm not asking for your permission. I'm telling you that I want the house. And I'll be damned if I let you stand in my way."

The words hung in the air like a threat.

I shook my head. "No, Joe. I can't agree to that."

He sat back in his chair and folded his arms across his chest. Then he got up. "Fine. Be like that. But I'm not giving up."

As I watched him walk out of the door, I felt a sense of

unease wash over me. Joe had always been stubborn, but I never thought he would be so unreasonable. We had agreed that the children should be with me for the biggest part of the time, and to try not to uproot them and make sure their lives didn't change drastically. And now this? This was a whole new side of him I didn't recognize. I knew he was having a hard time, but that didn't mean he got to walk all over me. I felt guilty, yes, but I still had just as much right to the house as he did.

I gathered my papers and headed toward the kitchen. I needed a cup of coffee to calm my nerves. As I waited for the coffeemaker to spit it out, I looked around the kitchen. This was the house that Joe wanted so desperately. The house that we had built together. It wasn't just a bunch of bricks and mortar to me. It was our home. A place where we had created memories and built a life together. With our three children.

I knew I couldn't just give that up.

When I heard the doorbell ring, I put down my coffee and went to answer it.

My new boss, the new Chief of police, was standing awkwardly on the other side of the door. She had taken over the Cocoa Beach police station just a month earlier. Her name was Becky Harold, and she was a former Marine and Air Force pilot before she started her career in the police. I had heard rumors that she didn't take any nonsense from anyone. She was a tall woman with short cropped black hair and piercing blue eyes.

"Detective Wilde, can I come in?" she asked.

I nodded and stepped back. I felt nervous for some reason. I had never had a Chief come to my house before. I had only met with her a few times since she got here, but I couldn't help but feel slightly intimidated by her. I could tell that she wasn't someone to mess with. She had an air of authority about her; from her perfectly shined boots to the fitness watch on her wrist, she seemed in control.

I wondered if there was a problem. We had been working

on a missing person case for a few weeks, but so far we didn't have any significant leads. A woman, Joanne Edwards, had been reported missing after a night out with her coworkers, and I'd spent most of yesterday evening combing through the interviews we'd already collected. Nothing new stood out. Did the Chief have news? Or was she frustrated with me?

"O-of course, Chief Harold. What brings you here?"

"I wanted to check in and see how you're doing. I just heard about the divorce from Tom and I wanted to offer any support you might need," she said, her voice softening slightly.

I stared at her, unsure of how to react. I mean I appreciated the gesture, but I didn't know if I wanted to share my personal life with my new boss just yet. "Thank you, Chief. I'm doing okay."

"Are you sure?" she pressed. "I know divorce can be tough. And I've been there, believe me."

I looked at her in surprise. I had no idea she had been through a divorce herself. "I didn't know that, Chief."

She shrugged. "It's not something I usually talk about. But I wanted you to know that you're not alone. If you ever need someone to talk to, I'm here."

I smiled faintly, and she placed a hand on my shoulder. I wasn't used to this kind of approach from my boss. This was definitely a first. "Thank you, Chief. That means a lot."

She nodded and removed her hand. "Now, I'm not just here for a social visit. I need you to come with me. I know it's Saturday and you're on your day off. But this is important."

I nodded with an exhale. I had a feeling that there would be more. I could tell by the look in her eyes. Something had happened. Something that required my attention. Chiefs didn't come to your house because of your personal life. They didn't show up due to a petty theft or domestic issue. This had to be something bad.

The Chief gave me a stern look. "We got a body. On the beach."

I looked at my watch. It was eleven o'clock, and the kids would be fine without me for a few hours. I could get my mom to come over if needed. Being nine, fourteen, and sixteen, they were old enough to be alone on a Saturday afternoon.

"All right. Let me get properly dressed, and I will be right there."

FOUR

Then

TRANSCRIPT OF INTERVIEW OF JOSEPHINE DURST

DEFENDANT'S EXHIBIT A

DURST PART I

APPEARANCES:
Detective Michael Smith
Detective Lenny Travis
Sergeant Joseph Mill

DET. SMITH: Could you please state your name for the record?
JOSEPHINE: Uh it's Josephine.
DET. SMITH: And what is your last name? Just for the record, please.
JOSEPHINE: (*clears throat*) It's uh Durst.
DET. SMITH: And how old are you, Josephine?
JOSEPHINE: I'm thirteen.

DET. SMITH: Okay, Josephine. Do you know why you're here today?

JOSEPHINE: (*long pause, then nods her head*)

DET. SMITH: That's good. Can you tell me why?

JOSEPHINE: Because of what happened to George.

DET. SMITH: And who is George?

JOSEPHINE: (*shakes her head*)

DET. SMITH: It's okay, Josephine, you can talk to me about what happened. I'm your friend.

JOSEPHINE: (*sniffles*) George is my stepdad.

DET. SMITH: Yes, that's true. And what happened to him?

JOSEPHINE: (*starts to cry*) He... uh... he...

DET. SMITH: It's okay, Josephine. I know it is hard to talk about. And you're just a kid. We understand that. But we are here to try and figure out what happened last night. In your home. Can you tell us a little about it?

JOSEPHINE: (*shakes head*)

DET. SMITH: I understand it is hard. Can we get you anything? A soda maybe?

JOSEPHINE: (*sniffles and nods*)

(*Detective Travis gets up and leaves the room. Comes back with a Pepsi that he hands to Josephine. He helps her open the can and she drinks.*)

DET. SMITH: That looks like it hit the spot, huh?

JOSEPHINE: (*nods and smiles vaguely*) Mm-hmm.

DET. SMITH: Now let's get back to my question, if you're ready. Do you think you are ready?

JOSEPHINE: (*shakes head*)

DET. SMITH: Well, that makes me sad, because—you see—I have to do my job here and that is to figure out what happened to your stepdad last night. And for that I need your help. Can you help me and tell me what happened to him? Please?

JOSEPHINE: (*puts down can on table and breathes rapidly*)

DET. SMITH: It's okay, Josephine. Take your time if you need to.

JOSEPHINE: (*cries and sniffles*) George... he... he was shot.

FIVE

BILLIE ANN

The beach was a hive of activity—a blur of blue flashing lights, the hum of voices, and an ever-growing crowd. Chief Harold moved through it with purpose, her uniform pressed and her cap low over her eyes. Chief Harold gracefully weaved her way through hordes of sunbathers, leading me to the police checkpoint. We paused briefly at the police blockage; she gave a few sharp orders to the officers there and then marched on. I followed in her wake, saying quick hellos to my colleagues as we passed by them before hurrying after her.

The air was humid and thick with the scent of coconut suntan lotion and salt, and the shoreline was adorned with colorful umbrellas and chairs. Most of them were empty as people gathered to see what was going on.

I made my way through the throng, the heat of the sand radiating through my sneakers with each step. In the summertime the sand could get so burning hot that unknowing tourists would end up having to receive treatment for burns underneath their feet, if they didn't wear shoes.

The Chief walked fast and determined on those long legs of hers. The sun was burning from above, and I regretted wearing a black shirt. I could feel the sweat trickle on my neck already. I wanted to call out to her, but she was too far ahead and I was too much in awe of her to make a sound.

Weaving through the crowds, she kept her eyes on the horizon, as if searching for something: a sign, a beacon. I followed two steps behind, wondering what we were looking for. But at the sight of the many people there, I knew it was something awful.

The Chief and I had barely spoken in the car on our way there, and it had become slightly awkward; she had told me only that she had received a call, that a boy had found a suitcase on the beach, and that it looked like a case for me. I had called my team, Big Tom and Scott, to come meet me there. They hadn't showed up yet, but I knew it wouldn't be long. They both lived close by.

"So, what are we looking at?" I asked an officer who approached us.

"It's right over here," he answered. "This kid is the one who found it."

I threw a glance around and saw a young boy with curly hair. He was crying, and his mother was loudly berating him, scolding him for what he'd done. The boy's mother turned to us. She was pretty out of it, and obviously scared.

"I can't believe this... what kind of a place is this... that my son can find something like this. Right here on the beach?"

She pointed toward the suitcase lying in the sand and explained that her son had found it on the beach, and that he had opened it. That's when she had called 911.

"Thank you," I said.

I approached the suitcase lying in the sand. It seemed out of place, with the beautiful blue ocean and white sand as its backdrop.

The suitcase was a hard case, and in a bright pink color that made it stand out. I could see that it had a lot of wear and tear;

the plastic part on the edges had been worn away and the aluminum had been dented and scratched. It was clearly well used. A sticker on the side read "Viva Mexico."

Heart in my throat, Chief Harold and I carefully approached the suitcase, both of us cautious. We bent over, then looked inside and gasped. There were body parts, mangled and bloody, inside of the suitcase, along with a thick pool of blood. It was disturbing and gruesome. The stench was also unbearable. I felt bile rising in my throat as I backed away quickly, turning away for a few seconds to compose myself.

We both stayed there in silence for a long moment, unable to process what we had seen or to utter words about it. Chief Harold finally spoke and called for backup on the radio. Moments later the beach teemed with forensic technicians and medical examiners, cameras flashing everywhere as everyone tried to make sense of the scene before us.

Dr. Phillips, the medical examiner, examined each body part thoroughly while my two detectives, Big Tom and Scott, arrived and started to question nearby witnesses in an effort to gather information. I couldn't believe anyone would do such a thing. Dismember a body and place it there, on the beach, where so many people could find it. It could only be deliberate.

But why?

Could it have been dumped in the ocean and then brought in by the waves? If so it would have algae and barnacles growing on it. Anyone who knew the waters around here knew that. I didn't see any of that on it. Plus it was located all the way up in the dunes. Not even during hurricanes did the water usually come up that far, and it definitely hadn't been rough surf last night. It looked more like it had been placed there. On purpose.

It was a gruesome discovery made even more chilling by its proximity to where families often come for vacation and relaxation—a reminder that evil can lurk anywhere regardless of how peaceful it may look on the surface.

I had taken my first step away from the suitcase to let the forensic techs get to work when something made me stop. I glanced back and noticed a tag on the handle, and without thinking twice, I leaned in closer. The letters were faded, but I could still make out the words written in black ink. A name and an address scrawled across the fabric in a neat cursive:

Danielle Simmons. 126 Deleon Road. Cocoa Beach, Florida.

For a moment, I couldn't move. My breath got caught in my throat, and my heart beat wildly against my chest. I had to read the words again and again, hoping that if I did, maybe they would change. But they didn't.

Suddenly, I could feel the hot tears streaming down my face and I doubled over, throwing up my morning coffee in the sand.

SIX

BILLIE ANN

I was struggling not to panic. My head was spinning, and my heart was pounding in my chest. Sweat beaded on my forehead as I attempted to remain calm and focused. I was fighting hard not to let my fear overwhelm me, but it seemed like the world was closing in on me and I was fighting just to breathe.

The air around me seemed to be growing thicker and heavier with every moment, pressing against my lungs like a hot, heavy blanket. My vision began to go blurry, vibrant colors swimming in front of my eyes like a brightly hued oil painting. I could feel my pulse racing faster with every breath, and I took long, deep breaths in an attempt to calm myself.

I focused on the sound of my own breathing, counting each inhale and exhale until the air around me started to feel a little less oppressive.

Danielle Simmons. Danni.

Chief Harold came over . "Are you okay?" she asked, her gaze as direct as an arrow. She looked concerned.

I looked up at her and opened my mouth, but no words came out. I was overwhelmed with emotions, and I felt certain that if I spoke, it would all come pouring out. I stared at her, still focusing on controlling my breath. Then I realized I couldn't tell her I had a connection to the suitcase... the victim. I couldn't be honest with her, since she would immediately take me off the case. Chief Harold took me aside.

"Yes, yes. I'm okay. Just a little feeble when it comes to scenes like this. It will pass."

She chuckled. "Between you and me then I threw up too first time I saw body parts like these. It's normal to have a reaction."

She tapped me on the shoulder, and I forced a smile.

"Just give me a minute," I said. "I'll be okay."

Her eyes grew concerned. "You don't look okay to me. You're all pale and sweaty."

She said the last part with a smile, trying to lighten the situation. But it didn't. Right now, I could barely think straight.

"You're the lead investigator on this case," she added more firmly. "I can't have you sick. I need to know that I can count on you."

"Of course," I said and stood up straight, realizing I couldn't let my own feelings get in the way of the investigation. I couldn't let her down. "Listen, the address on the suitcase. I'm gonna go check it out. It's right down the street from here."

The Chief nodded. "Sounds like a good initiative. Keep me updated with what you find and let me know if you need me to send Tom or Scott with you."

"They're of better use here," I said. "Talking to witnesses. I can take this one alone."

"As you wish."

Then I left the scene.

I walked all the way across the sand toward the parking lot, then continued down the main street, Minuteman Causeway. I didn't stop at my own street, but continued forward, my heart throbbing in my throat. I picked up my phone and called a number but there was no answer. I cursed and called it again, till I reached Deleon Road, and walked down to number 126.

Please let it not be true. Please let it not be her.

I walked up the driveway and found the doorbell. Danni's husband, Mike, opened the door.

"Billie Ann? It's been a minute. Where have you been? Busy with work I take it?"

I could barely speak. "Is-Is Danni okay?"

He smiled. "Yes, of course. Why wouldn't she be? She's sitting on the back porch, reading as usual."

I breathed in relief. "Are you sure?"

That made Mike laugh. "I should be, I was just with her before you rang the doorbell."

"Who is it?" a voice said, coming up behind him. The sound of it was soothing to me, and I smiled. "Who are you talking to?"

"Ah there she is," Mike said and stepped aside so Danni could come to the door. "I'll leave you two to catch up. Don't be a stranger for this long again," he said and left.

Danni came closer. Her big green eyes stared at me, her long brown hair was pulled back in a ponytail, and she was wearing yoga pants and a tank top. She was the most endearing sight I had seen in a long time. My best friend. And the greatest love of my life. The very reason I had realized I was gay.

"Billie Ann?" she said. "You look like you've seen a ghost."

"For a minute there, I thought I had seen something awful," I said. "I mean I did see something terrible... but it wasn't... I mean... Can I come in? Do you have minute?"

She smiled and laughed lightly. "Of course. Let me get us some wine. You look like you need it."

SEVEN

RANDY

Randy Edwards was sitting on his porch, a cold beer in hand, watching the cars drive by. His street was usually quiet for a Saturday in the midday heat, the sound of cicadas and the occasional car passing the only signs of life. Most people went to the beach on a day like today, or on a boat on the Intracoastal, or stayed indoors in the AC, escaping the scorching heat.

But this day was different. He could hear a distant commotion, and as it drew closer, he was alarmed to see his neighbor, Arlene, running up the street toward him, her bangs falling into her face, soaked from the heat. She was waving her hands wildly, and the closer she got the more he could make out what she was saying.

"Randy! Randy! Have you heard?!"

Randy stood up, setting his beer aside and walking toward her. She was panting heavily, her face flushed from exertion and excitement.

"Heard what? What's going on?" he asked and approached her.

Arlene was panting agitated. "I just heard... My neighbor came over and told me that—"

"That what? Dang it. Say it."

"They found human remains."

Randy stopped breathing. He couldn't speak. Arlene noticed, and paused. She was trying to catch her breath from running in the dense heat.

"Where?" he finally asked. "Where did they find them?"

"On the beach," she said, speaking fast, her voice pitchy. "Some kid found them. In a suitcase or a bag or something. That's all I know."

Randy's heart dropped into his stomach, and he sprang down the stairs, grabbing his bike, and hurrying down to the beach.

When he arrived, he saw that the police had already cordoned off the area where the remains had been found. In a daze, Randy walked up and down the beach, searching for a way to get closer, but the crowd was big and still growing. He was desperate to discover what the remains held.

Finally, he found an area that was less guarded. He quickly slipped through the crowd and started walking toward the crime scene, walking with his feet in the water. The farther he walked, the more he felt a strange sense of calm come over him.

Randy watched the detectives as they carefully combed the area, feeling a chill of dread run through his body with each step. He couldn't help but think of Joanne, fiddling with his wedding ring as he did.

The sun was burning from above, and not a wind moving, enveloping everything in an eerie stillness. There was no sound except for the gentle lapping of the waves against the shore.

Randy got as close as he could, then stood on the edge of the beach for hours, watching; his eyes trained on the scene ahead of him. Beachgoers were slowly leaving, and the sun setting behind the beach houses, while police continued their work into the late hours. Randy stared at them, at the scene. He felt powerless, as if he were watching from a dream. He knew that he was too far away to discover the truth of the human remains, but he stayed there anyway, ignoring the sunburn he had gotten earlier, from being out too long with no sunscreen.

As the night wore on, Randy grew tired, but he refused to leave. His mind was racing with thoughts of Joanne and where she could be. He remembered the last time he saw her. They had had an argument and she stormed out of the house, slamming the door behind her. Randy had thought nothing of it at the time; they had argued before. She was going out with friends, she said. Alexis, Jolene, and Jessica. They were coworkers from the law firm, and he didn't want her to go out with them. He didn't care much for any of those women and he wanted her to spend time with him instead. That was their argument. So naturally he had assumed she just went with them to spite him. But Joanne didn't come back that night, and that was unlike her.

As he watched the scene now as the only spectator, one of the detectives approached him.

"Sir, I'm sorry, but you need to leave. This is an active crime scene."

Randy nodded silently and turned to go. As he walked away, he couldn't help but feel a sense of emptiness wash over him.

The night was dark and quiet as he made his way back to his house. The moon cast a pale light over the streets as he rode his bike, lost in thought. His mind kept replaying the scene on the beach.

When he got home, he sat on his porch, staring out into the darkness. The world around him was silent, except for the cicadas and treefrogs. He thought about Joanne, about the life they had together, and the future they had planned. It all seemed so far away now, like a dream he could barely remember.

The night dragged on, and Randy couldn't find any peace. He paced back and forth in his living room, unable to sit still. His mind kept returning to the beach, to the detectives and the remains they had found. He felt a strange sense of foreboding, as if something terrible was coming.

EIGHT

Then

TRANSCRIPT OF INTERVIEW OF JOSEPHINE DURST
DEFENDANT'S EXHIBIT A
DURST PART I

APPEARANCES:
Detective Michael Smith
Detective Lenny Travis
Sergeant Joseph Mill

DET. SMITH: Thank you for telling us that, Josephine.
JOSEPHINE: You're welcome.
DET. SMITH: Now I am going to need to ask you some more
questions about what happened. Is that okay with you?
JOSEPHINE: (*whimpers slightly*) Sure.
DET. SMITH: Okay. Now let me know anytime you need a
break. If you need anything to eat or drink, you let me know. Or
if you just need to breathe a little. We are in no hurry.
JOSEPHINE: Okay.

DET. SMITH: Okay, so we know that your stepfather was shot last night. And you also know that he died, correct?

JOSEPHINE: (*nods her head*)

DET. SMITH: All right. Now I want you to tell me a little bit about your stepfather. When did you first meet him?

JOSEPHINE: When I was eight years old.

DET. SMITH: How did you meet?

JOSEPHINE: He came to my house. To pick up my mom.

DET. SMITH: And why was that?

JOSEPHINE: They were going out.

DET. SMITH: On a date?

JOSEPHINE: Yes.

DET. SMITH: And who was taking care of you and your brother?

JOSEPHINE: We had a babysitter.

DET. SMITH: Did George say hello to you?

JOSEPHINE: Yes. He came inside and my mom went "this is George" and he shook first my hand then Bobby's.

DET. SMITH: And Bobby is your younger brother, Robert, am I correct? How old is he now?

JOSEPHINE: He is ten years old.

DET. SMITH: So, he was five when he met George, am I correct?

JOSEPHINE: Yes.

DET. SMITH: Did you like him when you first met? Did you like George?

JOSEPHINE: Not really.

DET. SMITH: And why is that?

JOSEPHINE: (*pauses and sighs*) He was weird.

DET. SMITH: How was he weird?

JOSEPHINE: I don't know.

DET. SMITH: Did he look funny?

JOSEPHINE: Yeah, he had a strange beard, and his eyes were all weird, the way he looked at us.

DET. SMITH: How did that make you feel?

JOSEPHINE: Awkward. I wanted him to leave. I didn't want him to be with my mom.

DET. SMITH: Were you maybe jealous?

JOSEPHINE: (*shrugs*) maybe.

DET. SMITH: That's okay. I got jealous when my dad got a new girlfriend too.

JOSEPHINE: Okay.

DET. SMITH: So, tell me how often did George come to your house to pick your mom up?

JOSEPHINE: They dated for some months and then suddenly he was there one morning for breakfast. After that he never left. And then they got married, last year.

DET. SMITH: How did you react to that?

JOSEPHINE: It was annoying.

DET. SMITH: What did your brother say to it?

JOSEPHINE: He liked George. He liked having him around.

DET. SMITH: But you didn't?

JOSEPHINE: No.

DET. SMITH: Was that why you shot him?

NINE

BILLIE ANN

We stepped out onto the porch as the sun was still giving off its last bit of orange and yellow light. I welcomed the cool evening breeze after the heat of the day. Danni settled into the porch swing, and I sat beside her. I stared at her, as if I was wondering if it was really her, or a dream. For one moment I had thought I had lost her. I tried to relax. The sky darkened, transforming into a deep navy canvas dotted with stars.

The cicadas and frogs began to sing, and the evening settled into a comfortable silence. The air was thick with the scent of jasmine and the distant hum of city traffic. I could smell Danielle's perfume, and the very feeling it left me with calmed me down. She was still here. She was right here in front of me. I hadn't lost her.

"What's been going on with you? I feel like I haven't seen you in forever?" she asked, handing me a glass of bubbling prosecco. I smiled, taking a big sip, and looked into her deep-set eyes. She wasn't wearing any makeup, but she didn't need it. She was gorgeous even without it. My heart beat faster as I averted her gaze.

We sat in comfortable silence for a few moments, enjoying the evening air. Then Danni spoke again.

"So, are you going to tell me why you're here?" She smiled.

I took a deep breath, contemplating how much of my recent struggles I wanted to share with her. I didn't want her to know how deeply in love I was with her. I believed she knew; we had shared kisses on numerous occasions, after a little too much wine or prosecco. But it had never been more than that. We were both married and had children to think of. But fact was, we had never talked about us or why it kept happening when we had something to drink. I knew how I felt, but I had never asked her. I feared she didn't feel the same.

"I was at a crime scene nearby," I said.

She gave me a disapproving look. "Oh, so you're not here as my friend?"

I smiled. "Of course, I am."

"'Cause I feel like you have been avoiding me."

I swallowed hard and drank again. I couldn't tell her that it was too hard for me to be around her. It hurt to be with her and knowing I could never have her. I could still feel her warm kiss on my lips if I tried, and smell her perfume if I closed my eyes.

"I'm sorry," I said. "It's just... there's been a lot." It was true that things had been chaotic—the case I'd just come off had enveloped me in a way no other case had. I'd been forced to face parts of my past I thought were dead and buried. I still hadn't healed from it. "We just got a new Chief." I said. "But more importantly I need to ask you something."

She gave me a look of curiosity. "What's going on?"

"Do you have a bright pink suitcase?"

She stared at me, startled. "That's an odd question. Yes, I do. I have a green one too. I used to have a black one but that got destroyed on our trip to Spain. I don't know what airport handlers do with luggage, but it was—"

I placed a hand on her arm. "Could you bring me the bright pink suitcase? I would like to see it."

She hesitated, while a frown grew between her eyes. "You're acting a little strange here today. Are you sure you're okay?"

"Positive. Just indulge me, okay?"

She threw out her arms. "Okay, if that's what you want."

She left to get it, and I sat back with my prosecco, thinking about the poor person who had lost their life on the beach. I had feared the bones were Danni's, of course I did, so seeing her alive and well had been the biggest relief. But now as the feeling subsided, I was beginning to wonder what the heck this meant. If she was alive and well, why was her name tag on the suitcase?

"It's odd," Danni said, coming back outside, a confused look in her eyes. "I can't seem to find it. Well, I haven't used it in a long time, as it is very old, so maybe I put it in the garage? I was so sure it was with the others up in my closet. Let me go check."

She came back once again empty-handed, a puzzled look on her face. "I can't seem to find it."

I nodded and finished my glass. "Have you had anyone break in to your house recently?"

That made her laugh. "And steal my old suitcase? No that's ridiculous."

I chuckled. "I guess so. Well let me know if you find it, okay?" I walked toward the door, passing her, taking in her scent on the way, when she stopped me.

"Wait a second. Can't you tell me what you needed it for?"

I paused. "I can't right now, as it is part of an ongoing investigation, I'm afraid."

She exhaled. "So will I see you soon? Or will I have to wait months before you show up again?"

I swallowed, feeling all the emotions well up inside of me, unable to hide them the way I wanted to. I blushed and felt myself become awkward, my eyes avoiding hers.

"I missed you, you know?" she said, her words barely a whisper. "How about we have Thanksgiving together. Like we did last year?"

I nodded. I so badly wanted to do this with her, but how could I? I hated how I felt when I was around her. Hated and loved it at the same time. It was complicated. I wanted so badly to tell her everything that had been going on. That I was getting a divorce, that I had come out to my family. But this wasn't the time. Not yet.

"I missed you too. I will be in touch, okay?"

"Please do."

And with that I left, almost storming out of the house, my heart beating so fast, I felt like it was going to jump out of my chest.

TEN

BILLIE ANN

I stepped into the house, my steps echoing against the wooden floor. I was carrying my laptop under my arm, planning to continue work from home. I had evidence to look over, interview with eyewitnesses I needed to read through along with studying photographs and video taken from the scene. There was a lot to do.

I could feel Joe's presence in the kitchen before I even saw him. I walked in and there he was, laptop placed on the counter, looking up at me with an unreadable expression. He got up when he saw me.

We stood there in silence for a moment, both of us unsure of what to say. I noticed Joe's clothes were different, slightly dressier than he usually wore. He had changed since this morning, and he was now wearing a button-down shirt tucked into a pair of jeans. He seemed more put together than usual. I was surprised to see him there, since he had been living at a small condo he rented since I told him we needed to separate and he was just there this morning. It was a little too much if you asked me. He approached me when I entered.

"Where have you been?" he asked, his voice accusatory.

"Working," I said, taking off my belt carrying my badge and gun. I was in no mood for him right now.

"The kids told me you weren't home, that they were all alone, when I asked how they were doing. I was supposed to be on a date tonight, but had to cancel when I realized. So now you just leave the children all to themselves on a Saturday afternoon to go working?" he said the last part while making quotation signs in the air. I was tired of him, and to be honest, not in the mood to fight with him again.

"They're old enough. Besides I was close by, right down by the beach, so I could have come home any time they needed me."

"I don't like this," he said, throwing out his arms.

"What don't you like?"

"This whole setup. You just walking out the door. No one keeping an eye on our children, this, entire... the lifestyle choices... all of it."

"Excuse me? The... what?"

"Yes, there I said it. I don't like how you're exposing our children to your lifestyle choices."

I couldn't believe what I was hearing. Joe had always been conservative, but I never thought he would stoop to using that kind of language. I took a deep breath and tried to remain calm.

"My lifestyle choices? You mean being with women? That's who I am, Joe. I can't change that."

"I know, I know," he said, his voice softer now. "I just worry about how it's affecting our children. They're still young and impressionable. I don't want them to be confused or think that this is the norm."

I rolled my eyes. "Joe, they're not stupid. They know that not everyone is the same. And besides, I'm not hiding anything from them. They know and they haven't said anything negative about it."

He groaned. "But what if they start asking questions? What am I supposed to say?"

"You tell them the truth," I said firmly. "You tell them that their mother is gay and that there's nothing wrong with that. You tell them that love is love, no matter who it's between."

Joe's gaze slowly shifted to meet mine, and he squinted as if to better understand what I had said. His brow furrowed, and he let out a long sigh before dropping himself into a chair at the kitchen table.

"I just don't want them to be bullied or teased because of it," he said, rubbing his forehead.

"I understand that," I said, sitting down across from him. "But the best thing we can do for them is to be honest and open. If we treat my sexuality like it's something shameful or taboo, then they'll think it is too. But if we show them that it's just a part of who I am, and that it doesn't change how much I love them, then they'll be more likely to accept and understand it."

Joe sighed heavily. "I just don't think it's healthy. They need normalcy."

"You're kidding me, right?" I said. "This is normal. Besides I am not even dating anyone right now. It's not an issue."

"But it will be. And you will fill them with all that woke propaganda, and I hate it. I absolutely hate it."

I shook my head. This was so not what I needed right now.

"I'm not trying to indoctrinate them, Joe. I just want them to know that they can love whoever they want. They don't have to be afraid or feel ashamed of who they are."

Joe leaned back against the chair. "I just worry that their thinking will be poisoned, that's all. I'm not saying that people like you are bad, but I don't know, I just feel like your lifestyle choices will have a negative impact on our children."

"Joe," I said, trying to keep my voice steady. He was going down a road I didn't want to go down. I didn't want to start arguing with him about our lives. I just wasn't up for it. I had a victim to identify; a killer to find, and I still had a husband missing his wife. I needed to find Joanne.

He continued, "I worry about who they'll be hanging out with. They'll have access to all sorts of information and people we can't control. I don't know if I want to bring kids into a world like that."

I scoffed. "Our world? A world where people can love whoever they want? That sounds pretty great to me."

Joe shook his head. "It's not just about that. It's about safety and security. I don't want them to be exposed to things they're not ready for."

"Joe, they're going to be exposed to things no matter what. We can't control everything. But what we can control is how we react and how we teach them to react to these things. We can teach them to be kind and accepting, and to stand up for what's right. That's what's important."

Joe looked at me for a long moment, then sighed heavily.

"I just don't know if I can do this," he said, his voice barely audible.

"Do what?"

"Let them be around someone who's... different. I don't know if I can handle it."

I closed my eyes and took a deep breath. This was what I had been afraid of. I knew that Joe had never fully accepted my sexuality, but I had hoped that he would come around eventually. But now, it seemed like he was more closed-minded than ever.

"I'm not asking you to let them be around someone who's 'different,'" I said, my voice shaking a little. "I'm their mother. The person you once fell in love with."

Joe shook his head. "It's not that simple, and you know it. You're asking me to accept something that goes against everything I was taught."

"I'm not asking you to change your beliefs, Joe. I'm just asking you to love and accept me for who I am."

"I do love you," Joe said, his eyes filling with tears. "But I don't know how to deal with this. I don't know how to make it work."

"I don't either," I admitted, feeling a lump grow in my throat. "But we can figure it out together. We can go to counseling; we can talk to people who have gone through the same thing. Talk to someone who can help us navigate this. But we can't just ignore it or pretend like it's not there. That's not fair to anyone, especially our children."

He rose to his feet and grabbed his laptop in hand. "Well life isn't fair. It's about time you realize that. And everything isn't about you."

With that he walked to the front door and slammed it shut behind him. He didn't see the tears that rolled down my cheeks. Joe had been my companion and best friend for so many years. I couldn't bear the feeling of losing him. It was simply too much.

ELEVEN

VIVIANA

The sun was beginning to set, the orange light flattening and spreading across the surface of the lake like a sheet of gold. Viviana panted, while wiping sweat off her forehead with her hand and removing her wild black curls that kept falling into her face. She had been at home all day and needed to get out of the house. Viviana's mom always said she had ants in her pants, a restless energy, and that she needed to get it out of her. And running with her dog Manny was a good way for her to do just that. As the two of them moved around the lake, she looked down at him with worried eyes.

Manny had been diagnosed with a tumor in his stomach recently, and the vet had to remove it by surgery. He hadn't been able to run with Viviana for weeks now, and she had missed it. She had been so scared of losing him. Being an only child could be lonely from time to time, and he had become her best friend over the years. He would sleep in her bed and always wake up with her in the morning, and they'd go for a walk before breakfast. He would follow her around the house everywhere, even the bathroom where he would simply sit by her feet. Only when she was at the high school, did she have to leave him at home, and he would look at her with big begging eyes as she left in the morning with a kiss on his nose, asking for her to please take him with her. For ten years he had been her closest friend, and now she was so scared of losing him. The vet had said the cancer hadn't spread, but there was no telling for sure yet. She didn't know how she would ever continue on without him.

Don't ever leave me, she thought to herself as she wiped more sweat off her forehead with her hand. Manny was panting because of the heat, but seemed otherwise to be fine. It had been so long since he had shown this much energy and actually been running, Viviana was beginning to think that maybe—just maybe—he was going to make it.

All she could do was hope.

Manny began to slow down, and she stopped running to give him a break. There was no reason to overdo things and wear him out completely. She petted his back, and he lifted his leg against one of the palm trees surrounding the lake. When he was done, he looked up at her again, and she smiled. She loved the way he looked at her. Like he understood and heard her thoughts.

"Come on, Manny," she said and was about to take off again, when she spotted something in the grass. It was a yellow bag of some sort.

Startled, she and Manny both stopped in their tracks. Viviana couldn't help but be curious—she had never seen a sports bag out here before. Had someone forgotten it? Maybe it had been stolen from somewhere and its owner really needed it back? After a moment of hesitation, she made her way over to the bag, calling Manny to follow.

As she got closer, Viviana noticed something even stranger. The sports bag had a strange yellowish-brown stain on it. It looked dirty and slightly disgusting. She approached it slowly, as if it were a wild animal that might turn and attack her. As she knelt down to look inside the bag, she had a strange and sudden feeling of dread.

Manny began to bark at the bag, backing away from it, and Viviana shrieked, startled at the sound. Manny never barked.

"What's wrong, boy?"

The barking continued, and Viviana felt anxious.

"Oh stop it," she said to the dog.

Viviana slowly reached down and unzipped the bag, her heart pounding in her chest. What could be inside? Who would leave something here, in the middle of the park? She was so afraid that she almost stopped herself from looking into it, but her curiosity got the better of her. Taking a deep breath, she opened it up and looked inside.

At first, she couldn't believe what she saw. Viviana screamed and scrambled back from the bag, grabbing hold of Manny's collar and pulling him away with her. She felt a sudden surge of terror rush through her body as she realized what it was.

Manny was barking furiously now, echoing Viviana's fear. She wanted to run away as fast as possible, but was too afraid to move. With shaking hands, she pulled out her phone and called 911. After explaining to the dispatcher on the other end of the line what had happened, they quickly promised to send out a team immediately.

Viviana closed up the bag again and stepped back even farther away from it, waiting for help to arrive, grabbing hold of Manny's collar and backing away in fear, holding on to the dog's collar as if he were her lifeline.

TWELVE

BILLIE ANN

I arrived at the police station a little past eight in the morning. The sun was hiding behind the clouds, and the sky was already a deep dark threatening gray, as if the heavens were trying to preface the heavy storms that were due later that day. It had been raining all night as a few thunderstorms passed through our area. The parking lot was glistening, and I had to pick my way through the puddles as I hurried across, my shoes splashing me with water.

Just as I opened the glass doors, a sharp lightning bolt hitting close by startled me, and Doris, the receptionist, let out a little shriek as I stepped inside.

"Oh dear," she said. "And they say it's gonna stay this way all day. Something about a tropical low pressure from the Atlantic coming in over us in the coming days. Might be a hurricane before it makes it here. Hopefully it won't make landfall. It's the last thing we need right now."

"Isn't it a little late in the season for this?" I asked. "I mean it's almost Thanksgiving."

She threw out her arms. "What can I say. This is Florida.

You never know. Last year we had a storm in November: Nicole, remember? It happens."

The elevator rumbled as it took me up to the Chief's office, and I rushed through the corridors, arriving out of breath and slightly disheveled. When I entered, the meeting had already begun. All attention was focused on the Chief, who stood at the center of the room, pausing dramatically.

"Now that everyone is here," she said and cleared her throat while giving me a glare.

I was late yes, but only because Zack had wet his bed again this morning and I had to strip it all off and put it in the washer. I had asked my mom to come hang out with the kids today so Joe didn't throw another of his fits on me for leaving them home alone.

"I might as well recap for those who just got here." She sent me a smile, and I felt bad. I wasn't making a very good impression on my new boss. "But so far we have three bags with human remains in them, and they have all been taken to the medical examiner, who is now trying to piece them together. We do believe it's of the same person, but don't know for sure yet."

"Three bags?" I asked.

"Yes, there was one found at Melbourne Airport at the very same time as one was found on the beach, and a third one that was found last night, by a teenage girl out running with her dog. This was a sports bag. What's odd about this whole thing, well what makes it even more strange, is that all three bags belong to the same person, or at least has the same name tag on them a"— she paused and looked at her papers—"Danielle Simmons. She is from Cocoa Beach. I have told Melbourne this is our case. We have spoken to her, or Detective Wilde has, so we can conclude that it isn't her body inside of the bags. And we still don't know who it is."

"But it's a woman?" I asked.

"Yes, the body is a female. Dismembered into sixteen pieces." She paused and took in a deep breath. I looked at the pictures on the whiteboard, and felt sick again. I thought about Danni and my meeting with her the night before. I had called the Chief afterward and told her the suitcase was missing from her home, but that she was okay and very obviously didn't know anything about the body. I just hoped they believed me and didn't see my best friend as a suspect. And I'd managed to keep my friendship with Danni a secret—if the Chief knew about it, she'd definitely take me off the case.

"We've done background checks on Danielle Simmons and her husband," Tom said, then began to read out loud. "Danielle Simmons is a forty-one-year-old white female, living at 126 Deleon Road here in Cocoa Beach. She's five foot five, 110 pounds. She's married to Mike Simmons, and the mother of two children, twins, both daughters. She works at Maxwell Law downtown, as a paralegal. She has no priors except a couple of speeding tickets, and the same goes for her husband.

"Danielle is connected to all three of the bags. It has to mean something significant and I need us to find out what it is. She has been willing to come in this morning so we can have a talk with her," the Chief added. "She was very surprised when I called her and told her this morning. She only knew of the one missing suitcase, but confirmed for me over the phone, as I asked her to go check, that two other bags were missing as well. A duffel bag and a sports bag. Billie Ann, I was thinking that you and I should do that interview?"

I sent her a nervous smile. "Uh... yes of course, Chief."

How are you gonna pull that one off?

Chief Harold went over some more details of the case, and she added that they were working with the theory that it might be the body of Joanne Edwards, who had been reported missing by her husband, Randy Edwards, four weeks earlier, and we would probably know pretty soon whether it was her or not.

Joanne Edwards' husband had provided us with hair from her brush and her toothbrush when she disappeared, so we had a DNA profile on her in the system.

As the meeting came to a close, I couldn't shake the feeling of dread that had settled over me. I knew there was no way I could interview Danni without my emotions getting the better of me. She was my closest friend, someone I had known for years and shared everything with, and the thought of having to question her in a homicide investigation was almost too much to bear. If I was going to do it, it needed to be alone. I needed to find out if Danielle was in danger. Three suitcases had been found with her name on them. That worried me. It was no coincidence. Of course not. But what did it mean?

I stepped out of the Chief's office and headed toward the break room, hoping a cup of coffee would help calm my nerves. As I poured myself a cup, I heard a ding behind me and turned to see Danni coming toward me as she walked out of the elevator. I couldn't help smiling when seeing her. I could tell she was nervous. I walked up to her and handed her my coffee.

"Here."

"Oh Billie," she said and took the cup. "What's going on? I don't understand any of all this. I'm scared, to tell you the truth."

I placed a hand on her arm. "Don't be. I'm sorry that you have been put in this situation, but I am sure we will work it out."

I tried to sound reassuring, but it was hard. I could tell she was trying to be brave, but the fear in her eyes was palpable. "So where do I go?" she asked and sipped her coffee.

"Don't mention to anyone that we know one another. They might take me off the case. Just go sit by my desk." I pointed at it. "And then I will be right with you, okay?"

She sniffled, then walked to my desk and sat down in the chair in front of it. I threw her a brief glance, sensing how anxious she was, then rushed into the Chief's office, poking my head in. She was on the phone.

"Mrs. Simmons is here," I said.

She glanced at her watch and bit her lip, then removed the phone from her ear and whispered: "I'm running late," she said apologetically. "But if you start without me, I'll catch up soon." She motioned to me with her free hand, as if to say, "Go ahead." Not wanting to hold her back, I nodded.

"Hey if you're too busy, then I don't mind taking this one alone," I said.

"That would actually be helpful. I got to do another call after this, so if you don't mind?"

I smiled widely. "Not at all."

She gave me a thumbs-up, then returned to her caller.

I walked back toward Danni with a deep sigh of relief.

THIRTEEN

Then

TRANSCRIPT OF INTERVIEW OF ROBERT DURST
DEFENDANT'S EXHIBIT A
DURST PART 2

APPEARANCES:
Detective Michael Smith
Detective Lenny Travis
Sergeant Joseph Mill

DET. SMITH: Hi there, buddy. How are you doing today?
BOBBY: Okay... I guess.
DET. SMITH: Can you state your name and age for the record, please?
BOBBY: Um... it's Bobby Durst, and I am ten years old.
DET. SMITH: All right, Bobby, now tell me, do you know why you are here today?
BOBBY: Because of what happened.
DET. SMITH: And what was that? Do you remember?

BOBBY: (*nods*) Yes.

DET. SMITH: Something happened to George, your stepdad, right?

BOBBY: Yes.

DET. SMITH: Can you tell us what it was?

BOBBY: He got shot.

DET. SMITH: That's right. He was shot and killed at your home, on Pinehurst Avenue, right?

BOBBY: Right.

DET. SMITH: Did you see who shot him?

BOBBY: Yes.

DET. SMITH: Who was it?

BOBBY: I can't tell. I'm not allowed to.

DET. SMITH: Is that so? Says who?

BOBBY: My mom.

DET. SMITH: Okay then, but the thing is, that we really need to know who did it, so that we can solve this case. Don't you think you can tell us?

BOBBY: (*sniffles*)

DET. SMITH: Bobby? Are you crying?

BOBBY: (*sniffles again*) No.

DET. SMITH: I think you are. I also think that you're protecting someone because you care about them a lot. Am I right?

BOBBY: Maybe.

DET. SMITH: Okay let's go back a little then. Tell us what happened last night. Who was in your house?

BOBBY: Me, my sister, my mom, and George.

DET. SMITH: Now George lives with you, right?

BOBBY: Right.

DET. SMITH: Did you have dinner?

BOBBY: We had turkey. It was turkey day.

DET. SMITH: It was Thanksgiving, am I right?

BOBBY: Yes, turkey day. That's what we call it.

DET. SMITH: Well so do we at my house, Bobby. But tell me did you sit in the dining room or in the kitchen and eat the dinner?

BOBBY: Can I get a soda?

DET. SMITH: Of course. We got one right here. Detective Travis will hand it to you.

BOBBY: (*drinks from soda*) Thank you.

DET. SMITH: So let's get back to the dinner. Where did you sit when you ate it?

BOBBY: In the dining room.

DET. SMITH: Is that where he got shot too?

BOBBY: No it was in the bedroom.

DET. SMITH: One of the bedrooms, right?

BOBBY: Right.

DET. SMITH: Whose bedroom was it?

BOBBY: Josephine's.

DET. SMITH: What was he doing in her bedroom?

BOBBY: (*shrugs*) I don't know.

DET. SMITH: Where were you?

BOBBY: I was in there too.

DET. SMITH: I think you were. Did you like George?

BOBBY: Not anymore.

DET. SMITH: I see. Was that why you shot him?

FOURTEEN

BILLIE ANN

As I stared across the table at Danni, her voice shook slightly as she asked me if I believed her. I had just repeated the fact that three of her bags had been used to transport or hide body parts —a gruesome detail that I had to actively push out of my head as I tried to focus on her and stay present—and her connection to the case, the crime scenes, was evident.

She reached her hand across the table and touched my arm. The touch made me feel warm and I wanted to close my eyes for a second, but I steadied myself, focusing on my task.

"I mean you do believe me, don't you?"

"Of course," I said. "But we need to figure out who did this, and why they used three of your bags to place the body parts in. We need to talk to your friends and family—anyone who could have had a grudge against you."

Danni sighed and looked away, her gaze resting on the walls behind me, across the room.

The walls in the interview room were bare and white, acting as a stark reminder of the gravity of the situation. Across from me sat Danni, her slim figure almost swallowed up by the uncomfortable wooden chair she was sitting on. Her delicate features had paled, and the shadows beneath her eyes were evidence of the worry and fear that weighed heavily on her shoulders. It made me feel bad. I knew her well, and I believed her when she said she had nothing to do with what was found inside of the bags. Despite my best efforts to reassure her, I felt unable to do so. I couldn't tell any of the other officers *why* I trusted her.

"I feel so awful," she added and looked down at her delicate hand and long fingers. "Devastated. What does this mean for me? Do you look at me as a suspect? Am I a suspect?"

"Danni," I said softly, trying to reassure her that I believed she had nothing to do with it. "Is there anything you can tell me that might help us figure out who did this?"

She bit her lip, then shook her head. "No, not really," she said. "I can't think of anyone who would have a reason to do this to me. To put me in this situation. It really doesn't feel good."

I paused for a moment, thinking about the next question I should ask. It was a delicate balance to try and get information from her, but at the same time not intimidate her. Seeing her sad and scared like this broke my heart. I wanted to hold her and help her through it. Danni took a sip of the water I had given her.

"When was the last time you used any of the bags?" I asked finally.

Danni thought for a moment before answering. "I used the suitcase and my duffel bag this summer when going on that trip to Paris," she said slowly. "With Mike."

She was silent for several seconds as she slowly ran through a timeline in her mind. I remembered her trip well, as she had asked me to go with her initially, but I had said no. Not that I didn't want to, there was nothing I wanted more in this world, but I hadn't figured things out with Joe yet and I needed to get things right on the home front first. She had ended up taking her husband instead, even if their relationship wasn't well, not since he cheated on her with a coworker. He had promised it wouldn't happen again. He wanted to make things work too. The trip had been good for them and their relationship, she told me when she came back, and she was determined to make things work. For the children's sake.

It had broken my heart.

"And the sports bag?"

"It's been a while," she finally said. "I remember taking it on a trip up to North Carolina to visit with my sister a few years ago."

I gave an understanding nod. "That's helpful. Did you let anyone borrow any of the bags recently?"

"No."

"Is it possible someone has broken into your house recently?"

Again Danni shook her head. "No, not that I know off at least. I think I would have noticed. Right? Oh God, what if someone did go into my home, and I didn't even know? And this person is a murderer? The children could have been home. That's scary, Billie. "

"Okay, let's not jump to conclusions. I'm sure we'll figure this out. We just have to stay calm and think logically."

I leaned back in my chair and took a deep breath. Danni's presence had a calming effect on me. Her fragile beauty and vulnerability awakened a protective instinct within me. I wanted to keep her safe, and I had a feeling that solving this case was the only way to do that.

"I'll take care of everything, Danni," I said, looking directly into her big green eyes. "I promise you that. I will have a tech team come to your house, hopefully later today, and dust for fingerprints and look for evidence that this person might have left behind."

"Okay. That sounds good."

She smiled weakly, then took another sip of water. I

watched her delicate throat move as she swallowed, and I felt a
sudden urge to kiss her. It was inappropriate, I knew that, but I
couldn't help the way I felt. She was like a magnet, drawing me
in with her softness and vulnerability.

Danni's eyes met mine, and I could see the glimmer of hope
in them. She seemed to trust me and that trust gave me a sense
of responsibility. I needed to solve this case for her sake. I could
tell that Danni was trying to be brave, but she was on the verge
of tears.

"This is awful, Billie," she said. "I'm seriously fighting not to
freak out here. To think that someone—"

Suddenly, there was a knock on the door, and Danni looked
at me with wide eyes, and for a split second she was scared. But
she remained quietly seated, her hands clasped tightly in her
lap. I walked over to the door. I opened it to find Chief Harold
standing outside. She looked at me with a raised eyebrow. My
heart sank.

"Everything all right in here?" she asked.

I walked outside, closing the door. I nodded, relieved.
"Yeah, we're just talking. Trying to get some information. Any
news on the forensics?"

"Still waiting on the results," she said. "But we got a lead on
a possible suspect. The staff at Sea Aire Motel said they saw a
man leaving the motel with the bags matching the description."

I felt a surge of hope. "That's great news. Let's follow up on
that lead."

I turned to Danni. "We might have something."

She shook her head, her eyes wide with fear. "I just don't
understand why anyone would do this to me."

"We'll figure it out," I promised her. "In the meantime, I
need you to stay strong for me. We'll get through this together."

Danni nodded, a small smile appearing on her face. "Thank
you," she said softly. "I wouldn't know what to do without you.
I'm so glad you're here to help me."

"Are you okay to drive? Or should I have someone to take you home?" I asked.

"I'm okay. I can drive."

I returned to Chief Harold outside of the door, who gestured for me to follow her back to her office. As we walked down the hallway, I couldn't help but feel a sense of dread. The situation was more complicated than I had initially thought. I had hoped Danni could tell us something useful; perhaps she'd sold the bags, or lent them to a friend. It made it harder to keep her from becoming a suspect. But I was determined to protect Danni at all cost.

I sat down, and the Chief closed the door. She walked to her chair and sat down. I watched her nervously.

"I just need you to go through our next steps, Detective Wilde," she said.

I cleared my throat and leaned forward. "Well I am going to send Scott out to talk to Danni's husband and look around the house, to see if there are any signs of a potential break-in and to get photos of where the suitcase and bags were taken from. He will bring a team out to dust for fingerprints and secure potential evidence."

"So you're not treating Danielle Simmons as a suspect?" she asked.

I swallowed, and my eyes grew wide. "No. At least not yet. She's a wife and a mother with a full-time job. The killer left that poor victim out for everyone to see; they're brazen and unlikely to be able to maintain that sort of lifestyle. I would expect them to spend a lot of time alone, to keep to themselves, their predisposition well hidden, or to be the complete opposite and have some sort of criminal record."

She leaned back in her chair and gave me a look. "Interesting. Continue."

"We're gonna need to look at all the bags for fingerprints and DNA. I have already told the lab to do that. Hopefully we can get a positive ID on our victim within the coming days, and that will lead us in the right direction."

"Mm-hmm, good, good," she said and nodded. "And what about the airport?"

"I have contacted Melbourne Police Department and they have promised to send me all reports on the finding of the bag at the airport, eyewitness reports and so on. I know that our medical examiner, Dr. Phillips, has received the bag and its contents, and hopefully he can give us some answers soon. I know it was a woman who found the bag, and I have asked Tom to read through her statements and together we can decide if we need to follow up on something there. I don't assume we will need to, as she was just a random passenger, being at the wrong place at the wrong time, as far as I understand. Same with the girl who found the bag by the lake. But if you want to we can take an extra talk with them both, if you need us to? I just don't want us to waste our resources."

"I trust your judgment, Wilde," Chief Harold said, then added. "Until you prove me otherwise."

"Okay, because I really want to follow up on the motel first. I think that is the first real lead we have gotten. Hopefully it will be fruitful. And we can stop anything else from happening."

FIFTEEN

TREVOR

Sunday night

I-95 in Rockledge, Florida

Trevor had been driving a semitruck since he was nineteen years old. It was the open road, the endless possibilities, and the freedom that had always appealed to him. He'd been driving for so long by now that it felt like second nature, and despite the many hours on the road, he'd managed to remain married to his beloved wife for eighteen years.

So far.

It hadn't been easy. His wife hated that Trevor was gone for long periods of time, and since their son Jasper had been diagnosed with autism, she said she needed Trevor home more, to help out, that it was too much for her to carry alone. She begged him to spend more time at home, to get a steadier job where he would be closer to home. But Trevor was a lonely rider, he didn't care for spending too much time with the same people, in the same place. He needed the road, he needed to go, and he had told her that numerous times.

Before he left for this trip to Oregon, she had said she wanted a divorce. He hadn't answered her, just left slamming the door behind him. Then he had cried inside of the truck, just for a few minutes, before taking off. He would never tell anyone he cried. There was no need to. He didn't need anyone. Just him and the asphalt was all he wanted. He loved his son and his wife, but not even they could force him to remain in one place. It was in his blood, just like it had been in his father's before him. Driving a semitruck was his escape, his way of life, and he loved it. Especially on evenings like today when there was no traffic on the roads.

Trevor had been traveling along I-95 for hours, listening to them talk on the radio about the storm in the Atlantic, filling people with fear as usual, thinking it would become a hurricane and make landfall. He shut off the radio and continued through the heat and the humidity of the swamplands, before he spotted her at the side of the road. He didn't see her till his headlights hit her, and at first he thought it was a big animal, like a deer, but soon he realized it was a woman. Her hair was a wild mess, her clothing barely there, her body bruised and skinned, like she had been through a hell of a fight.

What on earth?

Trevor pulled over, and she slowly made her way toward his truck, looking exhausted and lost in her own world. He opened the door and asked her to come in, and she did, barely saying a word.

"What's your name?"

No answer.

He cleared his throat, attempting to get her attention. "What are you doing out here all alone? There isn't a house or town for the next fifty miles or so. Where did you come from? What happened?" he asked, but she remained unresponsive. She gripped onto the door handle tightly with her small hands, her face expressionless as she stared out of the window. There was a hollow look in her eyes, almost like she had seen something that had taken away her will to speak.

He tried again to talk to her, asking her where she had come from, what had happened, but she seemed too dazed to answer. She just sat there, clinging onto the handle of the door, staring out the window, her eyes vacant and cold.

Trevor finally gave up trying to make conversation and allowed her to stay in silence. He drove on, and the girl stayed like that the whole journey, lost in her own thoughts, until they reached the next town.

Trevor pulled into a gas station, and he turned to look at the girl. She looked thin, malnourished, and her eyes looked sunken in. He realized that he couldn't just leave her there, so he offered her a ham sandwich and a bottle of water. At first, she didn't move or acknowledge him, but eventually, she reached out to take the food and water from him. He watched as she ate hungrily, as if it had been days since she had eaten a meal.

Finally, when she finished eating, she looked up at him, and for the first time, he saw a flicker of emotion in her eyes. A small smile tugged at the corner of her mouth, and she said, "Thank you."

It was a small gesture, but it was enough for Trevor. He felt like he had done something good today, even though he didn't know anything about this girl. He felt like he had helped her in some small way.

"My name is Joanne," she finally said. "I think I need to go to the hospital."

SIXTEEN

BILLIE ANN

Scott, Tom, and I arrived at the motel and immediately began asking questions around the lobby. The staff were friendly and confirmed that they had seen a man with a bright pink suitcase, fitting the description we had provided, along with two other bags. One black and one yellow.

We followed the staff member to the surveillance room, where we were shown a grainy video of the man leaving the motel. The footage showed him dragging a suitcase and carrying two bags. The footage was in black and white so we couldn't make out the colors of the bags. It was also difficult to make out any distinguishing features of the person on the video, as he was wearing a baseball cap, covering the face, but it was a solid lead, nonetheless.

I noticed he had a big tattoo on his shoulder, and even if I couldn't see it very well, mainly because he was wearing a T-shirt that covered half of it, I believed it was of a bird, maybe an eagle. They had no name on him and said he had paid with cash when renting a room just for the night. He had checked in under the name M. Smith, but that didn't exactly help us much. Chances were it was an alias, or even if it wasn't then it was too common for us to be able to track down. He was alone, though, they could tell us that much. He stayed one night there. He checked out of the motel the day before the first bag was found in the airport. Now we needed to take this photo and go to the Melbourne Airport and see if we could find this man on their surveillance cameras there. I asked Big Tom to do that. He complained that it was a long drive and he had to pick up his son, Elliot, after baseball practice today. He had promised his wife, Gale, since she had gone out of town for the day for work. I told him he could make it back in time, and that it was important. It wasn't a big lead, but it was at least something to go by. I asked Scott to talk to the tech guys and ask them if there was any way of making the picture better, or enhance his face. Maybe even run a face recognition scan, but I knew it was going to be hard to do, since you couldn't really see his face properly in the footage.

The motel was old and worn down, and hadn't changed their cameras in twenty years. That's why the quality was so terrible. But if anyone could persuade the tech guys to at least try, it was Scott. He had a way with them. He had a way with most people. He was just nice to be around. He never had any children, at least not yet, and I felt bad for him. I knew him and his wife, Maddie, had been trying for more than a year now and it was getting to him that nothing was happening. I knew he would be an excellent father. Some people just radiated that about them.

I spent a couple of hours going through the reports from Melbourne Police Department, reading the eyewitness statements again, even if Tom had already done so and not come up with anything. I still wanted to go through the details of the findings of the bag in case anything had been overlooked. No detail was unimportant at this point. Most of the eyewitnesses were of people who had panicked when seeing the police come for the bag, thinking it might have been a bomb. One of them

stood out, as this woman said she had seen someone carrying the
bag as she passed this person by the sliding doors, leading
outside, but she didn't get a good look of the face, since it was
covered by a cap. But she did think that this person seemed
nervous and anxious and slightly suspicious to her.

Tom returned to me from the airport way faster than I had
anticipated, and he said the footage from there wasn't showing
much. I asked him to show it to me, and I watched it with him. I
saw a person arriving with the bag and placing it quickly by the
wall, before leaving in a hurry, but you could only see this
person from behind. The person was wearing a baseball cap but
I couldn't see if it was the same as in the motel, nor could I see a
tattoo since this person was wearing a jacket, covering both
arms.

It was frustrating.

I decided to go talk to the tech guys myself in the morning
and figure out if there was any way we could compare the two
people on the footage, and see if they bore any similarities. I
would have done it right away, but they had all left for the day. I
decided there was nothing more I could do, even if it bothered
me to let go and leave the case.

It was dark by the time I made it home. My phone had been
bombarded with text messages from my children all day. They'd
been asking me when I would be home and what was for
dinner. They were often so self-sufficient these days. I realized
that my kids needed me and I needed my kids. It was as simple
as that.

I made dinner, deciding on spaghetti and meatballs, since it
was my youngest, Zack's, favorite, and it was hard for me to get
him to eat these days. Being nine years old—and slightly spoiled
especially since the separation was announced and I was ridden
by guilt—he thought he could survive on a diet of chicken

tenders and hot dogs. Charlene, who was sixteen, and William, who was fourteen, were slightly easier to please. At least when it came to food. Being teenagers, they had other issues that were hard to deal with and that made me miss those days when it was just about the food. Charlene had been freaking out quite a bit when realizing I was gay, and I had caught her running away from home and drinking recently, and even getting into her truck while intoxicated, but lately she seemed to have been relaxing a bit more. She had gotten a boyfriend, Nathan, and he didn't like to drink as far as I knew, so that had stopped, much to my joy.

As I called their names, they came down the stairs, running fast, then gulped down the food in less than five minutes before they left the table again and went back to doing whatever it was they were doing in their rooms. It made me feel a little sad. I had thought they would at least talk to me, but perhaps all the messages during the day had been out of fear than anything else. Perhaps they just wanted me in the house. I'd been hurt in a case that had turned deadly not that long ago, and it seemed they still bore the marks of that.

I stared at the mess in the kitchen and thought about the time when they were younger and they enjoyed spending time with me. Okay maybe I was romanticizing things a little. If I remember right then they would chat my ear off and call for my help every two minutes, and I would never have a second to myself. Was I possibly missing those days? I guess so. I was missing them needing me, I guess. Only Zack would still hang out with me, sometimes, and watch a movie, and I clung onto that time with him like it was my last.

Was I lonely? I guess so. I had been married for eighteen years and was used to always being with the same person, so it was odd when they were no longer around. It wasn't that I missed Joe, I did some days, but I just wasn't used to being alone.

Joe had been my constant companion in life. I was used to his presence in my daily life, the way his smile always nudged me to get going and the way his words always soothed me like a balm. I had believed we were soulmates, but now I felt like I barely knew the man.

You were also lonely in your marriage. Don't forget that. Remember when you dropped to the floor in the kitchen, crying, asking him to love you, and he just stood there, then left you? Saying he believed you needed to be alone? Remember how you would scream at him to react, to see you, to hold you, and he still didn't do it?

I sighed and cleaned up after dinner, then decided to scan through local social media groups to see if anyone had said anything interesting about the cases. The local news stations had already caught wind of the police cordons at the beach and the suitcase at the airport. I was hoping someone would say something in a comment on a news site that they had no way of knowing; incriminating themselves. Or maybe someone would post photos of the crowd on the beach. And maybe the killer's face was among them? That I'd recognize him in an instant and give the poor victim's family swift justice. It wasn't unusual for a killer to be interested in his own work, especially when it was that sort of horrid attack and placement in public. This killer could very well obsess over the investigation, visit the scene, or discuss it online.

I woke up at midnight to the sound of a rocket launch going off from Kennedy Space Center at Cape Canaveral, then walked to my window and watched it from there. It was one of the big ones, a Delta IV Heavy rocket, and it lit up the entire sky looking like the sun rising. It was beautiful. But as I watched it, I couldn't stop worrying about Danni. Was she in danger? I would never forgive myself if anything happened to her. Never.

SEVENTEEN

Then

TRANSCRIPT OF INTERVIEW OF ROBERT DURST

DEFENDANT'S EXHIBIT A

DURST PART 2

APPEARANCES:
Detective Michael Smith
Detective Lenny Travis
Sergeant Joseph Mill

BOBBY: I can't tell you who shot him.
DET. SMITH: Well someone did. Who was it?
BOBBY: I can't say. I'm not allowed to.
DET. SMITH: Says who, Bobby? Who told you not to say?
BOBBY: I don't want to talk to you anymore.
DET. SMITH: But I want to talk to you, Bobby. It's my job to
figure these things out. Now the gun had been wiped clean so
there were no fingerprints on it, and none of you three had gun
residue on your fingers, so you must have washed them. And

one of you must have pulled the trigger. I need to know who it was. And why.

BOBBY: (*shrugs*) I don't know.

DET. SMITH: For crying out loud. Of course you do. You were there when it happened.

BOBBY: (*sniffles*) I wanna go home now.

DET. SMITH: Well you're not going home any time soon. The state attorney has decided you and your sister should be tried as adults, if it turns out to be one of you who did kill him.

BOBBY: (*cries*) Please let me go home.

DET. SMITH: I can't do that. Unless you tell me the truth about what happened. Who shot George?

BOBBY: I can't say.

DET. SMITH: (*sighs deeply*) For Christ's sake. Who are you protecting? Your mom? Your sister?

BOBBY: (*sniffles*) I wanna go home.

DET. SMITH: Did he make you angry? Huh? Is that why you did it?

BOBBY: (*sniffles*) I don't know.

DET. SMITH: Because I can understand that. By all means I have a temper and lose it from time to time. I take it out on people around me too. What did he do that made you so mad?

BOBBY: Nothing. I'm hungry.

DET. SMITH: Did he hurt your mother? Is that why?

BOBBY: I'm hungry.

DET. SMITH: Okay, then we will get you something to eat. Detective Travis can pick up something for you. What do you like? A peanut butter and jelly sandwich, huh?

BOBBY: (*nods*)

DET. SMITH: Okay then. That's what we will get you. While we wait maybe you can take me back to last night. You were eating turkey, and then what happened? What did you do after?

BOBBY: I don't know.

DET. SMITH: You can tell us, Bobby. The way I see it you

have done nothing wrong. And I am sure that if you did shoot George then you had good reason to, am I right? Was it an accident maybe?

BOBBY: I don't want to talk about it.

DET. SMITH: Okay let's just talk about the dinner then. Do you like turkey?

BOBBY: I love turkey. It's the best meal of the year. Pie too.

DET. SMITH: And what about your sister, she likes it too?

BOBBY: Not as much. She used to but not anymore.

DET. SMITH: Ah because of George? Because he is there now?

BOBBY: I don't know. Maybe.

DET. SMITH: Okay, nothing wrong with that. So tell me, did you go to the living room afterward?

BOBBY: (*nods*)

DET. SMITH: Did you watch TV?

BOBBY: Yes.

DET. SMITH: What were you watching?

BOBBY: *Finding Nemo.*

DET. SMITH: Oh I love that one. What is it she says again? Just keep...

BOBBY: Swimming, just keep swimming.

DET. SMITH: That's right. You know your movies, huh? Big movie fan?

BOBBY: Yeah I guess so.

DET. SMITH: So how were you sitting while watching this movie? Were you all on the same couch?

BOBBY: Yeah.

DET. SMITH: Who did you sit next to?

BOBBY: Josephine.

DET. SMITH: And on the other side of you?

BOBBY: George.

DET. SMITH: And then your mom sat at the other side of him?

BOBBY: Yeah.

DET. SMITH: Were they holding hands? Did they kiss during the movie?

BOBBY: No.

DET. SMITH: They never do that?

BOBBY: Not really.

DET. SMITH: So then what happened? Did you watch the entire movie?

BOBBY: No.

DET. SMITH: Why not?

(*Detective Travis enters and brings a sandwich.*)

BOBBY: Thank you.

DET. SMITH: Guess it is time for a little break, huh. I'm gonna get some more coffee. Anyone else needs some? But Bobby, we were doing so great just now. I don't want you to forget that. When I come back, I want you to tell me why you never watched the rest of the movie, okay?

BOBBY: (*chews loudly*) Okay.

EIGHTEEN

BILLIE ANN

The conference room was eerily quiet as Chief Harold stood in the center of it with her arms crossed over her broad chest. Her lips were pursed as her gaze swept across each of the officers and detectives in the room. No one dared to blink, and the stillness was thick with anticipation. Her face was stern and her voice carried an air of confidence that filled the space. Each one of her officers had their eyes locked on her, and I could feel the tension in the room building with every passing moment. It was clear this was going to be a huge announcement. Something big was happening. With a deep breath, she opened her mouth and declared, "Joanne Edwards was found last night." Her voice was strong but tinged with sorrow. "She was picked up by a semi and taken to the hospital."

My heart sank. We had been looking for Joanne for weeks, ever since she disappeared on her way home from a night out with her friends. Her husband had called us every day to ask for news, and at this point we barely knew what to tell him. She had gotten into a Lyft and that was the last anyone had seen of her. Our team had tried to trace the Lyft driver, but it turned out it was another car that she got into, and that the real one arrived a few minutes later and waited for her but she never showed up. We had believed that maybe she had decided to leave her husband. There had been a fight, and it wasn't unusual that someone decided to split. If anything, then I would suspect him of having done something to her. We had been told that they weren't doing very well in their marriage, that they had been having a lot of trouble. But we never could find anything that pointed us to him. He had been with a friend all night, who confirmed his alibi. If she was in hospital, it meant we had failed.

Chief Harold looked around the room before her eyes settled on me. I could feel my heart rate increase.

"Detective Wilde," she said, her voice a low rumble, "I want you to go and talk to Joanne."

My mouth stayed still, my tongue stuck to the roof of my mouth, as I listened to her instructions.

"Of course," I replied. "Has she said anything so far about where she has been? Any details I should know?"

Chief Harold shook her head and narrowed her gaze, her brow furrowed in determination. "No," she said. "Not to my knowledge."

"And the truck driver who picked her up?"

"He waited for the patrol to get there last night and told them he found her walking on the side of I-95 in Rockledge. He said that she seemed disoriented and that it took her a long time to even tell him who she was. She didn't say anything else, according to them, but I have put the report on your desk so you can read through it before you go and see her."

"And the husband?"

"He's been informed. He's at the hospital with her now."

"How's her condition?"

"She hasn't said much. She's badly bruised and beaten, that was all that they told me when I spoke to the hospital this morning. They're still running tests on her today."

I nodded, I was relieved she was alive, but my heart was weighed down by the heaviness of this case. Joanne's disappearance had been causing me trouble for weeks, and I had been hoping against hope that we would find her alive. Now that she had been found, but in such a terrible state, I knew that the road ahead was going to be tough. It was not easy having to juggle two cases at the same time. And it annoyed me slightly that it was taking focus away from Danni's. I knew I was biased but to me her case was the most pressing right now. I couldn't stop thinking about her, and worrying about her. I kept asking myself if I was doing the right thing hiding the fact that I knew her well? Would it become a problem?

It has nothing to do with me. If they take me off the case, I can't help protect her.

I was pulled out of my train of thoughts by Chief Harold's sharp voice.

"Could you give us a quick update, Wilde, on the Suitcase Murder?" the Chief asked. "Before you leave?"

"We still don't have an ID on the body parts, I'm afraid," I said. "Dr. Phillips called me this morning and said it's gonna take a little time to piece together."

The image left us all in silence.

"Any news from forensics? Neighbors? Surveillance footage?" she continued.

I cleared my throat. "Just that the suspect seen at the motel with the bags, and at the airport, was wearing a baseball cap and had a big tattoo of an eagle on his shoulder. We're assuming it's the same person. The bag at the airport was placed there at 8:16, and we are working with the theory that the suitcase was placed on the beach and the bag at the lake first, and then he took off to the airport."

"And why is that?"

"Because the footage of the guy leaving the motel with the bags was taken at 7:10 that same morning, and it takes half an hour to drive from the motel to the airport, or rather thirty-two minutes, if we're precise. It leaves him enough time to place both bags and then leave for the airport."

"All right," Harold said, nodding. She didn't look too happy, and that frustrated me. I wanted to have more to give her, I really did.

"I'll head to the hospital now," I said, already moving toward the door. "I'll let you know what I find out."

I left the room, while Chief Harold addressed my colleagues one last time before dismissing them all. She reiterated how important this case was and how we needed to do everything in our power to find out what happened to Joanne Edwards and to "track down this infamous suitcase killer who had destroyed the peace of our small paradise town."

As I left the station and got into my car, I felt a sense of dread creeping over me. Joanne's case had been one of the ones that kept me up at night. At least we knew now that it wasn't her body parts that were found, but I couldn't help but wonder. Could all of this be connected? I wasn't one to believe in coincidences much. I drove to the hospital, my mind racing with questions.

NINETEEN

RANDY

Randy's fists tightened and his knuckles whitened with rage as he fell to his knees beside his wife's hospital bed. The surge of anger that filled him was almost too much to bear.

He felt her soft hand in his and he slowly raised his gaze. Her eyes were filled with pain, and she was gripping his hand tightly as if to reassure him that everything would be all right. Randy nodded, willing himself to stay strong for her. He could not let himself break down. Not yet.

Randy leaned in and tenderly kissed his wife's forehead. He then gently brushed away a few tears and whispered to her softly.

He had never felt such rage before, and yet, in the back of his mind, there was a presence of calm.

He would never give up.

His trembling hands strayed around her battered body, examining every bruise, scrape, and cut. He touched her face— so soft despite its wounds—and looked into her eyes, still filled with love but now dulled with pain. She closed them again, as if keeping them open was too hard, required too much strength that she didn't have.

The door opened and a nurse came in. He looked to her for answers, but she just strode past him, then checked the IV drip and the monitors.

"Is she going to be okay?" he asked.

The nurse smiled. "She seems to be stable. But the doctor wants us to run more tests, just in case."

"But... but she's okay, right?"

"I'm sure she will be, Mr. Edwards. In time. The doctor will come talk to you a little later."

Then she left, her shoes clacking on the floors. But Randy couldn't wait till later. He wanted answers now.

"I won't let anyone get away with this—not ever—no matter what happens," he whispered to her softly.

Randy stayed by her side, refusing to move until he had answers. The room was silent, except for the beeping of the monitors and the sound of her shallow breaths.

His thoughts were interrupted by a loud knock on the door. He looked up to see a woman in a blue suit with a white shirt standing in the doorway. She had buzz-cut blonde hair, but carried it well with her small slim face. She still looked feminine.

"Detective Wilde," he said, recognizing her from when she had come to his house interviewing him about Joanne earlier on, when they were searching for her. They had believed she had taken off on her own. They had never believed him when he said something had happened to her, that he was certain of it. He had never liked her much, and he gave her a guarded look.

"I certainly hope you're here to tell me you've found out who kidnapped and hurt my wife?"

She stepped forward. "Mr. Edwards, I'm—"

"Look at her, woman. Look at her for crying out loud. Look at her bruised face, her swollen eye."

"I am looking at her, and that's also why—"

He threw out his arms. "You people are useless. For weeks

now I have begged you to find my wife. And what did you do? You didn't believe me. You thought she had left me. Because of the fight we had. Meanwhile she was with her kidnapper and look what this bastard did to her! And what did you do? Nothing. Absolutely nothing."

"That's not true, Mr. Edwards, and you know it. We have had search parties out; we have done everything—"

"In your power blah blah blah, yes I know the speech by now." He shook his head and looked at his wife. "I can't even imagine what you must have been through, my love. But you did it. You found your way back to me, all by yourself, and you were brave enough to do it. Joanne dear, can you hear me?"

She opened her eyes and nodded. Then she looked at the detective. "I want to talk to her. Alone."

TWENTY

BILLIE

"I'll be right out here, okay? If you need me, I'm right behind this door, okay?" Randy Edwards stared at his wife, then at me, like I was the enemy. I knew in his opinion I hadn't done enough to help him find his wife, and the way he looked at me made me feel like a failure.

Plus, I imagine he'd got the impression I considered him a suspect. I often found it hard to hide my feelings. From the very first moment I met him, I couldn't get it off my mind. When I'd interviewed him, when he seemed to squirm in his seat, not wanting to answer me directly when I asked about how their relationship had been. I couldn't ignore the red flags.

Had they been on good terms? No answer, just a shrug. Did they fight a lot? Another shrug. Did she have an affair? Did he? He said he hadn't but he didn't know about her. He gave me nothing during those interviews, and it had been very suspicious to me. But seeing him now made me realize that I probably hadn't done him justice. He wasn't the man I had thought. He looked distraught while standing there in his cargo shorts and bare feet in sneakers.

Randy's brow furrowed and his eyes darted around the

room, as if seeking a way to escape the situation. He was obviously not comfortable leaving her side. He shifted from one foot to the other, unwilling to go. He couldn't seem to tear himself away from her side.

"I'll be right out here, okay?" Randy repeated, his voice gruff yet subtly pleading. He turned his gaze to me, his eyes narrowing in accusation. Then he looked at her again.

"If you need me, I'm right behind this door, okay?"

Joanne nodded silently, her gaze on Randy, both of them obviously aware that this was an emotional moment and things were somehow changing. I felt like an intruder in this instant, witnessing the raw emotions between them without being able to do anything about it. So many times I had spoken to Randy as he begged me to do more. I wanted to say something, for them, for their family, but I couldn't find the right words.

The air in the room seemed to crackle with the tension of the moment, the uncertainty of the future. I finally spoke, my voice trembling as I chose my words carefully.

"It won't take long," I said, trying to convey empathy through my tone.

Joanne nodded.

"Okay so I am leaving now, all right?" he added. "But I'm still here."

She nodded again. "Yes. Thank you."

Finally, he left and closed the door behind him. I took a chair and sat next to Joanne, then served her a weak smile. I wanted to tell her that I felt so guilty for not being able to find her and get her home. I felt like I had done what I could, what I had the means to, but it just wasn't enough. I had searched for her everywhere, day and night, after she was reported missing. I had talked to everyone who knew her, family, friends. I had arranged search parties who combed the beach and the river. I had interviewed her husband again and again yet gotten nowhere. I had talked to each of her coworkers who were with her on the night she went missing. She had gotten into a car that wasn't the Lyft she had ordered. That's all we knew. Because the Lyft driver arrived afterward and waited for her, but she never showed up. No one had seen the car she went into, and no one knew where she could possibly have gone to. There was no CCTV, no witnesses. She hadn't seemed depressed, nor frightened for her life in the days before. Seeing her in this state made me realize I hadn't done enough. She was alive, yes, but that wasn't because of me.

"Joanne?" I said. "You don't know how glad we are to see you and have you back with us. We've been looking for you for a very long time."

She cleared her throat and nodded. "I'm just glad to be back."

I smiled, feeling relieved. She didn't seem to be upset with me. "So are you ready to talk about where you have been? Do you think you can handle that?"

Joanne's eyes flickered as she looked away from me. She twisted her fingers together, wringing them tightly. "I can't," she whispered. "It's too hard. I can't talk about it."

I leaned in closer to her, trying to offer her comfort. She had just said she wanted to talk to me alone. The will was there, but maybe not the courage. It wasn't unusual that somebody who went missing or had endured something terrible suddenly regretted offering to speak about it. Once she realized how difficult it was to talk about it, to face all those memories again.

"Joanne, we need to know what happened to you so we can help you. I want you to know that you're safe now." I felt more certain than ever that she hadn't left of her own choice. "If you do help us find the people who did this to you, then we can prevent it from happening to someone else. I'm sure you'd want that," I said, hoping I had assumed correctly.

She shook her head, and her eyes filled with tears. "I know you want to help, but you can't. No one can. Not anymore."

"What do you mean?" I asked, feeling a knot form in my stomach.

"I'm broken," she said, her voice barely above a whisper. "I'm not the same person I was before. I don't think I'll ever be that person again."

I felt a pang of sympathy for her. Whatever had happened to her had clearly taken a toll on her mental and emotional well-being.

"I'm so sorry," I said, feeling inadequate. "Let's just try again from the beginning. Can you tell me what happened on the night you disappeared?"

"I-I was out with my friends from work, we had a few drinks."

"Where exactly did you go, do you remember?" I asked, even if I knew from talking to her coworkers, I needed her account of every detail as well.

"The Alibi. We love going there. I had a couple of espresso martinis. And then a lemon drop. I didn't feel so good after that, so I told the others I was heading home. I ordered a Lyft in the app, and then walked outside to wait for it. I got into the car, or at least the one I thought was my Lyft, and took off. The person in my car locked the doors and just... took off."

"Did you see anything of him?"

"Her. It was a woman, and no she was wearing a mask, but I just thought she was worried about germs or Covid. It's not unusual these days for people to wear masks."

"So it was a woman?" I asked.

"Yes. She had long black curly hair, falling out of the sides of the mask, and was wearing hoop earrings, big round ones."

I looked at Joanne intently, scribbling down notes on my pad as she spoke. Her lips trembled and her face flushed with emotion, though she seemed to be struggling to maintain her composure. Every few sentences, she paused and took a few deep breaths, releasing them with a shudder before continuing.

Though I kept my questions brief, I could see the deep pain in her eyes. There was something about her story that wasn't just heartbreaking, it was also deeply troubling. I could tell that something wasn't right, and I was determined to get to the bottom of it.

"I remember that—"

Suddenly, her voice broke and she fell silent. She looked away, and I sensed that she didn't want me to ask any more questions. I knew that if I pushed for answers, it would only upset her further, so I let the silence hang between us.

Finally, after a few moments, she looked up at me. "I'm sorry," she said softly. "It's just hard to talk about."

"That's okay. Take your time."

I nodded in understanding, and she put her face in her hands. I waited patiently, giving her the time and space she needed to compose herself before we continued.

"Do you remember anything else about the woman who drove the car?" I asked gently.

Joanne shook her head. "It was dark, and I was drunk. I have to be honest and say I wasn't completely there. I didn't get a good look at her. And she never spoke to me, not once. She just drove and drove. I dozed off for a few minutes, maybe more. I was so tired. I thought she was just taking me home. When I woke up I didn't know where I was. I didn't recognize the streets. It took me a while to realize that we weren't driving toward my house. I asked her where we were going, and she didn't answer, just accelerated the car."

I could feel my frustration start to mount. I needed more information, there had to be something that could tell us where she had been.

"Do you remember anything else? Any landmarks, or street signs, anything that might help us track down where you were taken?" I pressed.

Again, Joanne shook her head. "I don't know. I just

remember feeling scared, and alone. And then... nothing. The next thing I knew, I woke up in that room."

"What room?" I asked, my interest piqued.

Joanne hesitated before answering, her voice barely audible. "It was a small, windowless room. There was only a bed and a bucket in there. No other furniture or decorations."

I felt my stomach drop. "Joanne, did anyone else come into the room while you were there?"

She shook her head slowly. "No one came in. I was alone."

But her eyes told me something different. I could tell she was holding something back. I could see the fear in her gaze, and the determination to keep it hidden.

"Was there any sound or noise coming from outside the room?" I asked gently.

She paused before responding, and I could feel her shaking. Finally, she said, "I heard distant voices sometimes, but I tried not to pay attention. I was too scared."

A chill ran through my veins. I knew that whatever had happened to Joanne in that room, it was much worse than she was letting on.

"Joanne, what are you not telling me?" I asked.

She nodded slowly, tears streaming down her face. "I lied."

"About what?" I asked.

"Someone did come in. He did."

"And who is he? Do you know?"

"I think it was her husband. He would come in and... hurt me. Over and over again. Him and sometimes the wife was with him."

"So there was more than one kidnapper?" I asked.

She was shaking, her delicate frame trembling as she spoke. Tears streamed down her pale cheeks, and her voice quavered in fear. "They beat me and he raped me, and... said they were going to sell me. They liked I was blonde and said they could get a lot of money for someone like me."

Her words echoed in my ears, and I felt my stomach drop. I had read about cases like this before—in remote areas, particularly, there were stories of kidnappings and trafficking networks. But here, in the quaint coastal town where I lived, such a thing seemed impossible.

Yet here she was, telling me this story. I wanted to reach out and hug her, to tell her that everything would be all right, but I knew better. All I could do for now was listen, and with each word, the horror and injustice of what had happened to her grew more and more vivid inside me.

I wanted to ask her more details on who these people were, what she saw while being kept there, and how she had escaped. But her lip began to tremble and she succumbed to her tears and stopped speaking. I reached over and touched her hand gently to offer support. We stayed there in silence for a few moments, me holding her hand, rubbing it gently to comfort her.

My heart broke for Joanne. I couldn't even imagine the trauma she must have endured. Despite the daylight streaming in through the window, the room felt as if it were cloaked in a blanket of darkness. I could hardly believe what she had told me. After all that she had endured, I could understand why she had trouble finding her words. She was trembling, her eyes wide and unseeing. I reached out and put my hand on her shoulder to reassure her, and slowly, she sank into me. She looked up and said nothing. The sorrow in her eyes made my heart ache. I wanted to give her some hope, some kind of assurance that it would all be okay. But I had nothing to offer her. No words to give her comfort. All I could do was be there for her in her time of need.

"Did they give away anything that might indicate who they were?" I asked. "Any accents or special signs of recognition? Maybe something that can give you any indication as to why they were doing this?"

Joanne nodded. "Yes, now that you mention it, they were wearing masks, but both had a Spanish accent when they spoke to me, and spoke in Spanish to one another from time to time. From what I could see of their hair around the masks, it was dark."

I wrote it down, nodding, "Okay, they're potentially Hispanic, that helps a little bit."

"They cut off my beautiful hair," she said, crying, and touched her blonde locks that were now just shoulder-length. "And they branded me, see. With some heated tool."

She turned her arm so I could see the mark on the inside of it. I stared at it and held back a small gasp. The area was swollen and was oozing something. It looked slightly infected. I couldn't make anything of the symbol. It looked like a letter or maybe two that were intertwined, like a brand or a symbol.

"Do you mind if I take a picture of it?" I asked.

She shook her head. I grabbed my phone and took one, then stared at it again, wondering what it could possibly mean. It had to have some significance to the kidnappers. Were there other women out there with the same mark? Being trafficked? Did we have any bodies found with this mark on them before?

"Is there anything else you can tell me. How did you escape?" I asked.

"I can't do this," she said, breaking down. "I just can't talk about it anymore. And I can't tell you where the place is, I don't remember. It's like... a big dark hole in my memory. I can't remember anything, I can't think of anything, I can't even think about it without..."

I nodded, knowing what she meant. Memories like these were triggering, they were traumatic events. "Okay, Joanne. That's okay. You don't have to talk about it anymore. Give yourself some time. We can talk again later so I can ask you some questions, maybe things will come back to you, maybe you will remember something."

"I don't think so," Joanne said, her voice so soft I could barely hear her. "I can't remember anything. I can't think of anything that can help you. I just want to go home, and for Randy to stay in the dark about this. I want to be left alone."

I reached over and held her hand gently, "I'm so sorry," I said, tears springing to my eyes. "You have no idea how sorry I am."

I walked out of the room and closed the door behind me with a deep sigh. Randy Edwards was standing right behind it and stormed back in as I came out.

I took the elevator down, while mulling this information over in my head and got back in my car. I sat there for a few moments taking notes and thinking about what I had learned so far.

I shook my head. The case seemed more hopeless by the minute. I tried to put myself in the mindset of the kidnappers and tried to go over what I knew.

I knew it was two kidnappers, a man and a woman, who seemed to run a sophisticated operation. They were well-organized, they had the means, they had the motive—these people had a lot of money and probably were running a sex trafficking operation.

I knew the woman who drove the vehicle was masked and possibly Hispanic. But I didn't have any leads to her identity nor to the kidnapper's.

I thought about the branding, and the two symbols. I wished I could find some sort of connection to them. Why take the time to brand her, and why use two different symbols? If they were going to sell her?

It made no sense.

TWENTY-ONE

Then

TRANSCRIPT OF INTERVIEW OF JOSEPHINE DURST
DEFENDANT'S EXHIBIT A
DURST PART I

APPEARANCES:
Detective Michael Smith
Detective Lenny Travis
Sergeant Joseph Mill

DET. SMITH: You still haven't answered us, Josephine. I asked you if that was why you shot him?

JOSEPHINE: (*sniffles and whimpers*) I don't want to talk about it.

DET. SMITH: I'm afraid you have to. We will find out somehow if it was you who shot George.

JOSEPHINE: (*cries*) I can't tell you, don't you understand that?

DET. SMITH: Josephine, I'm not here to hurt you. I just want to know the truth. You're not doing yourself any favors by refusing to talk.

JOSEPHINE: I just can't.

DET. SMITH: (*sighs*) Okay. But can we go back to last night then? Before the shooting. You were watching a movie in the living room?

JOSEPHINE: Y-yes. *Finding Nemo*. It's my brother's favorite.

DET. SMITH: Hey, mine too. I admit that.

JOSEPHINE: (*chuckles lightly*) That's funny.

DET. SMITH: But I understand that you never got to finish the movie, is that correct?

JOSEPHINE: Yes.

DET. SMITH: Why not? What happened?

JOSEPHINE: (*moves in chair*) I-I don't know.

DET. SMITH: Come on, Josephine. I think you do. You can at least give me that. Can't you?

JOSEPHINE: (*fumbles with soda can between fingers*) I guess so.

DET. SMITH: Okay. So what happened? Did you get tired of it and just stopped watching it?

JOSEPHINE: N-no.

DET. SMITH: Then what happened?

JOSEPHINE: I-I don't think I... can

DET. SMITH: (*slams hand on table*)Yes you can, Josephine. I know you can tell us. Just try at least.

JOSEPHINE: (*whimpers*) I...

DET. SMITH: Okay let's try this. Who stopped the movie? Who pressed the remote and stopped it?

JOSEPHINE: M-my mom.

DET. SMITH: Okay so she grabbed the remote and paused the movie. Did she say why?

JOSEPHINE: Not really.

DET. SMITH: Did she say anything else?

JOSEPHINE: She-she looked at George and my brother.

DET. SMITH: Was she angry? Or happy?

JOSEPHINE: She was angry. Very angry.

DET. SMITH: About what?

JOSEPHINE: She-she asked what they were doing.

DET. SMITH: What they were doing? Weren't they watching the movie?

JOSEPHINE: N-no.

DET. SMITH: Then what were they doing?

JOSEPHINE: They... they had taken the blanket and covered their bodies. Bobby was... in his lap.

DET. SMITH: Bobby was in his lap?

JOSEPHINE: Yes.

DET. SMITH: And then what happened?

JOSEPHINE: My mom walked over and grabbed the blanket.

DET. SMITH: Did she pull it off?

JOSEPHINE: Y-yes.

DET. SMITH: And what did she see?

JOSEPHINE: (*clears throat*) His hand.

DET. SMITH: George's hand?

JOSEPHINE: Yes.

DET. SMITH: What was he doing with the hand?

JOSEPHINE: Touching him.

DET. SMITH: George was touching Bobby? Where?

JOSEPHINE: In his pants.

DET. SMITH: He had his hand inside of Bobby's pants?

JOSEPHINE: Y-yes.

TWENTY-TWO

BILLIE ANN

The sun was just beginning to set as I arrived at Danni's house. On the drive there, I had felt a tinge of nostalgia at the familiar sights and sounds of her neighborhood. The winding street, lined with Victorian-style homes, seemed to transport me back in time.

She was the one who had asked me if I could come over for dinner, like old times, and I had agreed to it. I had been excited too. I was looking forward to catching up with her, since it had been forever, and I missed her deeply. I missed our conversations that would venture into the night and involve a lot of prosecco or chardonnay. I missed talking about everything in my life with her, all my worries and concerns, and she would listen to me, actually interested, and not emotionally distant like my husband Joe, who would usually just dismiss my feelings. Danni was the one who encouraged me to start working out, who helped me feel confident when I was first promoted and had no idea how to manage Tom or Scott.

I missed her. Just her simple presence, her smile, her eyes, and her hugs. Being close to her made me feel at home.

I drove past the small Sunoco on the corner and noticed a

line to get gas. People were filling their cars up and filling gas
cans that they placed on the back of the pickup trucks. It always
happened at this point once they started to talk about a possible
storm coming. People panicked and started to fear there
wouldn't be gas enough for them to get away or to fill up their
generators for when they lost power. I bet there was already
people hoarding toilet paper and bottled water at Publix.

I parked in the driveway, then corrected my shirt and my
hair while looking in the rearview mirror. Then I sighed. I
would never be enough for a woman like Danni. I had to take
what I could get, which was our close friendship, a bond I
enjoyed more than anything.

I received a text from Big Tom, saying that the search for a
man with an eagle tattoo in the database hadn't given any hits.
And the tech crew wasn't able to make the surveillance footage
better so we could see anything else, or even see if it was the
same man. We were nowhere closer to finding him. I had
finished my report on my interview with Joanne Edwards
before I left, and told both Tom and Scott to please read the
interview to stay updated, and tell me if anything stood out to
them. I needed fresh eyes on it.

I also needed to check up on Danni, as she had been on my
mind all day. I didn't need her to feel suspicious, or even
anxious, so I pretended like this was a normal visit. Us catching
up.

I made my way to the door. I was suddenly overcome with
butterflies in my stomach. I had been so looking forward to
catching up with Danni, but I couldn't help feeling a little
anxious.

I had brought a bottle of prosecco, just to not get there
empty-handed, and a small toy for each of her twin girls, who
were just four years old. For some reason they loved me, I never
knew why. Maybe because I often brought them something,
maybe just because I enjoyed their company so much.

I rang the doorbell, which was unusual for me. Back in the days when Danni and I were always together, I would just knock fast and then open the door and announce my presence. But times were different now, and I no longer felt comfortable doing that.

Instead, I waited.

The door opened slowly, and I saw Mike's face peering out from the darkness. His forehead was furrowed and his eyes were glassy. I felt my heart sink as I looked at him. His eyes were filled with worry and fatigue as he stood in the doorway, his arms limp at his sides. This was very unlike him.

What's going on?

"Hey, Mike. Is Danni here?" I asked, trying to sound casual. But I instinctively knew something was wrong. Something was very wrong. I had never seen him look like this. Those eyes and the way he glared at me.

Mike's face twisted into a frown. "No, she went for a run a few hours ago and she hasn't come back yet."

I furrowed my brow. She knew I was arriving. A shiver went up my spine.

"Have you tried calling her?" I asked.

Mike sighed. "Yeah, but she's obviously in the zone."

"Did you leave a message?" My voice conveyed my concern for Mike, and I knew that if his wife did not answer the phone, it was not because she did not want to: something had happened.

He paused before answering. "No... are you concerned?" he asked.

I regretted my insistence; I didn't want to worry him. "Maybe something came up? Maybe someone needed her? Like a friend? You know how she is," I said, knowing Danni was always there if you needed her; she would throw everything she had in her hands to come to your rescue. During Covid she had been the one to always make meals for people, if they were in quarantine with their children, and leave it on their doorsteps. It was always in her nature to help other people out. Especially if there were children involved. She had that kind of heart and compassion.

"But why didn't she shoot me a text? Or you? To let us know she was being late?" he asked.

He was making a good point. We both stood in silence for a moment, unsure of what to do next. Then Mike spoke up. "My mom is here and can look after the littles. Perhaps we should look for her? She might have fallen... sprained her ankle?"

I nodded immediately. My heart was racing rapidly in my chest. I kept thinking of the bags and the suitcase that all had been in her name, and maybe a warning? But had to push that thought aside. I simply couldn't go there.

No need to freak out just yet. There might be a reasonable explanation. Please let there be a reasonable explanation.

"Of course, let's go."

As we stepped outside, I glanced around, trying to figure out where Danni might have gone. She usually ran on the trail by the lake, but it was getting dark and it wasn't safe anymore. Black clouds carrying thunderstorms were approaching and would make the outdoors unsafe any moment now. I could hear them rumbling in the distance, and I had gotten an advisory on my phone as well. It was severe storms that could produce tornadoes, if the right conditions were present. If she had fallen down, and was lying somewhere, then finding her before the storms got here was important, maybe even vital. Mike and I decided to drive around the neighborhood, calling out her name and checking the local park.

As we drove around, I couldn't help but feel anxious. Something didn't feel right. We had been searching for almost twenty minutes when Mike suddenly slammed on the brakes. My heart raced as I looked out the window, trying to see what he had seen.

There, lying on the ground, in the light from the streetlight was a phone. Mike parked the car and we both jumped out, rushing over to it. I recognized it immediately since Danni had a very distinct cover, with red and green flowers on it.

"Danni would never leave her phone like this," Mike muttered, his voice trembling.

"Could she have dropped it?" I gasped. "While running?"

He whimpered. "But it was hours ago. She would have realized it was gone by now, wouldn't she?"

As his steel gray eyes bore into mine, my heart sank like a stone in quicksand. Panic surged through me as I realized the truth. Danni was glued to that phone; it was her connection to the world and to her children. She would never leave it like that on the ground. Never. And if it had fallen by accident, she would have immediately noticed its absence upon returning home. The possibilities of what could have happened drained all color from my face and made me lightheaded like I had just been sucker punched in the gut. But the fact of the matter was that she hadn't come home, and that's what terrified me to my core.

Where in the world was Danni?

TWENTY-THREE

BILLIE ANN

The sky above us crackled as lightning hit nearby. Rain soon poured on us, and every inch of my body was soaked, but I barely noticed, while I picked up Danni's cell phone from the street. It was dead, and I couldn't start it up.

Every step I took after that was like walking through water. I tried my best to stay calm, but I didn't even notice the rain; I didn't even notice when the winds picked up and lightning struck nearby. All I cared about was Danni. What if she had been injured or even killed and there was nobody around to help her?

But I had to remain cool, keep my thoughts gathered so I could think straight and not let the fear and anxiety get the better of me. The neighborhood where we found Danni's phone looked pristine. Rich people lived here. That's when I saw something under the light of an outdoor lamp attached to a house that made me start walking. Behind me, Mike ran a hand through his hair.

"Where are you going?"

I didn't answer. I didn't have time to think about him. There was only one thing on my mind: finding Danni, and fast.

I approached the front door of a small house covered in deep purple flowers, a Ring doorbell attached to it. As I reached out to press the bell, my heart was pounding, hoping that the homeowner could help me in my search.

I pushed the doorbell and waited, listening to the familiar chime ringing inside the house. The doorbell was a Ring model, which I knew had motion-activated cameras that could record activity and even send push notifications when the doorbell was pressed.

I waited a few moments before the door finally opened. A woman with graying hair stood in the doorway.

"Yes?" she asked, looking up at me expectantly.

"Good evening," I said politely. "My name is Detective Wilde with CBPD," I said and showed her my badge.

She smiled and nodded. "I know who you are. I know all of you from the station, as I bring you pizza or sandwiches with my volunteer group every Friday."

I smiled and recognized her. "Ah yes, Mrs. Francine. I'm sorry for barging in on you like this. But this is urgent."

"You look like it's urgent," she said. "How may I be of help?"

I tried to breathe to calm myself down. "I'm looking for a woman named Danielle Simmons, who may have dropped her phone near here earlier today. She was out running. I noticed you have a Ring doorbell and wondered if I could see the recordings from earlier today? It might help me locate her."

The woman stared at me for a moment, the surprise evident on her face. After taking a second to process my request, she nodded and said, "Yes, of course you can. Come in."

I followed her inside and she led me into the living room, where an iPad was connected to the Ring doorbell system. She opened the app and pulled up the recordings from earlier in the day. The camera was a motion sensor, and only reacted if someone passed by in the street. We watched as Danni came jogging past their house, my heart dropping as I saw her face. The time on the footage was 2:35 p.m.

Please let her be okay. Please dear Lord let her be okay.

Then something happened that made my heart stop: a car drove up on her side and lowered the window. I couldn't quite make out who was inside, but it looked like there was somebody talking to her. Then the door to the backseat opened, and that's the moment the clip ended.

Everything screamed inside of me.

What just happened?

"I'm sorry," Mrs. Francine said. "It only records sixty seconds at a time after being activated. This is all there is."

"Can I watch it again. Please?"

She looked at me, surprised, then nodded. She pressed the link in the app again and played the video for me. I saw it all happen again, and it wasn't easier the second time. I watched Danni walk toward the car again. I asked the woman to send it to me, to airdrop it to my phone, and she did. Then I left, blood draining from my face quicker than I could walk, feeling sick to my stomach.

Mike spotted me from the sidewalk as the door opened and came closer. I walked down the driveway toward him, barely able to say anything. I tried to but no words formed through my lips. It angered him, and he threw out his arms with a grunt.

"What is it? What happened? Talk to me, darn it."

I looked at him, my voice shaking as I said the words.

"I believe Danni was taken."

"What do you mean taken? I don't understand?"

"I think she was kidnapped. I have a video on my phone of it happening. She was talking to someone in the street, in a car. Right here where we found her phone. She must have dropped it when they dragged her into the car."

"I... what? I can't believe it. What are you saying?" he stuttered.

"I'm saying someone took her, Mike. That's what I am saying. And if we don't act fast, her life could be in great danger."

I grabbed my phone and reported it to dispatch. A person of interest in a murder case had gone missing and we needed a search party out. ASAP.

TWENTY-FOUR

RANDY

Randy Edwards had his back to the wall, his heart beating fast as he tried to avoid the shadows cast by the harsh fluorescent light. He forced himself to keep his composure, exhaling slowly as he gingerly opened Joanne's laptop and began to scour her files, desperately searching for anything that could help him. He was breathing hard, but tried to steady himself as he started going through it. He had done it before, and so had the police when she disappeared, but this time he was more focused.

He knew what he was looking for.

He had listened at the door as she spoke to the detective, and to the details she had given them. It had led him to an idea, a suspicion even. One he probably should take to the police, but what good were they anyway? No, he was better off taking care of this by himself.

He shook himself from his thoughts, turning his attention back to the laptop. His hands moved feverishly as he clicked on each folder, quickly scanning through the documents inside. He felt his pulse quicken at the thought of what he might find, if it fit his theory. He almost wanted it to, even if it filled him with terror. But at least he would have some answers, and he had been looking for those for weeks, while she was gone.

Randy's hands shook as he scrolled through Joanne's emails and documents. He was desperate to find some sort of clue that would lead him to whoever had hurt her. He had gone down this road before, but never thought it was actually possible—that what had happened to her, could reach that far back into her former life.

The life she had put behind her years ago.

But as she had spoken to the detective it had struck him. This could very well be connected to her past.

Come on, Joanne. You got to have something in here that I didn't notice before. An email, a direct message, something.

He pressed his lips into a tight line and moved on to the next file, determined to find something that could help him in his search. But the next file, and the one after that, were all empty. He slumped against the wall, feeling despair creep in. As Randy clicked through Joanne's computer, his eyes darted across the screen, scanning for anything that could lead him to the answers he needed. His mind raced with possibilities, each of them more terrifying than the last. He knew he was taking a big risk by going through Joanne's things, but he couldn't shake the feeling that she was trying to tell him something, something important that the police had missed.

Then, he saw it. An email from an unknown sender, with a subject line that sent shivers down his spine. Words that meant nothing for most people, but to him, they meant everything. Randy's heart raced as he clicked on the email, his eyes devouring the words on the screen.

The message was short, but it was enough to confirm Randy's worst fears. It was hidden who it was from, but he knew. This was from someone he thought she had left behind years ago. As he read on, the implications of the message became clearer, and he suddenly understood everything much better.

He also knew what his next step had to be.

And it wasn't going to be pretty.

TWENTY-FIVE

BILLIE ANN

My tires screeched and I jerked the steering wheel as I raced down the empty downtown street. The city was asleep, and there wasn't a single car in sight. My foot pressed the gas pedal flat against the floorboard of my cruiser. I had no clue where the night would take me, but I knew where I had to go. I had called for the K-9 unit and they had been out with the dog, sniffing the area where Danielle was last seen. But the track stopped where she spoke to the person in the car. I had let everyone know. The Chief, Big Tom and Scott, and the entire station was on high alert.

Yet we found nothing. No trace of her anywhere.

Tom and Scott didn't know that I knew Danni well, and I didn't want them to know either. Not now. It was hard for me to keep my emotions at bay and act completely professional.

"Are you okay?" Tom asked as I grabbed a cup of coffee and gulped it down all at once. "You seem a little... different. Almost hectic."

I nodded and threw out my plastic cup in the trash. "Just haven't had a proper night's sleep in a long time."

"Take care of yourself, please," he said and placed a hand on my shoulder. "Don't overwork yourself. You have a family to think of."

"I'll try," I said. "But not making any promises."

I had taken Mike with me back to the station for questioning, and we sat down in the small interrogation room. I cleared my throat then looked at him. I knew Mike had a tendency to be controlling with Danielle. She always made excuses for him, saying he was just insecure, but I had always been a little wary of him and the way he always checked in on her, and always needed to know where she was at all times. They had been doing better lately, she told me. After the trip to Paris things had changed, but I wasn't sure I believed her. I had told Mike I needed him in for an interview, that it was all protocol, and it was, but I had to also make sure he hadn't hurt Danielle.

"Okay, Mike. I know we've already been through this, but for the purposes of the tape, when was the last time you saw Danielle?" I said.

"She... she went for a run around three p.m."

"And you didn't worry about her till five thirty when I came to the house?" I asked, deciding to press him. "After two and a half hours?"

He seemed taken aback. "N-no. I didn't. Sometimes she runs for a long time, like she will do these fifteen K's. She's nuts like that. Wanting to stay in shape." My experience told me he was telling the truth; his concern was palpable, but I continued.

"But Mike, this is two and a half hours. That's a very long jog. Does she usually stay away that long?" I asked, knowing the answer.

"I guess not. I was concerned, but thought that maybe she had run into someone she knew, or maybe stopped at the beach and stayed there for a while, watching the ocean. Something like that."

"I see. And where were you while she was out jogging?" I asked.

He shrugged. "At the house."

"Can anyone confirm that?"

"My kids can," he said. "I was with them. And then when she didn't come back I called my mom and she came over to look after them."

I wrote it down, nodding, trying to calm my rapidly beating heart. I was so worried about Danni, I could barely control myself. My hands were shaking.

"Did she say anything to you before she left on her jog?" I asked.

He shook his head. "No. She just said she was going for a run."

"No kiss? No 'I love you'?"

He shook his head. "No."

"Were you guys fighting?"

He sighed. "Listen, am I a suspect here? 'Cause then I will need my lawyer. I just want you to find my wife. I worry something happened to her."

"So do I. That's why I need to get the real picture of what happened."

He stood up. "Well I don't have time for this. My wife is missing and this is a waste of precious minutes we could be out there searching for her. Either you read me my rights and arrest me or I'm leaving now."

I threw out my hands. "I can't prevent you from that. You're free to go."

"Good," he said and moved toward the door. I stared at his arm and the tattoo sticking out under his T-shirt.

"Can I go now? Or do you want to ask me anything else?"

I shook my head. "You can go."

Then he left. I sat back looking at my notes in my office feeling heavy with worry. The footage from the Ring camera was hazy, but I couldn't find anything else of importance in the images. My eyes burned with exhaustion, my skin itched with nerves, but I couldn't tear my eyes away from it, hoping I might uncover a hidden clue.

I had my mother stay with the kids—I could no longer pretend I could focus on both my family and the cases on my desk, not with Danni missing. It was terrible timing, what with Joe's comments, and it was Thanksgiving break so they didn't have school all week. I had to call Joe and let him know.

"Are you kidding me?" was his reply. "You haven't changed at all, have you? It's still the same with you. I can't believe you."

Then he hung up. I didn't even get to tell him what was going on, that Danni was missing. I stared at the phone as it went dark, surprised at his reaction. He used to care about the victims in my cases and wanted to help them as much as I did.

I shook my head in disbelief. It was so unlike him. But perhaps it had less to do with me and more to do with what I had done. I'd had him arrested when my car was connected to a hit-and-run in the local area. It had been crucial he took the fall at the time, but I knew he was angry at me still. I couldn't deal with him right now. There was too much to do.

"Come on, show me something I can go after, just one single little lead," I mumbled into the darkness of the office. Tom and Scott had both left. Scott had a yoga class that he was teaching at the local studio, and Tom's son had a baseball game. The station was quiet as I sat there with my head in my hands, watching the events from earlier unfold in grainy black and white. It felt like a dream, like it wasn't really happening. I had gone from looking forward to a nice dinner with my favorite person, to sitting alone in a police station, searching for my missing friend. The woman I so dearly loved. It was surreal, but I was determined to find her. There was no one else in our department there, only downstairs, where the officers and night shifts hung out. It was eerily quiet and all I could hear was my heavily beating heart.

"Give me anything," I pleaded.

I watched the clip over and over again. Trying hard to see a license plate or make out the brand of car, but it was hard to see properly. The footage was all in black and white so I couldn't even make out the color of the car. But it seemed to be a light color, like gray or white. I was able to zoom in the footage but the more I did, the grainer it got. Still I tried. Over and over again, trying to get to see the face of the person sitting in the car, the one rolling the window down and calling out for Danni, causing her to stop.

What were they talking about? She seemed familiar with this person, I thought to myself. She didn't hesitate for even a second to go to the car and talk to this person. Not even a little bit.

I leaned back in my chair and rubbed my eyes, feeling the exhaustion setting in. It had been hours since I first arrived at the station, and I was no closer to figuring out what had happened to Danni. The person behind the wheel, driving this car, was wearing a mask, so I couldn't see much there; everything went by pretty fast it was hard to see anything. But I did notice this person looked to have dark hair, maybe black or at least brown. But this person didn't seem very large in stature, or at least not the arm that was visible as the window came down. The small shoulders pointed in a different direction than I had initially thought?

Was it a woman? *Could it be the same people who had taken Joanne?* But why? And how were those two cases connected?

As I continued to examine the footage, I noticed something peculiar about the car too. There was a small sticker on the side of it that I hadn't noticed before. It was too small to make out from the previous zoomed-in footage, but now that I was paying closer attention, I could see it clearly. It was a black and white sticker of a skull with dark eyes. I made a mental note of it, maybe anyone recognized it? Maybe if we asked around in the neighborhood? Ask if they had seen it before? Or maybe even send it out to the media, and ask for them to ask the public for help.

But then again. There could be others with the same sticker. It was probably pretty common.

I sighed and rubbed my exhausted eyes. Staring at the screen and the grainy parts made them tired. But I wasn't going to give up. I couldn't find rest as long as Danni was missing.

Not ever.

I stayed glued to my computer as people began to trickle in to the morning meeting in the conference room. Glances were exchanged with furrowed brows and frowns of empathy as they passed by; they all knew what it was like to fall asleep at their desks.

Scott came up to me, looking annoyingly well rested and tanned. He placed a recyclable to-go box in front of me.

"The Montaux," he said. "I bought you one, when getting mine, thinking you probably had stayed here all night. This should help you feel better. It's vegan, with house made coconut bacon, spinach, and tomato, and I also got you a bowl of fresh fruit for a side."

I stared at the to-go box from Café Surfnista, the local health café where Scott always went for his acai bowl in the morning after doing yoga on the beach or surfing. He had to watch the sunrise every morning in order to begin his day right. He called it doing the dawn patrol.

"You don't have anything stronger?" I groaned and stared at

the food that made me feel nauseated by the very thought of eating. I pushed it away. "And caffeinated?"

Finally, the elevator dinged, and the Chief stepped out. She walked out on her long legs, clad in a dark business suit, and shot everyone a sharp gaze. In her hand, she carried a briefcase, and her steps were purposeful and certain as she strode across the room. When she reached my desk, however, she stopped. Her expression was stony, but it softened slightly as her eyes met mine.

"Any news?" she asked, then tilted her head. She smiled compassionately at me. "Have you been here all night?"

"Yes," I said and looked up at her. My eyes jerked away from the grainy pictures that had filled my vision for what felt like an eternity, and I blinked rapidly as they adjusted to refocus on her standing in front of me. She moved closer, and I could see water glimmer on her forehead, probably from rushing through the parking lot, getting from the car to the entrance as fast as possible in the pouring rain.

The winds had picked up outside, as the tropical storm, which they had now named Oscar, inched closer every day. It was going to be a major hurricane as it came closer, but they expected it to stay out in the Atlantic Ocean. It left us in this humid atmosphere that seeped through everything. Even if they said the storm would stay off the coast, we still never knew for sure. These things had a mind of their own and, sometimes, they took a sudden turn. Since we lived on a barrier island we were in a mandatory evacuation zone, and if it did decide to suddenly turn, it would make it hard for us to get over the bridges in time, and not get stuck in traffic while trying to get away. As cops some of us were told to stay behind and ride the storm out along with the firefighters and paramedics, in case any locals hadn't evacuated and needed help. Everywhere at the station I heard colleagues preparing each other for it. They were having a meeting later with the mayor to prepare an emergency response team.

"I still think she was kidnapped. You don't see it happening in the video, but I think that's what happened."

She looked pensive. "Hmm, do you think they are the same as took Joanne as well? That it is all part of a bigger operation?"

I nodded, rubbing my temples. "It's very possible."

She exhaled. "Maybe because Joanne escaped, they decided to take Danielle instead?"

"I don't know," I said. "It's a little odd, isn't it? It seems to run deeper than that. With the body parts in the suitcases and all that. It seems so calculated, if you ask me."

She cleared her throat and nodded. "Perhaps they couldn't sell our victim—the one in the suitcase. Something went wrong and they needed to dispose of her. Perhaps when they stole the suitcases from Danielle's house they realized they could target her next."

I nodded, but wasn't convinced. "I don't know," I said. "It seemed to me that the bags and suitcases were on display. We were supposed to find them. Besides, I don't really believe in coincidences."

"I heard that about you," she said with a soft smile.

I gave her a look. I hadn't exactly gotten along with her predecessor. He had turned out to be a kidnapper and a murderer and had nearly killed me, so my trust in my superiors was all but gone. I didn't know how seriously she was taking her own theories; they were clearly conjecture. Maybe I didn't even care. I was here to do a job, and if she didn't like the way I did it, then that was her problem. That's how I operated. I got the work done, but I did it in my own way. But I did want to get along with her. I liked her, even if I didn't trust her yet.

"So what is next?" she asked right as my phone rang. It was the medical examiner's office.

"I will pick up this call," I said and showed her the display. "Hopefully they have a lead we can go by."

"I will leave it in your capable hands then," Chief Harold said and left with a smile on her lips.

I watched her go before I picked up the phone. "Dr. Phillips? What do you have for me?"

TWENTY-SIX

Then

TRANSCRIPT OF INTERVIEW OF CAROL DURST

DEFENDANT'S EXHIBIT A

DURST PART 3

APPEARANCES:
Detective Michael Smith
Detective Lenny Travis
Sergeant Joseph Mill

DET. SMITH: State your name and address for the record, please.
CAROL DURST: I... um... it's Carol Durst. I live at 246 Pinehurst Avenue, Melbourne, Florida.
DET. SMITH: (*clears his throat*) All right Mrs. Durst
CAROL DURST: You can call me Carol.
DET. SMITH: All right, um, Carol, do you know why you're here today?

CAROL DURST: (*sniffles*) Well because of what happened to
my husband. Last night.

DET. SMITH: And what happened to him?

CAROL DURST: He was shot.

DET. SMITH: And where did this take place?

CAROL DURST: In our home. On Pinehurst.

DET. SMITH: All right, thank you.

CAROL DURST: You're welcome.

DET. SMITH: (*clears throat*) Okay let's return to the events on
Thursday, November twenty-sixth, Thanksgiving Day. What
can you tell me about what happened to your husband?

CAROL DURST: (*sniffles*) I-I didn't see it myself. I was downstairs when I heard the gun go off. I ran up to the bedroom and
saw him on the bed, a bloody wound on his forehead. It was a
terrible sight.

DET. SMITH: That must have been awful. Now, who was
holding the gun?

CAROL DURST: I don't know. It was on the floor, on the
carpet.

DET. SMITH: So no one was holding it? But who was in there?

CAROL DURST: Both of my children. Josephine and Robert.

DET. SMITH: You don't seem upset over this?

CAROL DURST: Oh but I am, Detective. It was the worst
sight of my life. I loved my husband dearly and my children as
well. I can't... I can't explain to you what a sight like that will do
to you.

DET. SMITH: Did it make you feel sick?

CAROL DURST: Yes. Of course.

DET. SMITH: And you didn't see who pulled the trigger?

CAROL DURST: I just told you I didn't.

DET. SMITH: Yes, you did. How did the children get ahold of
the gun? Whose gun was it?

CAROL DURST: (*breathes heavily*) It was George's own gun. I
never wanted that thing in the house, but he insisted that it was

for our protection. I worried about having a firearm around my children. You hear all these stories you know? Of two year olds getting ahold of them and then shooting their mother or themselves or a sibling. But he assured me it was safe.

DET. SMITH: Where did he keep it?

CAROL DURST: In a safe in our bedroom.

DET. SMITH: Did the children know how to get into that safe?

CAROL DURST: I didn't think so. But they must have seen him do it, or figure it out somehow. Children can be sneaky like that, you know?

DET. SMITH: I don't know a lot of sneaky children, if I am being honest with you, Carol.

CAROL DURST: Well my children can be very sneaky and devious once they put their minds to it.

DET. SMITH: So you're saying they planned to shoot their stepdad?

CAROL DURST: (sighs) I don't know what to think anymore.

DET. SMITH: Would your children be capable of planning something like that?

CAROL DURST: I don't know. Maybe?

TWENTY-SEVEN

BILLIE ANN

I walked slowly down the long, white hallway of the medical examiner's office. My footsteps echoed in the otherwise silent corridor, clanging against the walls like a funeral bell. Every step seemed to take forever as I inched closer and closer to the foreboding office of Dr. Phillips.

Finally, I reached the door. Taking a deep breath, I pushed it open and walked in. The room was sterile, containing only a couple of chairs and a long metal table. The only sound in the room was the faint hum of the air conditioner. As I looked around, my eyes finally came to rest on the face of Dr. Phillips. He was an older man, with a tired, lined face that seemed to have seen too much. His eyes were deep and unfathomable, revealing little of what he was thinking.

"Detective Wilde," he said quietly, his voice barely a whisper. "Always good to see you."

"Likewise, Dr. Phillips," I said.

I meant it, because I always enjoyed his company and I admired his passion for his work, the way he always catered so intensely to details, which was essential in our line of work. But of course, I wasn't happy about the circumstances in which I usually met him.

He gently guided me toward a long table, which was covered with bloody fragments of what used to be a human being. The floor was slick with fluid and strewn with bits of flesh, clothing, and organs. Fractured bones and torn skin were carefully arranged in an effort to bring the woman back together again. The pieces had been arranged in a human shape, though not quite symmetrical. It was obvious that it had taken hours of painstaking work for someone to assemble such a macabre display.

"There she is. Our mystery woman." Dr. Phillips sighed. He had a solemn expression, and he didn't speak for a long time. Dr. Phillips' gaze was heavy as he slowly walked around the remains of the skull. He paused in front of the face, his expression solemn as he took a deep breath before speaking. The woman's features were unrecognizable, and there were still fragments of bone scattered around her like a broken puzzle. He pointed a trembling finger at it and shook his head slowly in disbelief.

"We found the cause of death to be a gunshot wound to the head," he said quietly. "See right here in the skull is where the bullet went through."

"So she was shot before she was... separated?"

"Yes," he said. "By a nine-millimeter. Shot and then dismembered into sixteen pieces."

I nervously cleared my throat and avoided looking at the doctor. I held my breath, hoping for a miracle for Danni, as I nervously bit my lip and forced out the words, "And do we have all parts of her or might there be more out there?" My stomach turned as I spoke the words.

"We have them all. I found most of the bones and were able to put them together. "

"How was she dismembered? With a tool?"

He nodded. I cringed as I watched Dr. Phillips carefully inspect the dismembered bones. He stepped closer, pointing to the disjointed pieces of bone scattered across the table like broken china. Dizziness swelled in my head as I realized the precision required for such an act. How Dr. Phillips was able to do this day after day with such masterful skill was something I couldn't comprehend.

"A chainsaw," he said. "The bones were cut into smaller pieces, as you can see here."

He showed me it, and I nodded, feeling lightheaded. I could see the marks from the chainsaw etched into them, and my stomach churned. He seemed to be completely unfazed by the task before him, and I felt admiration for his dedication. How Dr. Phillips did his job every day, was beyond me. But I was glad that someone had that passion. So I didn't have to.

The room began to spin as visions of Danni flashed before me—her name echoing in my mind like a funeral march. In my mind's eye, I could see Danni in danger, hear her cries for help as she faced whatever fate this evidence foreshadowed for her if I didn't locate her soon. And I could hear the sound of a chainsaw in the back of my head. Would this happen to her if I didn't find her soon?

"How long has she been dead?" I asked.

"A few months," he said as he peered through the magnifying glass at the body pieces lying on the gurney. "Her skin is severely decomposed, but I have a feeling she's been kept somewhere cool, to slow down the decomposition. There isn't the usual amount of insect activity or pungent odor that you expect with normal decomposition. I can't say precisely how long she's been here, but my guess is no more than three, maybe four months."

I swallowed hard. "When you say somewhere cool, do you mean in a freezer?"

"Yes, that would be a good place to suggest." He paused.

Why had no one reported this person missing? "But we were able to get a positive ID from the DNA," he continued. My eyes lit up. "She was already in the system when they ran it," he said.

"That's amazing. Who is she?"

"Her name is Carol Durst. She's a sixty-eight-year-old woman from Melbourne, Florida."

TWENTY-EIGHT

BILLIE ANN

The wind hit my face as I walked out of the car. It felt as if the air was thick and heavy and full of moisture. Jagged bolts of lightning split the black sky as I made my way to Danni's childhood home. After a forty-five-minute drive south, the sky had turned into a stormy gray.

I looked at the pastel-colored house and exhaled, remembering the countless stories Danni used to tell me about this place. All the long afternoons Danni spent playing hide-and-seek in the backyard, and the lazy Sundays when her mom would whip up breakfast burritos with chorizo, potatoes, cheese, salsa, and scrambled eggs.

I could almost hear her laughter from that time, and it filled my heart with both joy and sorrow. I had called ahead and told them I would stop by. I was praying that they could provide me with something—anything—useful that could bring me closer to finding Danni. I was desperate for answers.

I got out of the car and walked up the steps, feeling a strange mix of anticipation and dread. Danni's mom answered the door, her face a portrait of worry. Her sister was right behind her, her eyes red from tears that had been recently shed.

"Come on in," her mom said. "We can sit in the living room."

I walked in and sat down on the couch, where her mom had put out coffee and cups. I looked around me and imagined seeing Danni there running around as a child. Silence filled the room as I took in the pictures of her hanging on the wall. I could see that same sparkle in her eyes, that same mischievous grin. I felt a lump in my throat as I tried to swallow past the sudden sadness that washed over me.

"Thank you for coming to see us," her mother said. "Can I offer you a cup of coffee?"

"Yes please," I said, and she poured me a cup. She signaled for sugar or milk, and I refused. "Black is fine."

I sipped it, and I studied her sister's face. She had Danni's same bright green eyes, the ones I used to look forward to seeing every day, but without the sparkle that made Danni so captivating. Her features were softer than Danni's: more delicate and subdued. I felt a pang of sorrow at the sight of those familiar eyes without their owner.

I slid a small, hardback-covered notepad out of my pocket and opened to the first blank page. I exhaled a shaky breath before looking up at the family. Her mother, sitting on the edge of her seat, stared expectantly at me. Her mother's eyes brimmed with hope as she asked, "Do you have any news you can share with us?"

I shook my head solemnly and met her gaze, feeling guilty for not having any news to tell them. I really wanted to. I really really did.

"I'm afraid not. But believe me I am working on it."

She reached out and touched my wrist. "We're so happy that you're on the case. She's always spoken so highly of you, dear. I know you two are close."

I smiled, thinking that I wouldn't be if anyone knew of my relationship to Danni. I had met her mother once before at her house for Thanksgiving dinner, while her sister had been with her husband's family, so I had never met her before. She lived in North Carolina, but had come down when hearing of Danni's disappearance.

"Do you know of anyone who may have wanted to hurt her?" I asked, my voice trembling slightly as I spoke. Danni's mother and sister exchanged a look and shook their heads sadly.

"No," her mother said, her voice quiet and sad. "Danni is always so full of life, and she always has others' best interests at heart. It's unfathomable to us that anyone would want to harm her. She trusts people, maybe too much sometimes, but she is a good person. You know how she is."

I did. I knew her exactly like that. Always thinking of others before herself. And funny. She and I would always laugh till our stomachs hurt. The memory made me smile.

"And her marriage? How will you describe it?" I asked.

The room went silent as her sister spoke, her voice low and filled with sadness. Her mouth moved silently for a few heartbeats before words slipped out in a rush. "Mike cheated on her," she said, her eyes downcast. Her words were heavy in the air—a weight that no one dared to fight.

"It was only that one time," her mother interrupted with a pained expression. Her voice was firm but gentle. She shifted in the armchair, clasping her hands together tightly. "It happened so long ago. They worked through it. She forgave him, and he promised it would never happen again. I don't believe he would have anything to do with her disappearance. He loves her too much. I can see how much he regrets that night."

I slowly nodded as I scribbled down the words in my notebook, recalling the stories they shared about their romantic getaway to Paris, which had reignited their love for each other.

Much to my regret. I mean, of course I was happy for them, and for her, if that was really what she wanted. If that's what made her happy. I just wasn't sure it was. Maybe I was just being selfish because I wanted her to myself.

"It's not easy with children, you must understand," her mother argued. "And especially twins. It can really take a toll on a marriage. You don't have any children, Lily, so you wouldn't know, but Billie Ann here knows. Right, Billie Ann?"

I exhaled and nodded, seeing how her sister felt embarrassed by her mother's comment about not having children. She was in her mid-thirties, and Danni had spoken to me about how her mother always was on her case about starting a family, before it was too late. But Danni wasn't sure that Lily even wanted them. She had a great career and enjoyed life the way it was, she always said.

"Yes that is definitely true. It can be very hard at times. I'm going through a divorce myself now," I said and sipped the coffee.

"Oh dear, sweetheart. I'm sorry to hear that," her mother said and placed a hand on my arm. "That's awful. Don't you think you can make things work perhaps? If you try again? No one seems to want to fight for their marriage anymore, do they? It's a shame. Such a waste. I really do hope that it works out for Danni. I mean when she comes home and all." She paused and I could see the worry in her eyes that she might not see her daughter again. "Life hasn't been easy on our poor Danni."

"What's that mean?" I asked.

"Well she lost her father, when she was just very young. When she was fourteen years old, I believe it was."

"I lost him too," Lily said, her voice complaining. "He was my dad too."

"Of course he was," the mother said. "But you were so young. You barely remember him. Danni was a daddy's girl. She was always clinging on to him and followed him everywhere he went. She was very upset when he and I divorced and she had to live with just me, but that's how it had to be."

"I was upset too," Lily said.

"Nonsense, you weren't old enough to dry your own behind by the time that happened," she said. She looked at me and smiled. "It was so many years ago. But Danni took it hard, especially when he died. She never really got over losing him."

Lily's eyes widened at the thought of it and she shook her head. "No, it's true. I wasn't that old. But Danni..." She trailed off for a moment before continuing. "Danni felt like a part of her had died along with him. She never really recovered."

I held both their hands and squeezed them tightly, looking into their kind faces until I felt my sorrow dissolve into strength.

I lingered as I said goodbye and thanked them for their time. I embraced them each in turn, noting how small I felt next to them. They were putting all their faith in me and my ability to bring back their sister, and daughter. It felt like a lot.

After releasing each other, I drove back toward home. The sadness that had clung to me as I arrived still lingered, but I felt more motivated than ever.

I stopped at Carol Durst's home on Pinehurst Avenue in north Melbourne on my way back. I knew the forensic teams were coming soon, and I wanted to meet them here and see the scene for myself, before they did. I put on latex gloves and plastic covers on my sneakers, so I wouldn't contaminate anything.

I stepped onto the small wooden porch of the bungalow. It looked almost untouched. An unnatural silence hung in the air as I closed my eyes and exhaled slowly before continuing.

The neighborhood felt one part abandoned, one part forgotten. I rang the doorbell and waited, we hadn't yet determined if anyone lived in the house, but no one answered, which made things a little easier.

I tried the door and, to my surprise, it opened without a sound. I stepped inside, letting my eyes adjust to the darkness. I couldn't help but feel a sense of unease as I wandered through the silent rooms. Everything felt still, like the whole house was holding its breath. I felt like an intruder, a trespasser in a sacred space.

The house was a time capsule, a snapshot of the victim's last moment frozen in time. Cold coffee cups sat atop the dining room table beside plates of half-eaten toast with mold growing around the edges. The remote control for the television lay abandoned on the armrest of a well-worn armchair in the living room. The seat cushions still showed the depression where she had been sitting before she vanished, but now they were covered in an inch-thick layer of dust. The scene was eerie and made my skin crawl. I took a deep breath. In the bedroom, I found a half-packed suitcase on the bed and a note on the pillow. It was clear that the victim had been planning to leave before her life was tragically cut short. The note simply read: "I'M SORRY."

Blood on the carpet and splatters on the wall behind told me this is where she was shot, and I had to step carefully to not ruin important evidence. The Chief's theory that Carol had been taken by the same people who had Joanne, that they'd failed to sell her and killed her to tie up the loose end couldn't be right.

I took out my phone and started to take pictures of the bloodstains on the carpet. Who could have done this to her? And why? She was trying to leave? Did she know someone was coming for her? What was she sorry about?

I made my way to the wall, stopping to examine the bullet hole. It was a clean shot, straight through the victim's head. Whoever did this had fired a gun before.

As I turned to leave the room, something caught my eye. A glint of metal on the floor. I bent down to pick it up and found a small, silver bullet casing. I put on a latex glove, before I carefully placed the casing in an evidence bag and continued my search of the house, but found nothing else. Maybe the techs would, once they got here. Hopefully they would.

As I made my way back through the house, I couldn't shake the feeling that someone was watching me. I slowed down and looked around. I walked quietly past the open doorways, glancing behind me, trying to avoid every creak in the floor. I quickly walked through the living room, the sense of being watched growing stronger with each step. I crept down the hallway, passing closed doors and peering into each room.

Just as I was about to step out of the front door, I heard the sound of a sharp crunch and scrape of gravel behind me. Instinctively, I swiveled around and reached for my gun, but it was too late. A dark figure lunged from the shadows, tackling me to the ground. Pain shot through my skull when my back slammed against the doorframe. My vision blurred as I fought to breathe. White spots swam in front of my eyes as I stumbled to stand up, but it was too difficult. I fought hard to free myself from their grasp, but they held on tight, pinning me to the ground.

I fought again to break free from my attacker's grip, but their strength was more than a match for mine. My head throbbed in pain from the impact of falling. I fought back as hard as I could despite the pain radiating from a cut on my head. But it was no use. I didn't have the strength. The panic that had seized me moments before suddenly shifted to exhaustion as I felt myself slipping into unconsciousness. My body felt heavy and my mind was growing foggy. The last thing I remember seeing was a black bird tattoo that glowered at me from my assailant's right shoulder. Poking its wings out from beneath the white T-shirt.

TWENTY-NINE

BILLIE ANN

I slowly woke up, feeling disoriented. My head throbbed and my eyes were heavy as I adjusted to the bright light hitting my face. It took me a few seconds to realize I wasn't at home in bed. I was lying on the floor, still in the victim's house. The place was being invaded by forensic techs all dressed in blue body suits. They were carrying in big lamps, and plugging them in, to light up the entire room. Big Tom was kneeling in front of me.

"What happened?" I asked groggily, my head still spinning.

Big Tom frowned, his brow deeply furrowed with concern. He watched me closely as I tried to recall what had happened. I could feel the pain in the back of my head like someone had clobbered me, but I still had no idea why I was here. With a deep sigh, I met Big Tom's gaze and asked again: "What happened?"

He sighed heavily, his brow furrowed with worry. "You don't remember?"

I tried to focus, but my mind was muddled. The last thing that felt clear was a sharp pain in the back of my head.

"No, not at all. What happened?"

His expression only grew more concerned. He gave me a

sad look. "I thought you could tell me. Looks like you hurt your head pretty bad. Can't you remember anything?"

"Not really."

Big Tom's face was grim as he crouched beside me, his calloused hand resting on my shoulder. "Looks like you were knocked out," he said softly. "We found you lying here when we arrived."

I tried to swallow down the fear that was rising in my throat. I desperately wanted Big Tom to have a name, a face for the person who had done this to me. "Did you catch the guy?" I asked, praying that the answer would be yes. He shook his head slowly and looked away, and I felt like my heart had sunk through the floor. All around me, his entourage of burly men stood still, nobody speaking a word.

Big Tom's expression darkened. "Whoever attacked you was gone when we got here."

I nodded, my mind whirling with questions. As I struggled to sit up, I felt a sharp pain in the back of my head and groaned. Big Tom put a hand on my shoulder to steady me.

"Take it easy," he said. "We need to get you to the hospital."

The thought of going to a hospital filled me with dread. I didn't have time for that. I had to find Danni, no matter the cost.

He must have seen the fear in my face because he said, "We'll go somewhere quiet. You'll feel better once you've had a chance to rest."

He helped me to my feet, and I swayed, unsteady on my legs. I was going to be sick.

A memory slowly began to surface. I remembered the sound of footsteps, followed by an intense pain as something collided with my head. An image flashed in my mind—of a large eagle tattoo.

"Someone attacked me," I said, my voice tight with fear. "I saw a tattoo, before I passed out, it was lit up by the streetlight outside, maybe it was a lightning strike, but there was a ray of light coming through the window and hitting the tattoo just before I passed out."

"Are you sure?" Big Tom asked, his expression serious.

I nodded, still dazed and confused. "Certain," I replied. "I remembered the tattoo on the man's right shoulder. It was definitely an eagle. It must be the same man as we saw in the surveillance footage from the motel. I'm positive it's the same."

Big Tom's face twisted with anger. "We'll find the bastard who did this to you. If we have to look at every tattoo in this town."

I nodded, grateful for his support. But I knew that finding the attacker would be difficult. There were probably hundreds of men around here with an eagle tattoo in this area alone. I needed to gather more information, and fast. I couldn't stop thinking of Carol Durst and what happened to her. I feared that the more time passed, the bigger the chances were that Danni would end up the same way. In a suitcase. The very thought filled me with fear and adrenaline.

"I need to find Danni," I said, breathing rapidly.

Big Tom sighed. "I know, but you need to rest first. I'll take you home. Once you're feeling better, we'll continue the search."

I reluctantly agreed, knowing that I wouldn't be much use in my current state.

THIRTY

Then

TRANSCRIPT OF INTERVIEW OF CAROL DURST
DEFENDANT'S EXHIBIT A
DURST PART 3

APPEARANCES:
Detective Michael Smith
Detective Lenny Travis
Sergeant Joseph Mill

DET. SMITH: (*sighs*) Listen, Carol. I have to be honest with you and tell you I think it all sounds a little... out there.
CAROL DURST: What do you mean?
DET. SMITH: (*clears throat*) Well, you're seriously telling me that you want me to believe that your children, who are what, thirteen and ten years old, that they planned to shoot their step-dad, and carried it out last night, on Thanksgiving.
CAROL DURST: I-I guess so. I know it sounds a little strange, but I don't know how else to explain it.

DET. SMITH: Well one idea could be that you shot him, and now you want the children to take the blame for it since they are minors and won't get the chair, but will just have to spend their childhood in prison, most likely.

CAROL DURST: No, no. I would never do that.

DET. SMITH: So you didn't tell them to not tell us who shot George?

CAROL DURST: N-no. I would never.

DET. SMITH: What if I tell you that I don't believe you?

CAROL DURST: But-but it's the truth. I came up there and they had shot him. They wouldn't tell me who did it.

DET. SMITH: Okay let's say I go with it. Why did they kill him?

CAROL DURST: Why? I... they didn't like him.

DET. SMITH: So they shot him? Why not just run away from home or go live with their dad? Like most children do.

CAROL DURST: Their dad died years ago.

DET. SMITH: Oh really? How did he die?

CAROL DURST: (*clears throat*) He shot himself.

DET. SMITH: He shot himself? Ah I see. And it wasn't the children who shot him? Or maybe you?

CAROL DURST: No. He shot himself in his office. The children were young. They barely remember.

DET. SMITH: (*clicks his tongue*) Let's circle back to the why. What reason could they have for wanting their stepdad dead?

CAROL DURST: I-I don't know.

DET. SMITH: But I think you do. You just don't want to say it because it might make you look like a bad mom, or even worse might give you a motive for wanting him dead too. Isn't that the truth?

CAROL DURST: What are you saying?

DET. SMITH: Didn't George molest Robert? Didn't he touch him on the couch that night? Before he was shot?

CAROL DURST: I... what on earth are you talking about?

DET. SMITH: He had his hand in his pants, didn't he? He was touching him. Underneath the blanket, while you were watching *Finding Nemo*.

CAROL DURST: He promised it would never happen again, or I swear I would have kicked him out.

DET. SMITH: So it happened before?

CAROL DURST: Y-yes.

DET. SMITH: How and where?

CAROL DURST: I caught him. Coming out of his bedroom at night. I woke up and couldn't find him, so I went into the hallway, and the door wasn't closed properly.

DET. SMITH: The door to Robert's room?

CAROL DURST: Yes. It was left a little open, and that's when I saw it. Through the crack. It paralyzed me completely. When George came out of the room, I started yelling at him, and that's when he broke down and cried. He promised me it would never happen again.

DET. SMITH: But it did.

CAROL DURST: Yes.

DET. SMITH: More than once more?

CAROL DURST: Yes.

DET. SMITH: How many times?

CAROL DURST: (*sobs*) I don't know.

DET. SMITH: No, because you closed your eyes, didn't you? You decided to pretend like you didn't know anything. You decided your relationship was worth more than what was happening to your poor little boy. Am I not right?

CAROL DURST: (*cries loudly*) Yes. I'm sorry. I never meant for it to go this far. I kept praying that it would stop. But it didn't. I'm so so sorry!

THIRTY-ONE

BILLIE ANN

I awoke with a start, my heart pounding as if it would break through my chest. Instinctively I reached for my phone, feeling the dread as reality set in—I had been asleep since Big Tom had brought me home the night before; I'd briefed him on everything I'd found at the scene, and he'd insisted I rest. Danni had been in my dream, and I thought I had found her, but now I remembered that she was still missing. I quickly scrambled out of bed as I heard the sound of my children downstairs.

I had been away from home for what felt like an eternity. My body still sore, and my head aching from the attack, I quickly threw on my clothes and rushed downstairs, determined to make amends for my absence.

The kitchen was bright and cheerful. My oldest, Charlene, was standing at the counter, measuring out coffee grounds for the morning. She smiled when seeing me.

"I'm making you coffee," she said.

I stared at her wondering if I was still sleeping. My sixteen-year-old daughter usually didn't do something like this out of sheer will to be nice. Something was up.

"Thank you," I said as she handed me a cup. I narrowed my eyes. "Do you need money or something?"

She shook her head lightly. "No, nothing."

"Ha. Good one. What is it?"

She rolled her eyes. "Okay. Me and my friends were talking about driving down to Miami for the rest of Thanksgiving break. Leaving tomorrow."

"No. Absolutely not. You have to be kidding me."

"Well why not?" she whined.

"First of all, it's Miami."

"So?"

"Way too dangerous a place to go for a bunch of teenage girls."

"Mom, you're overreacting. Brenna has an uncle down there that we can stay with. We're basically visiting family." She chirped like that settled it. But not for me.

"No. No, and no."

"Ah but why not?"

"You're not going to Miami all by yourself, young lady. It's a three-hour drive, and too dangerous."

"That's not fair. You're never here, and I take care of my siblings all the time these days. I do that for you. You could at least do something for me."

I shook my head with a chuckle. "Don't try and guilt-trip me, Charlene. I don't do guilt."

She growled. "Can we at least go to Orlando then?"

I thought it over for a minute, then caved in a weak moment. "Okay you can go to Orlando. It's only an hour away. That's doable."

Her face lit up. "And spend the night?"

I exhaled. "Yes, you may. But I need the address of the place you're staying at, and I need you to check in with me every day. And you're not going till Friday. Thursday is Thanksgiving and we're having dinner here. Together. Your father is coming. I have promised that we will celebrate it all together this year, maybe for the last time. For you and your brother's sake. So you better be here."

She smiled and sipped her own coffee, with a shrug. "Okay."

Then she swirled around and left. I sat behind feeling like I had just been taken advantage of. Did she just ask me about Miami so I would say yes to Orlando, and that was the plan all along? I chuckled and shook my head. Of course, she did. Sneaky little thing. I guess I had to let her go now.

I had finished my cup when Joe appeared. He walked straight in through the front door, even if I had told him numerous times that he needed to text me first so I knew he was coming, or at least have the decency to knock. What if I was naked? What if I was with someone? Apparently he didn't care. He had that look on his face, and I knew he was angry.

"Oh you're here. For once. How nice of you to stop by your own home and check on your children," he said.

I rolled my eyes and stood up, bracing myself for another argument.

"Joe, let's not do this," I said calmly, trying to defuse the situation before it escalated. But it was too late for that. He was already on a roll.

"I mean, seriously, how long has it been? I'm starting to think you don't even care about them anymore," he spat out, his face turning red with anger.

I took a deep breath and counted to ten in my head. I had heard this all before. "You know that's not true, Joe. I'm doing the best I can," I replied, trying to keep my voice even.

"The best you can? Is that what you call it? Leaving them alone for the entire day while you go off and do God knows what? They need a mother, not just some absentee parent," he sneered, his words cutting like a knife.

"That's not fair, Joe. You know I'm working. Besides my

mom has been here. They're fine. They're on break now and barely notice that I'm not here."

"Oh they notice, because they tell me. When I call and ask, they tell me you're not home, again, and that they don't know where you are."

I sighed. "Again, Joe. I have been working."

"Oh so that makes it okay, I guess. You're the one ruining their family; the least you can do is to be there for them."

I exhaled, tired. I was sick of having to listen to the blame being put on me again and again. Yes, it was me who wanted the separation; yes I was the one who found out she was gay. Could we move past that soon, please? How long was he going to throw that in my face?

Till he felt like I had suffered as much as he did, probably.

"Listen, Joe. Danni is missing. That's why I have been a little crazy here."

He paused. "Danni?"

"Yes. She was kidnapped. I saw it on a surveillance camera. So now you understand why I am working extra hard?"

His expression changed. "Yes, yes of course. What does Mike say?"

"He's worried, of course."

Joe made a grimace.

"What's that face about?" I asked.

"Well it's just... How long has she been gone? I saw him last night, down at Coconuts on the Beach, and he was with some woman. I just figured that maybe they had split up. He didn't seem very sad if you ask me. He was drinking heavily, sitting in the tiki bar, yelling out loudly, putting his arm around this woman."

I frowned. "Really?"

"Yeah, really. I mean, I could be wrong... but he didn't seem too upset."

I felt a pang of unease, but tried to push it aside. "Well,

maybe he's just trying to cope. People react differently in situations like these."

"Yeah, maybe," he said dismissively. "Anyway, I just came by to drop off some paperwork for the divorce. I need you to look through it."

I groaned inwardly. The last thing I wanted to deal with was more legal drama. "Can't we just do this later, Joe?"

"No, we need to get this settled. Get the process started. You're the one who wanted this, remember?"

I sighed and took the papers from him, scanning them quickly. "Fine. I'll look through them."

"Good," he said, turning to leave. "And maybe you should think about being a bit more present for your kids. They need you more than ever right now. It's always the children that gets hurt in a divorce. Remember that."

I watched him go, feeling a mix of anger and frustration. Yes, maybe he was right. Maybe I did need to be a bit more present, but it wasn't as if I wasn't trying. I had a lot on my plate right now with Danni missing and all the legal drama that came with the divorce. I couldn't just drop everything to be there for my kids all the time. I was doing the best I could, and that was all I could do.

I sat back down, the paperwork still in my hand, and tried to focus on it. But my mind kept drifting to Danni and Mike and the woman Joe had seen him with. Was he really cheating on Danni? Again? And if he was, did that mean he had something to do with her disappearance? The more I thought about it, the more my worries grew.

I resolved to call Mike later and see what he had to say about it. But for now, I needed to focus on the paperwork. I took a deep breath and started reading, hoping to get it over with fast. I stared at the first page. This was Joe's suggestion for a settlement. I turned another page, then paused.

"You've got to be kidding me, Joe. You've got to be freaking kidding me." Then I grabbed the papers, and threw them all in the trash, muttering under my breath. "Over my dead body."

THIRTY-TWO

BILLIE ANN

I strode into the police station, my shoes clicking over the scuffed tile floor. The fluorescent lights hummed, and in a nearby corner, Scott and Big Tom sat huddled over their computer screens. "I need everything we have on our victim Carol Durst," I announced to them, both of whom were hunched at their desks, peering at computer screens. They lifted their eyes from the glowing monitors to look at me.

"Good morning to you too, boss," Big Tom said. "How are you feeling today? Is your head okay?"

"There is absolutely nothing wrong with my head," I said and sat down at my desk.

"That's good to hear," he said.

I crossed my arms and shifted my weight impatiently while I waited for him to speak again. His hazel eyes were framed with a charming smirk, but today his usual charms wouldn't work on me—I wasn't in the mood for it.

"Well, then, what have you got?"

"Okay so Carol Durst, sixty-eight, lived in Melbourne on Pinehurst Avenue."

"I know all this," I said. "I was there. What else?"

"I'm getting to it," he said. "She was a retired water treatment plant manager. She leaves behind two grown children, Josephine and Robert Durst."

"Why do I know those names?" I asked, feeling my eyebrows furrow together as though searching for an answer. "They sound familiar."

He nodded. "Thirty years ago, they were both convicted of killing their stepdad, George Andersson. It made national headlines, because they were the youngest in American history to have been tried as adults and be sent to adult prison for murder."

"That's right," I said snapping my fingers, remembering the case. It had been covered in all the news outlets. "How long did they get?"

"They both got fifteen years," he said.

"So they have been out for quite some time."

"Yes, actually, another fifteen years."

"So if they somehow wanted to get rid of their mother as well, they would probably have done it earlier. I mean why now?"

He nodded. "You make a valid point, boss."

"They're still interesting, though," I said. "So make sure to find out more about them and track them down, so we can have a chat with them."

He nodded again. "Of course. Working on it as we speak."

"What else have we got? Anything on the Joanne Edwards kidnapping?"

"We had a drawing made that we are going to send out to the media today," Big Tom said. "Of the two kidnappers, the way she described them."

"Can I see?"

"Sure," he said.

I walked up behind him and looked over his shoulder as he opened the drawing. It was of two Hispanic-looking people, a man and a woman. Both had long hair, and the woman was wearing the hoop earrings that Joanne had told me about. Both were wearing masks in the drawing. Joanne hadn't mentioned any tattoo, but couldn't say if any of her kidnappers had one or not, so I wanted there to be a separate drawing of that as well going out to the public once more, and Tom had made sure of it.

"That looks good," I said. "Let's get it out there and ask the public for help."

"You know it's gonna blow up our phones, right?" Scott said. "They're pretty generic."

"I know, but it's better than nothing, and remember time is of the essence here. Danielle Simmons' life might depend on it."

"Right," he said. "I will be by the phone the next couple of days in case you need me. Talking to every racist in town who has seen a suspicious-looking Hispanic couple. Fun."

"Where are we on the guy with the eagle tattoo?" I asked, ignoring his remark. "We've already had this one out in the public. Did we get any hits?"

Big Tom looked at the stack of notes next to him. "Got a lot of heat on that one, boss. Lots of people out there with an eagle on their shoulder. I will run through them today and get back to you if anyone seems interesting."

"Perfect," I said. "I want us to look at Danielle Simmons' husband as well. He's been seen downtown getting drunk with an unidentified woman. Not the behavior you'd expect from a man grieving his wife's disappearance."

"Sure thing, boss," Scott said. "I already sent you background checks and info on him. It's in your inbox."

I sat down at my computer and opened my emails, but it was hard to concentrate. My thoughts were constantly straying to Danni, and I had a knot of worry deep in my stomach. I clicked open one of the emails but couldn't focus on the words as my mind kept returning to her.

I closed my laptop and got up from the chair, pacing around

the room in an attempt to contain my agitation. Nothing felt real and my skin felt heavy, like I was wearing a costume made of lead. I couldn't shake the feeling that, if I stayed still long enough, I'd find out this was all just a dream and my life would be restored to normal. Danni would call or stop by and I would be able to hug her again.

I didn't know what to do or how to get through this. All I could do was try my best to cope. But then again, I couldn't just sit there and wait for a miracle. It wasn't my style. I had to make it happen myself.

I decided to pay Joanne Edwards another visit. She had seen these kidnappers. She had to know more than she was telling us. The way I saw it, she was the key to finding Danni.

THIRTY-THREE

RANDY

Randy sat at his desk, his hands trembling with nerves as he typed out the email. He kept rereading it, debating whether the urgency he felt would be conveyed in the words he had chosen. His mind was caught somewhere between anxiousness and anger.

Randy took a deep breath and pressed send, feeling a sense of relief wash over him like a cold shower. He leaned back in his chair and closed his eyes, letting out a long exhale. This was it, he thought.

But as he sat there in the silence of his office, Randy's mind began to wander. He thought about the past, about all the things he hadn't wanted to think about for so long. He felt himself clench his fists.

He took a deep breath and tried to calm down, reminding himself that he needed to keep his composure. But as he read the email again, he could feel his blood starting to boil.

He waited. He felt like the seconds were dragging on forever. Then, the notification came back: the person had replied.

Randy opened it.

No. We can't meet. It's too dangerous.

Anger surged through him. He began typing again, his hands shaking even more with each keystroke. He couldn't believe the audacity of this person. He gritted his teeth and hit send on the scathing response he had just written.

We have to. It's important.

He hit the send button and waited again, his heart pounding in his chest. He leaned back in his chair, closing his eyes once again. He took a few deep breaths to keep the furor at bay. He kept breathing, trying to collect himself. He knew he couldn't lose his cool now.

The waiting was unbearable. He knew they had probably seen the email by now, but were they considering it?

The reply finally came.

I can't keep doing this with you. Please stop.

Randy continued. He began typing with purpose now, his fingers flying across the keyboard as the words poured out of him.

I need to see you. Face-to-face. It's very important.

He hit send, not caring anymore about the consequences.

The seconds ticked by, and Randy felt like he was holding his breath, waiting for a response.

It took a while before the reply finally came:

Okay. Let's meet at the Pig and Whistle, tonight.

A wave of relief washed over Randy as he settled into the

realization that he had finally made it. He pushed away from his desk, standing on unsteady legs that shook with a mix of excitement and dread. He regarded himself in the mirror mounted on the wall, noting the anxious sheen on his forehead and drawn cheeks, and the tremble of his lips and hands. Taking a deep breath through gritted teeth, he steeled himself for what was to come. He checked himself in the mirror one last time, then wiped his sweaty hands on his jeans and took a deep breath before leaving the room.

THIRTY-FOUR

BILLIE ANN

As I entered her hospital room, I found Joanne asleep. I sat down and waited for her to wake up. I stared at her, wondering what her and Danni could have in common. Why did the kidnappers choose these women out of anyone around here? Was it the long hair? Joanne had said they cut her hair, so it couldn't be that important? But maybe they were looking for a certain type? If it was trafficking, then maybe they knew that whoever they were selling them to searched for a particular look? Was it that simple? But how was it connected to Carol Durst? The woman they had murdered? She was older and had short red hair? She was completely different than they were. Danni and Joanne were both in their early forties. Carol was in her late sixties. Maybe they were chosen based on their person-alities? I had heard that argument before when working on similar cases. They needed them to be easy to break. To be vulnerable.

I still hadn't learned how Joanne managed to escape, and I needed to hear that. I was hoping she could remember more details.

Though I was sure I had not made a sound, she seemed to

know I was there, and as soon as she opened her eyes they fell upon me. She sat up in the bed, with her hands clenched on top of the covers. Her eyes shone with anticipation as she glanced up at me. "Hello, Detective Wilde," she said softly. "Are you bringing any news?"

I could see the fear in her gaze. I gave her a gentle smile and asked, "How are you feeling?"

She paused for a moment before replying, "I'm okay. Better at least." Her voice was tinged with exhaustion, but there was still hope in it. She hesitated, and then continued, "I just can't wait to go home."

A wave of determination came over her face. She straightened her posture and squared her shoulders before asking again, "So do you have any news for me?"

"No," I said. "At least not yet. We're working on it. But I'm gonna need you to try and remember more about your kidnapping. I need more details. I know it's horrible to relive what's happened, but we're concerned your kidnappers have taken someone else, and any detail you can give—large or small—might help us find her."

Joanne nodded. She closed her eyes again, and I could see the strain of concentration on her face as she tried to conjure what she had endured. I waited in silence.

Joanne's eyes fluttered open, and she began to speak.

"The car was a dark-colored sedan; I don't remember the exact make or model," Joanne stammered, her throat dry. "It was winding and unfamiliar—the road was—so I couldn't keep track of where we were going. I was very confused. I didn't know what was going on."

Her eyes darted around the room as she racked her brain, desperately searching for answers. She bit her lip, tears welling up in her eyes, and I could feel her frustration. Her hands forming fists. A tear slid down her face, and I knew this was taking a toll on her emotionally.

"There was just the woman in the car with me. The one with the earrings. I started to cry and asked her to stop the car. She kept threatening me, telling me that if I didn't cooperate, I would never see my family again."

Joanne swallowed hard before continuing on. "They kept me at an old motel, and there were several other women who had been kidnapped the same way as me. At least I think so. I could hear them crying at night. It was very scary. They warned me not to attempt to escape, or else they would kill me. They knew where I lived, they said. They would find me if I tried to leave. I belonged to them now. That's why they branded me. That's what they said." Joanne paused for a moment before adding softly, "I still can't believe I managed to get away…"

"Could you tell me more about how you escaped?"

She took a deep breath, her chest expanding, her shoulders rising. Joanne's lips trembled, all the wind escaping her in one breath.

"The kidnappers let me go to the bathroom, and I noticed a window in the bathroom that was unlocked. I waited until the guards had their backs turned and then I climbed out through the window. I ran as fast as I could, but I didn't know where to go. I was lost and scared, but I knew I had to keep moving."

She lifted her eyes to mine. She was exhausted—the kind of tired that goes beyond the physical—and I could sense her desperation as she told me her story.

Tears pooled in the corners of her eyes, threatening to spill over onto her cheeks. She swallowed hard before she continued to speak.

"I-I don't know how I did it, but I somehow managed to hide and evade them for days. I hid in the swamps; under deep foliage, listening out for the sound of voices. When I was certain they hadn't come after me, I ventured farther, and that's how I made it to the road."

I nodded. "You were gone for weeks, Joanne. Did you stay at the motel all that time? Or did they move you?"

She opened her mouth to speak, then quickly closed it. Her jaw worked up and down as she searched for the right words, but it was like her mind was a blank sheet.

I paused and looked at her. "Just to be clear, you weren't alone? 'Cause I remember you said in the first talk we had that you were all alone in a barren room. If I recall correctly you said it had no windows and just a bed and a bucket."

She paused, her eyes scrutinizing me. I could tell she was trying hard to recall everything. I knew it couldn't be easy.

"Yes I was at first, but... I don't remember to be honest what came first and next. I was so scared I thought I would never see my husband again. Or the rest of my family."

She smiled weakly, her eyes filled with tears, then added: "I just want this nightmare to be over."

"Of course. That is totally understandable. But we need to make sure this doesn't happen to more women and to help find the women that were left behind who weren't as lucky as you to be able to escape. So tell me about the other women who were with you, were they all the same age?"

"I never saw them. Just heard them." She paused and teared up. "Through the walls."

I nodded, feeling compassionate for her. This had to be a nightmare. To think that this was where Danni might be right now, made me want to scream.

Joanne's story gave me much to think about in regard to Carol Durst's murder and Danni's disappearance. It seemed clear that the kidnappers were targeting women. Maybe it was a question of being in the wrong place at the wrong time, which made it harder for me.

I thanked Joanne for her help and left the hospital room, feeling shaken by her story. I was in deep shock at the thought that Danni could be going through the same thing. I left the hospital room, slightly stunned by the details she suddenly provided. This opened up possibilities of new leads, and I couldn't stop thinking about the fact that the man with the eagle tattoo and Danni's pink suitcase had also stayed at a local motel. I was definitely on to something even if I still had no idea what the picture looked like. Some of the pieces were beginning to fit, and that made me feel hopeful.

THIRTY-FIVE

Then

TRANSCRIPT OF INTERVIEW OF ROBERT DURST
DEFENDANT'S EXHIBIT A
DURST PART 2

APPEARANCES:
Detective Michael Smith
Detective Lenny Travis
Sergeant Joseph Mill

DET. SMITH: So, Bobby. We just talked to your mom for a little while, and she said that you shot George. Is that true?
BOBBY: No.
DET. SMITH: It's not?
BOBBY: No.
DET. SMITH: And you're sure about that?
BOBBY: Yes.
DET. SMITH: So it was your sister?
BOBBY: I can't say.

DET. SMITH: But it was only the two of you in the bedroom, so if it wasn't you then it had to be her, right?

BOBBY: I don't know.

DET. SMITH: I think you do. Just tell us Bobby. It's okay. We know George did stuff to you.

BOBBY: (*sniffles*) Oh yeah? What stuff?

DET. SMITH: He put his hand in your pants, right? And your mom saw it and that's why she stopped the movie, right?

BOBBY: I don't know.

DET. SMITH: I think you do, but you're just protecting her. And that's okay, Bobby. I can understand why you want to protect your mom, and your sister.

BOBBY: Okay.

DET. SMITH: (*sighs*) Did you and your sister plan to do this? Did you talk about it before it happened?

BOBBY: What do you mean?

DET. SMITH: Like did Josephine talk to you about the gun in the safe? Did she maybe say that she knew how to get ahold of it?

BOBBY: Maybe.

DET. SMITH: Okay. That's something. Did she suggest that you shoot him?

BOBBY: (*holds a long pause*) He touched me.

DET. SMITH: Yes, he did. And that made you angry at him, right?

BOBBY: Yes.

DET. SMITH: So you and your sister planned to shoot him?

BOBBY: No.

DET. SMITH: So you never talked about killing him for what he did to you?

BOBBY: I don't remember.

DET. SMITH: Okay. Do you remember who grabbed the gun from the safe?

BOBBY: No.

DET. SMITH: Was it Josephine?

BOBBY: I don't know.

DET. SMITH: When did you see the gun the first time that night?

BOBBY: In the bedroom.

DET. SMITH: In Josephine's bedroom?

BOBBY: Yes.

DET. SMITH: Who brought it in there?

BOBBY: I don't know.

DET. SMITH: What happened after your mom stopped the movie? Did you all go your separate ways? How did you end up in Josephine's room?

BOBBY: Josephine and I were hiding in there.

DET. SMITH: You were hiding? Why? From whom?

BOBBY: From them. They were fighting in the living room. They were yelling at each other. So we hid in her closet. Like we always do. We can close the door. We sit on the floor and play with our toys. We can't hear them in there.

DET. SMITH: That's good. So they were fighting and you guys hid in there. And then what happened? Did George come in and find you?

BOBBY: Yes.

DET. SMITH: And then what?

BOBBY: He told us to come out. He wanted to talk to Josephine. Alone.

DET. SMITH: Why did he want to talk to her alone?

BOBBY: I don't know.

DET. SMITH: I bet that scared you, huh?

BOBBY: A little bit.

DET. SMITH: Were you afraid he might do to her what he had done to you?

BOBBY: Yes. He liked to touch me.

DET. SMITH: I know. And that's why you shot him then? So he wouldn't touch her too?

BOBBY: I don't know.

DET. SMITH: You don't know? But you were there, Bobby. You either shot the gun, or Josephine did.

BOBBY: No.

DET. SMITH: What do you mean no?

BOBBY: Our mom shot him.

DET. SMITH: Excuse me? Your mom shot him?

BOBBY: Yes. She told me not to tell you.

DET. SMITH: Really? That is very interesting news. Thank you for sharing this, buddy.

BOBBY: You're welcome.

DET. SMITH: Tell me, Bobby. Did your mother also tell you to take the blame?

BOBBY: What do you mean?

DET. SMITH: Did she tell you to tell us that you did it?

BOBBY: Y-yes.

DET. SMITH: Thank you, Bobby. Thank you for telling us this. This was a huge help for us. You can be very proud of yourself.

BOBBY: Okay.

DET. SMITH: I know it doesn't feel like it, but you did something good.

BOBBY: Okay. Can I have another soda now? I'm thirsty.

DET. SMITH: Of course, buddy.

THIRTY-SIX

BILLIE ANN

I was driving down A1A, when I called up Big Tom and asked him to run some checks on the local motels, particularly in the area close to where Joanne had been found. I also asked him to look into any recent missing person reports or suspicious activity involving women of all ages. I asked him to search for branding in any other murder cases recently, especially unsolved ones.

"That was a lot. But I'm on it," he said.

"How's it going with Scott?"

He chuckled. "As expected. He's been on the phone all day. Talking to every Tom, Dick, and Harry who has seen anyone Hispanic. Nothing useful so far though. We're also getting a lot of heat on the eagle tattoo, and I am going through all the people who've been identified now."

"Sounds good. Keep up the good work."

I hung up the phone just as I turned into the driveway of the Sea Aire Motel. It seemed natural for me to begin here, since this was where the man with the suitcase and eagle tattoo had been seen. The gravel crunched under my tires. It was a quiet little motel on the beach. The Sea Aire Motel was once a sparkling blue and white motel, but time and neglect—not to mention the hurricanes—had taken their toll. The paint was faded and flaking, the roof fissured and cracked. The once ocean blue facade of the Sea Aire Motel was now stained and dingy. The colors almost completely washed away.

I parked my car and stepped out into the warm salty air. It was still windy and the palm trees swayed heavily, but the rain seemed to have stopped. At least for a little bit. Dark clouds on the horizon told me that it wouldn't be long before the next thunderstorm hit. My phone kept dinging with rip current notifications and warnings to stay out of the ocean as the storm approached. There was always one surfer who thought it would be great to surf the hurricane waves, who ended up dying while doing it.

As I made my way to the reception desk, I couldn't help but feel a sense of unease. The motel seemed deserted, and I couldn't spot a single guest or staff member. The front desk was empty till suddenly someone came out from the back. The receptionist, a young blonde woman, greeted me with a smile.

"How can I assist you?"

I showed her my badge.

"I'm looking for any information on a recent guest of yours. We have a surveillance camera photo that you provided of him leaving with the suitcase and two bags."

I unlocked my phone with a practiced flick of my thumb and found the photo nestled among the hundreds of others stored there. I turned the screen to face her, holding it out like a peace offering. "This was taken last week," I said, my voice low and urgent. "I was informed that he went by the name of M. Smith, and that he paid cash. But could you maybe provide me with more information?"

The receptionist's expression turned somber as she met my gaze head-on, and I felt a small sense of relief that she seemed to take me seriously. "Like what?" she asked softly.

"I need to see the room he stayed in. I know it was looked through earlier in our investigation, but I would like to see it again."

She shook her head. "I don't think... I need to ask my manager first. There might be someone staying in it now."

I nodded. The receptionist hesitated before reaching for her phone.

As she talked to her manager, I pretended to fiddle with my phone, looking around the room as I did so. The motel was eerily quiet, and it seemed like it had been that way for a while. The floors were old, and the wallpaper was faded. There was a musty smell everywhere, like the place hadn't been aired out in a while, or maybe the AC just didn't work properly.

Finally, the receptionist put the phone down and turned to me. "Okay, my manager said I can show you to the room. But it's occupied at the moment, so please be discreet."

I nodded and followed her down the hallway, my hand resting on the gun in my holster. As we walked, I noticed that the doors to some of the rooms were ajar, and I could see inside. They were all empty.

When we got to the room in question, the receptionist knocked softly. "Housekeeping," she called out.

There was no answer.

She knocked again, a little louder this time, and called out, "Excuse me, sir? We have a request from the management."

Again, there was no response.

The receptionist turned to me. "I'm sorry, ma'am. Maybe they're not in."

I nodded and pulled out a pair of gloves from my pocket. "Do you have a spare key?"

She nodded and fished out a key card from her pocket. "Here it is. But please be careful. I don't want to get in trouble with our customers."

I took the key card and slid it through the reader, until I

heard a click and I could slowly push open the door. The receptionist watched me with a frown as I stepped inside. The room was shrouded in darkness; heavy curtains were drawn shut and only a faint sliver of light shone through. A musty odor filled my nostrils as my eyes adjusted to the gloom.

The sparsely furnished room was cramped, but functional; a queen bed with a sagging mattress and thin blanket, a scuffed dresser, and two chairs surrounding a wobbly wooden table that had seen better days. A beat-up suitcase lay sprawled open on the bed, half-filled with clothes still wrinkled from being stuffed hastily inside. Two duffel bags were slumped against the door, overflowing with what appeared to be more of the same.

I approached the suitcase and peeked inside of it. Inside, I found women's clothing. Dresses, tops, underwear. Nothing unusual. I closed the suitcase and moved on to the duffel bags. I looked inside the first one and found makeup, a hairbrush, and various toiletries. The second duffel bag contained some lingerie and a set of handcuffs. I closed it swiftly, then left the room, closing the door behind me.

As I walked down the hallway, I spotted someone walking through the lobby. Two people, a man and a woman. The man had his arm around her shoulder. I watched them for a few seconds as they turned the corner, then followed them down the hallway and watched them go into the room I had just been in.

Then I felt sick to my stomach.

The man was Mike. Danielle's husband. The woman was someone I had never seen before, but I guessed it was her belongings I had just looked through.

THIRTY-SEVEN

BILLIE ANN

"Have we talked to her coworkers?"

My voice was echoing off the gray walls of the police station office. Scott stared blankly at me, while Big Tom scratched his stubbled chin, perplexed. I drummed my fingers against the desk, looking between Scott and Big Tom. Both men squinted, as if they didn't understand the question. I had gone back to the station after seeing Mike at the motel and now I couldn't stop thinking about him, and what the heck he was doing there. Why was he with that woman? I couldn't believe it. Why would he do this to her? Wasn't he at all concerned that she was missing? Was he just having a blast while I was awake tossing myself in my bed worried night after night. Something was wrong with this picture. Something was very wrong. I didn't want to think the thought but couldn't help it.

Was he happy she was gone? Had he something to do with her disappearance? If he did, then I would make sure he didn't get away with it. Even if it was the last thing I did on this earth.

"Danielle Simmons," I added. "We need to talk to the people she worked with again. There must be something we have overlooked. I also want her husband in for questioning

after seeing him today at the motel with another woman. But I
need some ammunition before I can take him on. Her coworkers
might know something."

"They did call from her work and say they were worried,"
Scott said and looked at his piles of notes. "The day after she
went missing."

"Who did?" I asked.

"I don't remember her name. Some woman. You can go
through the pile there and find her name and number."

"You can't help me?" I asked.

Scott lifted his hands, resigned. "I got my hands full with all
these people calling about Hispanic criminals in their neighborhood. Just saying."

"Me too," Big Tom said. "People from all over are calling
about the eagle tattoo. WESH 2 News also wants a statement
from you as soon as possible."

"Let the Chief deal with that one," I said. "I'm no TV
personality."

"As you wish."

"All right, I'll go then," I said and threw myself at the piles
of notes of calls coming from the public. I found it after a few
minutes and pulled it out. On it was a name and a number. A
woman named Mrs. Pena had called and said that Danielle
seemed in distress.

"Why is this the first I hear of this?" I asked, holding up the
note. I received shrugs for answer as they were both on the
phone, calling back possible witnesses.

I walked up the steps to Danielle's workplace, a small law
office tucked between other bustling buildings downtown.
Inside, the reception area was filled with shelves of legal books
and the pungent smell of freshly brewed coffee. My eyes swept
over the dark mahogany walls and spotless marble floors.

There was no one in sight until, after a few moments, a tall brunette woman came out from the back room with a friendly smile.

"Can I help you?" she asked.

As I flashed my badge, the woman's face twisted in surprise. "I'm Detective Wilde," I said. "I'm investigating the disappearance of Danielle Simmons."

The woman's expression changed to one of concern. "We've been so worried," she gasped. "It's all anyone can talk about around here. We know Danielle was taking the entire week off for Thanksgiving, like she does every year. Is there any new information you can share with us? Any news?"

"We're still searching for her," I replied. "I was hoping to get some information that might help us find her. Is Mrs. Pena around?"

The woman nodded. "Of course. I'm Danielle's superior, Alexis Maxwell. This is my law firm. I was just about to leave for the day, but I guess it can wait. Danielle is my paralegal. I care about her very much and have been so concerned. If there's anything I or this company can do to assist you, let me know. Follow me."

She strode briskly through the maze of desks, her heels clicking against the floor. I followed close behind as she weaved her way to a small conference room with frosted windows. Inside, three women sat around a mahogany table, their eyes trained on an open folder.

"Ladies, this is Detective Wilde," Alexis said. "She's working on finding Danielle. She has some questions for us."

The women in the office had a collective look of dread on their faces, and I could feel the tension and fear radiating from them. They refused to make eye contact with me, instead looking down at the table, as if hoping the disappearance of their coworker was all a bad dream.

"We were just talking about it," one of them said, and

finally they all looked at me. "Do you know what happened to her?"

"Not yet," I said.

"Mrs. Pena," Alexis said. "Detective Wilde was especially asking for you. Mrs. Pena is Danielle's assistant here. She joined our firm less than a year ago. But she was very close with Danielle. Right, Jolene?"

The youngest looking woman, with long hair and a pierced nose, looked up at me. She seemed nervous and I tried to soften my face so that I did not intimidate her.

"I understand you called about Danielle on the day after she went missing?" I asked.

Jolene sniffled and nodded. "Yeah. I don't know if it's of any help, but I just noticed that... well she seemed a little off lately, like something was bothering her. I don't know. I just worked the closest with her, and thought you should know. She was always on edge and seemed to be hiding something. I have been very worried."

I looked at her. This was certainly news to me. This wasn't the Danni I knew? She was usually so calm and collected, like nothing could throw her off balance? But again I hadn't seen her these past months. Maybe things had gone really bad at home? With Mike?

"I noticed she would take a lot of breaks and go outside to vape," a woman named Jessica Olson added. "But I'm not sure if that's relevant."

I knew that Danielle vaped, and she had actually told me she had stopped, but apparently without success. I wrote it down in my notes.

Alexis chimed in next. "Danielle was a hard worker, but she did seem preoccupied lately. She even missed a few important deadlines, which is really unlike her."

I scribbled down notes as they spoke, thinking of her marriage. Did she know something was wrong? "Did she mention any specific issues or problems she was dealing with?" I asked, looking up from my notebook. "Did any of you address this with her?"

The three women shook their heads in unison, and that's when I noticed something. Jolene had a small tattoo on her wrist that looked eerily familiar. It caught my attention right away.

There was something about this tattoo that I couldn't stop thinking about as I thanked the women for their time and left the law office, feeling more confused than ever. That's when my phone rang.

It was the Chief.

THIRTY-EIGHT

RANDY

Randy took a seat in the corner of the pub, away from the prying eyes of others, and ordered a beer. He didn't have to wait long. Only seconds went by before he came in. He saw him walk through the door and scan the bar with a cursory glance, his eyes adjusting to the darkness, not realizing Randy was lurking in the shadows. He sat down at a table for two, seemingly unaware that he was there to meet someone else.

For the next forty-five minutes Randy watched and waited. His teeth were gritted and his hands clenched into fists as he observed every move the man made, sizing him up as if preparing for a fight. He was taking in the way his broad shoulders stretched his shirt, and the way his hands moved as he talked to the waitress. His heart began to race, thinking of Joanne.

This is for you my love. For us.

The minutes ticked by slowly, and Randy felt his patience wearing thin as he watched from his silent corner. Just when it seemed like he was never going to leave, his mark stood up and headed for the door. Taking one last swig of his lager, he stepped outside into the night.

Randy drained the last drop of beer from his pint glass and signaled to the bartender for his tab. Sliding a few bills across the counter, he stood and stepped out into the night air, looking around for his target. His mark was a silhouette in the street-light, moving slowly through the parking lot toward their car. Randy followed cautiously, keeping a safe distance.

The man never saw Randy coming. He was still walking through the parking lot, his head buried in his phone, when suddenly Randy pounced on him from behind. The impact of the sudden attack knocked the wind out of him and he stumbled to the ground, screaming in terror as Randy pounded away at his face and chest with a flurry of punches.

Randy's rage was uncontrollable; every blow seemed to be harder than the last. The man attempted to fight back, but his efforts were feeble and ineffective against Randy's onslaught. With each blow, Randy seemed to be fueled by a greater rage, his muscles tensing and his teeth gritted together. Randy felt a sense of satisfaction as he watched his mark's face contort in pain beneath the force of his blows. Each punch was a release of pent-up anger, a way of purging his soul of the hurt he felt inside.

The terrified victim begged for mercy as he fell to the ground, but Randy merely sneered and continued to rain down blows upon him. The man cried out in pain and terror as he curled up into a ball, trying desperately to protect himself from Randy's relentless attack. Finally, after what felt like an eternity of unrelenting violence, Randy stepped back, panting heavily with exertion from the savage beating he had just inflicted. He looked down at his victim—a bloodied mess lying motionless on the cold asphalt.

Without another word or backward glance, Randy walked away into the darkness, leaving his victim lying in agony on the asphalt. As Randy faded into the night, all that remained was the sound of his footsteps and the man's broken cries of anguish echoing through the deserted parking lot.

THIRTY-NINE

BILLIE ANN

"Hello?"

I heard my Chief's voice on the other end of the line.

"Hey. It's me. Sorry for the late call, but I thought you should know."

My heart skipped a beat. "What is it? What's going on?"

She sighed. "It's your son. William. He's been taken in to the station tonight."

My throat went dry, my mind racing with worry. I hurried to my car, phone pressed against my ear. What the heck was this? William? Arrested? It couldn't be.

"What happened?" I asked, scared of the answer. This was the kind of phone call a mother dreaded to get. A thousand scenarios rushed through my head. William had told me he was sleeping over at a friend's house. I had texted him good night. Had he been in an accident? Was he hurt?

Chief Harold cleared her throat. "He was caught smoking weed behind Publix with some friends."

I shook my head in disbelief, then closed my eyes briefly, steadying myself.

William, I thought. *You're fourteen.*

My Chief's voice interrupted my thoughts. "I thought you'd want to come down and get him. I'm still here wrapping things up."

I nodded, my mind already set on getting to the station as fast as possible. "I'm on my way," I said and hung up the phone.

My heart heavy, I quickly got into the car and started the engine. As I drove toward the station I couldn't help but think back to the days when William was just a sweet, innocent child. Where did I go wrong? Was this my fault? Was Joe right? Had I lost touch with my children? Were they acting out because of me? Because of the divorce?

Don't go there. You're only guilt-tripping yourself. Don't let Joe make you feel like a bad mom.

I pulled into the police station's parking lot, and I got out of the car and walked inside, my heart heavy.

My Chief was waiting for me, her expression grave. "He's in the holding cell," she said, leading me down a hallway. "I've talked to him, and he seems remorseful. But we have to go through the proper procedures."

I nodded, my thoughts still jumbled. When we arrived at the cell, I saw William sitting on the cot with his head in his hands. My heart broke at the sight of him like that. I opened the door and walked in.

"William," I said softly, trying to keep my voice steady. "What were you thinking?"

He looked up at me with red, puffy eyes, tears still streaming down his face. I sat down next to him.

"I'm sorry, Mom," he whispered. "I didn't mean to cause any trouble."

I sighed, feeling the weight of the situation. I was trying to keep the guilt at bay, but it was easier said than done. Me coming out as gay and their dad leaving the house, had to take its toll on them. Of course it did. I was a fool if I thought it wouldn't. Charlene, my oldest, had been the first to act out, starting to drink and run away at night. Now William was doing his thing. As the middle child, he had always been slightly overlooked. Maybe especially because there was never any trouble with him. He got good—or at least decent—grades; he never skipped school, and had always been the quiet one among them, whereas both Charlene and Zack always made sure to get what they wanted and make us aware of their presence and if they needed anything. William never did. Not in the same way. I would have to remember to ask him if he was hungry when he was younger. He would rather go without than ask me for it. One time, he threw up in school, but told the teacher that it was just because he had been drinking too much water, so she didn't send him home. When he came home he had a high fever and was throwing up all night. I asked him why he never told his teacher he wasn't feeling well, and he simply said he didn't want to be a bother. That was William for you.

Not this.

"I know, Will. But you know better than this. You're better than this."

We sat in silence for a few moments, the only sound in the room the soft hum of the fluorescent lights. I took a deep breath, steeling myself for what I had to say next.

"Listen, Will. I'm not going to sugarcoat this. What you did was wrong. You're only fourteen, and there are rules in place for a reason. You need to understand that your actions have consequences, and this is a serious matter. You could have gotten hurt, or worse, hurt someone else. You need to start making better choices and thinking about the consequences before you act."

I paused, taking a deep breath. "But I still love you, William. And I'll always be here for you, no matter what."

William looked up at me with tear-filled eyes, and I could

tell he was really feeling the gravity of the situation. "I'm sorry, Mom," he said again. "I didn't mean to disappoint you."

I put a hand on his shoulder, trying to comfort him. "I know you didn't, Will. We'll get through this together. Come, let's go home."

FORTY

RICK & MAGGIE

Rick and Maggie stepped out of the Pig and Whistle, laughter spilling out behind them. They had enjoyed dinner together—Rick a classic burger with a pint of beer, Maggie savoring her fish 'n' chips and an equally large mug of bitters. The evening was still fairly young, and the two of them could not contain their joy.

They had won the lottery. Literally.

Maggie grabbed Rick's arm and pulled him along into the night. He felt warmth spread from where she touched, and he followed her in a daze, ignoring the rain that had started to pour once again, as they stumbled through the parking lot toward their truck, parked behind the pub.

"We're gonna need a new one soon," she said with a grin, covering her head with her hand to shield herself from the rain.

"You can get any car you like from now on," he said, almost yelling against the howling wind. "'Cause we just won the lottery."

She giggled and covered her mouth with both her hands. Her hair was soaked, and so was her shirt. "We did. We just won the lottery. Can you believe it?"

They had bought the Mega Millions ticket as a second thought the day before at the gas station, not thinking much about it. Both of them had grown up poor, never having much, always dreaming of a better life. Winning the lottery was a dream come true for them. They had always bought a ticket, thinking "someone had to win, right?" But they never actually thought they would.

"Seven million dollars. I can't believe it," Maggie said again. "We're rich!"

Rick grinned, feeling a sense of pride and relief wash over him. No more struggling to pay the bills or worrying about making rent. They could finally live the life they deserved.

Maggie leaned in close to Rick, the scent of her perfume intoxicating him. Their wet soaked bodies, sticking to one another. They didn't care about the wind or the rain at this point. Nothing else mattered right now. "What do you want to do with all that money?" she yelled, wiping rain from her face.

"Anything you want," he replied, his voice husky with desire.

Maggie's eyes sparkled with mischief. "Anything?"

Rick nodded, his heart racing. He knew exactly where this was going.

Maggie pressed herself against him, her lips brushing his ear. "Then let's go on a world tour. Just you and me. We'll see everything this world has to offer."

Rick felt chills run down his spine at the thought of traveling the world with his beautiful and adventurous girlfriend. "Yes," he whispered, his hand sliding down to her waist. "Let's do it."

"Maybe we shouldn't drive home," Maggie said. "Especially not in this weather."

Rick laughed. "So what if we get stopped? We'll just pay the friggin' ticket, ha!"

She laughed, carefree, happy. Feeling like nothing could ever get them now. They were invincible.

As Maggie stepped toward the truck, her feet stumbled slightly, and her heel squelched into something wet. At first, she thought she had stepped in a puddle. She paused and looked down at her shoes and had to blink to properly focus. Was she seeing right? Or was she so drunk she was seeing things? What was that? Was it...?

Blood!

Her breath caught in her throat, Maggie looked down to see where it came from. She gasped for air as she saw a dark crimson pool expanding on the asphalt, leading up to a man's lifeless body. The blood was being washed away by the heavy rainfall, and it was beginning to soak into the cracks of the pavement.

Maggie froze. The stench of iron and death hit her like a punch to the gut, and bile rose to her throat. Her hand flew to her mouth as she stumbled backward, shaking her head in disbelief. Tears streamed down her face as the reality of what had happened sunk in, striking her like a hammer—and instantly all thoughts of being an invincible millionaire and of unreachable dreams coming true were completely forgotten.

FORTY-ONE

BILLIE ANN

The call came as soon as I got William home. A body had been found. Taking a deep breath, I told my son to go to bed, that I would be back a little later, and then we would talk in the morning about what happened. He nodded without looking at me, then trotted up the stairs to his room. I then grabbed my belt with my badge and gun and headed toward the Pig and Whistle.

While I drove, I tried to shake off the feeling of dread that was settling over me. *Please let it not be Danni. Please dear God.*

As I came around the corner of the old English pub, I saw a chaotic scene. In front of the building were police cars, firetrucks, and an ambulance, all with their lights on and sirens blaring. Their red and blue lights reflected off the palm trees surrounding the parking lot. I quickly made my way toward the scene, past the onlookers and the curious bystanders who had sought shelter for the rain underneath the roof on the porch of the restaurant. I put on my CBPD rain poncho and put the hood over my head. I tried to put up an umbrella but it was no use with the strong winds. I had to get wet, there was no way around it.

When I came through the police blockade, I saw the paramedics collecting the body on a stretcher and surrounding them were the police, all asking questions and taking notes. I looked around, surveying the scene before making my way up to the Chief.

She nodded at me and gave a slight smile. "Billie Ann, it's bad." She gestured toward the body on the ground. "He's been attacked, and it looks like it happened right here. There are traces of blood splatter on the car and asphalt over here, but a lot has been rained away. It still looks like it was a fight of some sort. I spoke to the waitress inside and she said the guy was there alone, like he was waiting for someone and then left. Another guy who was sitting in the corner left right after him. That could be our attacker."

I nodded and began to look around the parking lot, surveying the area. There was a camera but it looked like it only covered the entrance not the parking lot. I stared at the crowd that had gathered. Lots of faces I recognized as locals, some were tourists who had probably been eating inside when it happened. Whoever did this couldn't be far away. It happened from time to time that they even came back to the scene of the crime to watch. I scanned their faces, but didn't see anyone behaving oddly, then decided it was useless.

I hurried toward the paramedics and looked down, seeing what remained of the man's face. It left me breathless for a second. He had taken a strong beating, and his T-shirt had been torn. There was no doubt he had been attacked. I stared at his face, and then at his red shorts.

I looked around me and noticed the couple in the corner under the shelter of the roof—a man and a woman, both looking pale and shaken. I walked up to them and asked what they had seen.

The woman spoke first, her voice trembling with fear. "We were just walking past to get to our truck over there, when we found him lying here." She hugged her partner close as she spoke, her body shaking from fear or shock, I couldn't tell which.

The man stepped forward then, his voice low but strong. "We tried to help him but he didn't respond at all..." He trailed off, unable to go on any further.

Just then there was a shout from the paramedics working on the body. "We got a pulse!" Then they quickly loaded him onto a stretcher and rushed him away.

I turned back toward my Chief who had been watching everything quietly from afar.

She caught my eye and gave me a nod. "Let's get to work, Billie Ann."

I followed her back to the Pig and Whistle, the entire journey consumed by thoughts of the beaten man. As we made our way inside, the atmosphere was thick with tension. The regular patrons were huddled together in groups, their faces pale and drawn. I could see the waitress from outside, the one who had spoken to my Chief earlier. She was sitting with another officer, both of them deep in conversation.

My Chief motioned me over to them, and I quickly made my way over. The waitress glanced up as I approached, her face twisted in concern. "I don't know what happened. That man, the one who was attacked... he was in here earlier. He had two beers, while he seemed like he was waiting for someone."

"How do you know he wasn't just there alone?" I asked.

"He asked for a table for two. But whoever it was, they never came, and he left after about an hour or so, alone. I didn't think anything of it at the time." She shook her head, looking close to tears.

"Tell me, the guy who walked out after him," I asked. "Can you describe him for me, please?"

"He-he was tall and blond, and wore camouflage cargo shorts, and... a yellow polo shirt... and uh yes he had bare feet in his sneakers. I remember that well because I never understood how people can do that in this heat and not get sweaty feet and smelly shoes, heh."

She gave me an insecure smile, and I wrote it down. I thought I knew exactly who she was talking about. I'd seen those bare feet in sneakers before.

It was time I had a serious chat with Randy Edwards.

FORTY-TWO

Then

APPEARANCES:
Detective Michael Smith
Detective Lenny Travis
Sergeant Joseph Mill

DET. SMITH: (*shuts door, chair screeches across floor*) I'm
sorry to keep you waiting, Carol, but I had to go talk to your son.
CAROL DURST: How is he? How's Bobby?
DET. SMITH: He's okay. Taking a little break now and having
a soda.
CAROL DURST: I can't believe he has to go through this, the
poor kid.
DET. SMITH: He's been through a lot, hasn't he?
CAROL DURST: Yes. I-I feel awful. Did he tell you what
happened with George? Was he honest about it? Did you tell

him that it was okay to talk about it, that he didn't need to protect me?

DET. SMITH: Yes, he was actually very honest.

CAROL DURST: Oh. That's good.

DET. SMITH: Yes.

CAROL DURST: I have a feeling there is something you're not telling me. I can see it in your eyes.

DET. SMITH: Bobby did tell us something very interesting.

CAROL DURST: H-he did?

DET. SMITH: Yes, and I wonder if there's something you want to tell me?

CAROL DURST: I-I don't know what you mean. I have told you everything.

DET. SMITH: Not exactly everything.

CAROL DURST: Yes, everything. I know what I saw, which was the kids alone in the room, and George on the bed, shot dead, and the gun on the floor. I don't know who pulled the trigger. I swear.

DET. SMITH: Really? Because Bobby seems to think differently.

CAROL DURST: (*sighs*) What did he say?

DET. SMITH: He told us you shot George.

CAROL DURST: (*scoffs*) No. He didn't. Tell me he didn't do that.

DET. SMITH: I can't I'm afraid. Because that's what he said.

CAROL DURST: And you believe him?

DET. SMITH: I do.

CAROL DURST: (*groans*) Of course you do. Because he's a child. But children can lie too, you know?

DET. SMITH: They generally don't lie about things like these. He was trying to protect you first but once he broke down, he told us this. Yes, I believe him.

CAROL DURST: Well, he is lying.

DET. SMITH: So, you didn't shoot George?

CAROL DURST: (*slams hand on table*) NO!

DET. SMITH: No need to get aggressive.

CAROL DURST: It's hard not to be when being accused of something you haven't done.

DET. SMITH: Why don't you just tell us the truth, Carol?

CAROL DURST: I am telling you the truth, dammit.

DET. SMITH: I don't believe you.

CAROL DURST: So, you believe a child over an adult?

DET. SMITH: Yes.

CAROL DURST: Well, I didn't do it. I told you my children are devious. Especially him, especially Bobby. You can't trust a word he says.

FORTY-THREE

BILLIE ANN

"I have no other choice but to ground you and take your phone away for a week. And those friends you hung out with last night while smoking weed. Not your friends anymore, okay? Find new friends. Ones that make better choices."

I stared at William. He looked tired, and I wondered how much sleep he had gotten. I hadn't gotten a lot, since I came home late and then I couldn't find rest. I was in no mood to deal with my son, but it had to be done. I had made him breakfast and while he ate, I drank my coffee and talked to him.

I could tell that William was upset, and I felt a pang of guilt in my chest. He deserved to be grounded, and I couldn't let him off the hook this time. I had just checked his grades for this semester and realized that they had been slipping lately, and his behavior had become more reckless. I had to show him that actions have consequences.

As he finished his breakfast, I stood up from the table and walked over to him. I placed my hand on his shoulder. "I know this isn't easy for you, but I have to do what's best for you."

He nodded; his eyes downcast. "I understand, Mom," he said, his voice barely above a whisper. "I'll try to do better."

I smiled, feeling a surge of pride in my son's willingness to change. "I know you will," I said. "And I'll be here to help you every step of the way."

With that, I took his phone and put it in my pocket. William didn't protest, knowing that it would only make things worse. As he got up from the table, I saw a glint in his eye, a look that I recognized all too well.

"William, what is it?" I asked, my voice tinged with concern.

"Nothing, Mom," he replied quickly, avoiding my gaze.

I wasn't convinced, but I didn't push him. Instead, I watched as he walked out of the kitchen and headed toward the stairs.

"William!" I called out, my voice now laced with urgency. "What have you been up to?"

He turned around, his eyes wide with fear. "I-I swear, Mom. I haven't done anything."

But I knew that he was lying. I could see it in his eyes. William was on something, and I had a pretty good idea of what it was. My heart sank as I realized that my son was not just experimenting with weed, but something much stronger.

"William, come here," I said, my voice stern. "Now."

He slowly made his way back to the kitchen, his head hung low. I grabbed him by the arm and pulled him close, searching his eyes for any sign of deceit. I knew that I had to act fast, before things got out of hand.

"William, I need you to tell me the truth," I said, my tone serious. "What have you been taking?"

He hesitated for a moment, before finally speaking up. "It's just some stuff that my friends brought over," he said, his voice barely audible.

"What stuff?" I pressed, my grip on his arm tightening.

"Xanax," he said, his eyes darting around the room. "Blake

gets it from his mom's cabinet. And Oxy. We crush it and sniff it."

My heart skipped a beat at the mention of the drugs. They were a highly dangerous and addictive substance that could cause severe damage to the brain and body. I felt my anger boil up inside me as I realized how reckless and foolish my son had been.

"You know that this drug is incredibly dangerous, William," I said, my voice shaking with anger.

"It's not that bad, Mom. You're overreacting."

"Are you kidding me? I will have you know that these drugs are highly addictive. It's not something to mess around with."

He scoffed. "Mom. Everyone does it. It's not that bad."

"William, do you even know what these drugs can do to you?" I asked, my voice shaking with anger and fear.

He looked away, unable to meet my gaze. "I didn't think it was a big deal," he muttered.

"Not a big deal? You could seriously hurt yourself or someone else," I countered, my voice rising with every word. "Do you want to end up in the hospital, or worse?"

"Come on, Mom. It's hardly that bad."

I stepped forward and grabbed his arm. This was way more serious than I had thought. I mean smoking a little weed, who hadn't done that as a teenager? But sniffing prescription drugs? This was bad. The very thought made me feel almost light-headed. How had I missed this?

"This needs to stop right now, do you hear me? You're fourteen years old. I need you to give me everything you have of this, and I need to know how you got ahold of it. Who gave this to you?"

He scoffed again. "As if I would tell you."

"You're kidding me, William?" I said as he ripped his arm loose and ran up the stairs, while my phone rang in my pocket. I knew I was wanted at the station for the morning meeting, and then I had to go get the turkey I ordered for Thanksgiving.

I sighed as he slammed the door upstairs, then decided I would have to get back to this and take it out with him later. I had to get to work.

FORTY-FOUR

BILLIE ANN

"Happy Thanksgiving, everyone. I know you're anxious to get home and be with your families, and eat turkey, so we will make this brief."

The morning meeting at the station was tense. Chief Harold informed us that the man who had been discovered in the parking lot the night before was alive and stable, but in a coma. When I asked if we could talk to him, she shook her head.

"His name is Adam Rodriguez," she said. "Thirty-five years old, from Cape Canaveral. Works as an electrician on the cruise ships. His family has been notified."

She paused, her brow wrinkling slightly with concern.

"He's not married. No children."

We all sat in silence for a moment, absorbing the gravity of the situation. Then Chief Harold cleared her throat.

"Right," she said. "Let's get to work. I assume we're still working with the theory that we're dealing with some sort of trafficking ring, right?"

I nodded, that was what we thought. "Three women that we know of have been kidnapped, one murdered, one escaped, and one not found."

I paused before continuing. "Joanne told us she was certain they were going to sell her. She overheard them say it, and she was transported to multiple locations and raped by various men that were brought to her by her Hispanic looking kidnappers. There were more women with her, so we must assume this is a bigger operation. And they were staying in motels across the county. That's what we know so far."

"Plus that you were attacked by one of them at the victim Carol Durst's house," Harold added. "And he had an eagle tattoo on his shoulder, right?"

"Yes, and that's also what we saw on the shoulder of the man at the Sea Aire Motel who had suitcases and sports bags similar to those that were found with Carol Durst's remains in them."

"I just don't get why she was shot. And what about the note? No one talks about the *I'm sorry* note? And the fact that she was packing up? Trying to get away? Did she know she was in danger?"

"The note was gone when we got to the house," Big Tom said. "We only know of it because you took that picture with your phone."

"So we must assume that whoever attacked me took the note, right?" I said. "This doesn't exactly fit the theory of a trafficking operation."

They all gave me a look. No one liked it when you shot down a theory, but I had to point it out.

"All right. The theory is getting a little thin, admitted," the Chief said. "But so far it's what we have to go by. We still don't know if the attack last night on Adam Rodriguez has any link to the rest, but if you do find anything, then let me know."

"I have to add that we are not done looking at Danielle Simmons' husband, Mike Simmons," I said. "He's been seen downtown with another woman, getting drunk, and that's suspicious behavior when your wife has gone missing. I want him taken in for questioning soon. I just need to gather some ammunition. So far all we have is the coworkers talking about her acting odd and like something was wrong, but it's not quite enough."

"Okay do that, as soon as you're ready for it," the Chief said. "Has anyone gotten to talk to Carol Durst's children?"

"We've been trying to track them down," Scott said. "But with no luck."

"All right. Keep trying."

"We talked to her friends and a couple of other family members, her sister, an uncle, and a niece," Tom said. "But nothing stood out. She didn't have a lot of people close to her, if any, and kept mostly to herself, the neighbors said. They said they never saw the children come to visit."

"That's a little odd," I said.

"Wilde is right. We need to find those children," the Chief added.

And with that, she began to assign tasks for the day. She called our attention to the video footage that had been taken from the front door to the restaurant and asked for volunteers to review it. Big Tom took that one. She then asked Scott to look into Adam Rodriguez's background, as well as any witnesses who may have seen something in the area the night before. Lastly, she gave instructions for the rest of us to talk to those closest to Adam, including his family and friends, and see what they could provide us with.

"Anything at this point," she said. "Anything will be helpful."

"I would like to bring in Joanne Edwards' husband, Randy Edwards, for further questioning," I said.

She looked at me, her eyes narrowing. "In Joanne's case?"

"No, in this case. Or maybe both. I think they're connected."

"On what grounds will you bring him in?" she asked.

"He fits the description the waitress gave us of the person walking out right after the victim."

Chief Harold nodded thoughtfully at my suggestion. "Randy Edwards," she said. "I see. Do you have any more concrete grounds for questioning him?"

I sighed. I knew what she meant, but I didn't have any hard evidence linking Randy to Adam's condition. All I had was a gut feeling, and that wasn't enough.

"No," I admitted. "Not yet."

The Chief gave me a long look before speaking again. "If you think you can find something," she said finally, "go for it, Wilde. Go find it. But it has to be good, Wilde. I won't tolerate mistakes. That's one thing you all might as well know about me. One strike and you're out. That's how I operate. I don't believe in second chances."

FORTY-FIVE

RANDY

Randy's heart raced as he pushed open the heavy doors of the hospital and walked toward her room. As he rushed through the hallway, hospital staff greeted him with warm smiles and waves, the nurses wishing him luck as he passed by. He told them how he felt an overwhelming sense of gratitude for the care that had been shown to Joanne, and to him, during this difficult time.

"Thank you to you all. And happy Thanksgiving!"

Finally, he reached the room where Joanne was staying. He closed his eyes and sucked in a deep breath before pushing open the door. The sight that met him made him smile: Joanne, as beautiful as ever, sitting up in bed with a smile on her face.

He rushed to her side, and embraced her gently.

"I'm so happy to see you," she said. "Finally, I get to go home."

Joanne was already dressed and ready to go. He grinned and took her hands in his. "You look beautiful," he said simply.

Joanne smiled, her eyes crinkling. "Thank you," she replied, her voice filled with emotion.

He helped her get into the wheelchair, then rolled her down the hallway, nurses waving at them, clapping at her fast recovery and of the love the two of them seemed to share for one another. He yelled another thank you to the staff, before getting into the elevator and once more to the women in the lobby downstairs, whose faces he all knew since he had seen them every day when coming to visit.

Joanne breathed relief as she felt the hot and humid air hit her face when exiting through the sliding doors. Luckily the rain had stopped for a while, even as the winds were still strong. She sighed deeply, then looked up at him as they reached the car.

Randy lifted Joanne carefully out of the wheelchair and into the car. She cried a little, then looked at him as he got into the driver's seat next to her.

"These past weeks have been a nightmare," she said. "I can't tell you how grateful I am to be going home."

He exhaled. "You have been through so much. I'm just grateful to be able to take you home, finally."

After settling in comfortably, Randy started the engine and drove away. They chatted easily as they passed familiar sights, discussing plans for the future—there were so many places they wanted to go and things they still wanted to do together.

"Let's promise each other," Randy said suddenly, "that we will always make time for us, no matter where life takes us. This experience has taught us to value us more, our relationship, I think."

Joanne smiled softly and squeezed his hand. "It's a promise," she said.

Before long, they pulled up outside their home, and Randy helped Joanne out of the car with gentle care. Carefully he escorted her up the stairs. She leaned into him, her arm around his neck for support.

At the top of the stairs, Randy paused and looked down at Joanne.

"Well," he said, "we're home." He opened the door and stepped inside with a sigh of relief.

She chuckled lightly, then teared up. "I'm just so happy to be home in time for Thanksgiving," she said. "I've been praying about that."

"I got the turkey," he said with a grin.

Joanne looked around the room, taking in all the familiar sights. Randy closed his eyes and took a deep breath, feeling a sense of relief wash over him. This was it. It was time.

Then he turned to Joanne, and for a moment, neither of them spoke. Finally, Randy broke the silence.

"I know everything," he said. His voice was firm, and his gaze was unwavering.

She stared at him, her eyes growing wide, her smile freezing at first, before turning into a frown.

"What do you mean by everything?" she asked, her voice shaking.

"As in *everything.*"

Then he reached for the door and locked it.

FORTY-SIX

"You were right, Billie Ann," Scott said from behind his computer screen. It was right around noon, and I had gone home to begin preparing the turkey. Meanwhile Scott had stayed behind doing research before going to his mother's for dinner, trying to figure out what happened to Adam Rodriguez and how it could possibly be connected to the disappearance of Danni. I couldn't for the life of me see the connection, but something told me that there was one, and to me that connection had to be Randy Edwards, the man whose wife was kidnapped and returned.

I lifted my gaze and looked out the window at the black clouds on the horizon. The storm would reach us by the weekend, they said, and they still expected it to stay out in the ocean, so we were praying for that.

"What about?"

"When going through the surveillance footage from the entrance to the Pig and Whistle, you do see Randy Edwards come in right after our victim, and he is seen leaving right after he does as well."

"Anyone else walk through the door after he does?" I asked, just to be certain.

Scott shook his head. "Not till about half an hour later, when a guy walks out, and then two hours later we see the couple who found him on the asphalt leave."

I nodded pensively. "So if it wasn't him, then it would have to be someone coming from the street side, or already waiting in the parking lot."

"Exactly," Scott said.

"What else do we have?" I asked. "What do we know about Adam Rodriguez?"

"I've gone through all of his social media and called around to talk to his friends and family," Scott said. "But mostly get the picture of a guy who lives a pretty quiet life. Not very social, his friends say. Stays mostly to himself."

"Any partners? Girlfriends? Boyfriends?" I asked.

"Not for years, his mom said. His best friend said the same. Some girl broke his heart like three years ago, and he hasn't dated since."

"So nothing recently?"

"No."

"Do the family or friends know of anyone who might hold a grudge against him? Who would want to beat him up?" I asked.

He shook his head. "No. According to them he's the nicest guy around and they can't understand why anyone would want to hurt him."

"And he wasn't involved in anything shady? Did he have like friends that seemed up to no good?" I asked.

"I asked them all about that too, and no."

"Did you ask them if he knew Randy Edwards?" I asked.

"None of them had ever heard that name before."

I wrinkled my nose and sipped my coffee. The turkey in front of me was big and juicy. "That gets us nowhere, then."

"Should we just take him in?" Scott asked. "On the grounds that he walked out of the pub right after the victim did?"

I mulled it over for a few seconds, then shook my head. "I need more. I don't want to mess up with our new Chief on the first case."

"I hear ya," Scott said. "We'll find it."

I hung up, then walked to the cabinet only to find we were out of coffee in the pot. I filled the coffeepot with water and spooned some ground coffee into the filter, then looked out the window. I had been looking forward to spending the day with my family, and I had planned to take the rest of the day off, and to spend some quality time with William especially, but how could I when the woman I loved was missing? How was I supposed to be thankful and hold hands with my family, and soon to be ex-husband, when she was out there somewhere, held captive? I could only imagine the horrors that were done to her. If it were the same kidnappers as had taken Joanne, then there was no telling what they might do. They had branded her, and beat her, and raped her.

I poured myself a cup as soon as it was done spluttering, then rushed back to my laptop. I checked my email and found that I had gotten the results from the lab of Adam Rodriguez's DNA sample. I opened the CODIS, the United States national DNA database, then ran for a match at both state and local levels.

What came up made me lean back with a puzzled sigh. Then I called the Chief.

"Sorry to disturb you on Thanksgiving, but there is something I need to talk to you about."

"What's going on?" Chief Harold said.

"I'll be... This is very odd indeed."

"What is?"

"It's just that... well, I ran a DNA match on our victim Adam Rodriguez."

"And?"

I bit my lip. I couldn't quite figure this out. How was this all connected?

"I... well it matches with the DNA sample taken from Joanne Edwards when she was found."

"He was the one who raped her?" the Chief said. "Is that what you're saying?"

"I mean that's what we'd normally assume, yes."

"But you don't?"

"Yeah, I guess I do."

"It would fit fine with the fact that he was beat up by her husband. Somehow he must have found out, right?"

I nodded, staring at the screen, and at the results. How on earth did this add up? "Right."

"So maybe Adam was a part of the trafficking ring?" she said. "He is Hispanic so that would fit Joanne's description. Even if it is a quite vague one. According to her there was a man and a woman who was in charge of it. My theory is that the woman is used to lure them into the car or to approach their victims, because they will trust her. So I guess now we just need to find out who she is."

Chief Harold paused, then continued. "Good work, Wilde. Now go have turkey. I'm sure your family wants to be with you."

"Sure I just need to..."

She cleared her throat. "Now Wilde. It's Thanksgiving. Take the rest of the day off. I mean it. I don't want to see your face or hear your voice till Friday. Is that understood?"

"Yes, ma'am."

FORTY-SEVEN

TRANSCRIPT OF INTERVIEW OF JOSEPHINE DURST

DEFENDANT'S EXHIBIT A

DURST PART I

APPEARANCES:
Detective Michael Smith
Detective Lenny Travis
Sergeant Joseph Mill

DET. SMITH: All right, Josephine. Sorry to keep you waiting, but we have found ourselves in kind of a pickle here. And we need your help to solve it.

JOSEPHINE: O-okay?

DET. SMITH: Are you feeling okay? Do you want another soda? Or maybe a sandwich?

JOSEPHINE: N-no. I'm good.

DET. SMITH: Okay that's great, Josephine. I want you to be comfortable, okay? So let me know if there is anything you need or want or if you just need to take a break, okay?

JOSEPHINE: Okay.

DET. SMITH: (*exhales*) The thing is, Josephine, that now we have talked to both your mother and your brother and they well —they're telling us different things. We need you to tell us who is telling the truth.

JOSEPHINE: (*nods*)

DET. SMITH: So here is the deal. Your brother says your mom shot George. Is that the truth?

JOSEPHINE: No.

DET. SMITH: Okay so it was your brother who shot him?

JOSEPHINE: No.

DET. SMITH: (*sighs*) Listen, Josephine. If they're both innocent then that must mean you did it.

JOSEPHINE: N-no.

DET. SMITH: Josephine. There were three people present when George got shot. You, your mom, and Bobby. One of you shot him. Who was it?

JOSEPHINE: I don't know.

DET. SMITH: Josephine. I know you know who did it.

JOSEPHINE: It wasn't me.

DET. SMITH: Okay, then. I believe you. So can you maybe tell me who it was?

JOSEPHINE: I-I can't.

DET. SMITH: Listen, Josephine. We know that your mother told you and your brother to not say anything.

JOSEPHINE: (*crying*)

DET. SMITH: Just be honest with us, and nothing will happen to you.

JOSEPHINE: (*cries louder*)

DET. SMITH: He was trying to rape you, wasn't he?

JOSEPHINE: (*crying stops*)

DET. SMITH: George was in your room, wasn't he? It's okay, Josephine. I understand it. He had been doing things to your brother and now he was moving on to you, right? That's why he was in your bedroom, right?

JOSEPHINE: (*sniffles*) Y-yes.

DET. SMITH: All right. So he was a bastard, a sick bastard. And then your mom came in, am I right?

JOSEPHINE: Yes.

DET. SMITH: And then what happened?

FORTY-EIGHT

BILLIE ANN

I took Zelda, my golden retriever, out for a walk, while the succulent aroma of roasted turkey drifted through the house. As Zelda and I circled the block, I couldn't help but remember last year's Thanksgiving when Danni and I had celebrated with our two families together. With light laughter and cheerful banter filling the room, Danni had served up her signature dish— a sweet potato casserole to die for. Her daughters had played tag with Charlene in the backyard, filling the air with giggles. My heart ached as I thought of her dear daughters, who would be missing their mother this holiday. I assumed that their father would be with them, and missing her too, but then I remembered the night I saw Mike at the motel with another woman and it made me so angry.

I saw one of the neighbors and waved and wished him a happy Thanksgiving, then went back inside as soon as Zelda was done with her business.

I started preparing the rest of the dinner for my own family, trying to forget my worries as I put my energy into creating the perfect Thanksgiving spread. I hummed softly to myself as I did the stuffing, my mind occasionally drifting back to thoughts of

Danni and where she might be. I basted the turkey, peeled the vegetables, and sat watching the meat brown, while thinking of the trip Danni and I had taken to San Francisco the year before.

The memories of that trip were still fresh in my mind. We had rented a cozy little Airbnb, and had spent most of our time walking around the city, taking in the sights, the sounds, and the smells. We had also visited Alcatraz and the Golden Gate Bridge. Danni had been so happy, carefree, and full of life. I remembered how the Golden Gate Bridge had looked as we walked across it, the salty sea air filling our lungs. I thought of how Danni had held on to my arm, her fingers interlaced with mine. It was a bittersweet moment, filled with joy and sorrow. Joy, because we had been together, but also sorrow, because I knew we could never be together. We had kissed that night after a few drinks, but then she had pulled away. She had told me she was attracted to me, but she didn't want to lose her family. I understood that more than anything, because I felt the same way. I hated the thought of breaking my family apart. But to me there was no choice. That was the moment when I knew I could never go back to my normal life with my family. I couldn't stay married to Joe. It was in that instant I knew I was gay and that I was in love with her. Madly in love. And there was a big part of me I had been ignoring, hiding even.

How am I supposed to do this? Have Thanksgiving with my family? With my ex? When Danni is missing?

As I peeled the potatoes and started to make the gravy, the aroma from the turkey filling my entire house, I decided to distract myself with some music. I asked Alexa to play my favorite playlist and tried to sing along. Zelda barked excitedly, wagging her tail, and that made me feel slightly better. Until the next song came on and I realized it was Danni's favorite.

"Alexa, stop!" I yelled.

I touched the bridge of my nose, trying so hard to compose myself. But all I could think about was her. Her face, her eyes, and beautiful hair. We used to sit outside on the porch swing and talk all night, and no one could make me laugh the way she did. Gosh how I missed the sound of her laughter. She was the one I would come to when in need. She always knew what to say to make me feel better. I opened a bottle of white wine and had a glass.

Where are you, Danni?

Suddenly, the doorbell rang, breaking me out of my reverie. I went to answer it. Outside stood Joe. I looked at my watch.

"I thought we said five o'clock? I'm not even halfway done with the—"

I didn't get to finish. His angry eyes stared at me and he stormed past me. I closed the door behind him.

This wasn't good.

"Joe?" I said, walking out to him in the kitchen. He was shaking his head.

"What's wrong, Joe?" I asked. I felt anger rise in me. I wasn't going to let him ruin Thanksgiving. No matter what he was angry about, it would have to wait.

"Why didn't you tell me?" he asked.

"Tell you what?"

"That our son was arrested? For smoking weed?" My heart dropped. "I have to hear about it from one of the other fathers?"

"Yeah, well, I'm sorry about not telling you. There has been a lot going on."

"Oh so much you can't even tell me that my own son, my flesh and blood, is arrested? For doing drugs."

I blinked, thinking I needed to tell him about the more hardcore drugs too. But I had hoped to do it after the holidays. I didn't want to ruin it. William had promised me he wouldn't do drugs again. I trusted him.

"Well there has been a lot going on, in case you didn't know," I said.

"Like what?"

"I told you Danni was missing."

"Yes? But how is that more important than our son?"

"It isn't, but I just—well I never got around to telling you."

"You have to tell me these things. I'm his father. I'm beginning to think you're unfit as a mother, how about that?"

"What?"

"Yes, you're never home. You have no control over the children, don't know where they are half of the time, and you're always drinking." He pointed at the bottle I had just opened.

I scoffed. With a desperate voice, I said, almost crying: "I told you, Danni is missing. She's been kidnapped. My best friend."

He threw out his arms. "And why is that so important? People go missing all the time. She probably just ran away from that idiot she's married to. Why are you freaking out so much about..." he paused and stared at me, a shadow rushing over his face as the realization sank in.

"She's the one you fell in love with." It was a statement. One intended to catch me off guard, but I couldn't help reacting. I let out a breath, almost as if it was a relief for him to finally realize. He ran his hands through his hair.

"Of course. It all makes sense now. It was always Danni this and Danni that, and she was there all the time or you were at her place, and the trips... you took so many trips together. She was the one you fell in love with?"

I stared at him, barely blinking. It wasn't what he had said about me being in love with Danni that had made me stop. It was the other part. About her running away. I took out my phone then opened Joanne's Instagram page and scrolled through her old photos. And there it was. Right in front of my nose.

Oh dear God, no.

I took off my apron, then threw it at him. "Turkey is done in forty minutes, take it out and then mash the potatoes and finish the gravy, please."

I ran for my belt with my gun and badge, then strapped it on. Joe came out after me, still holding the apron in his hand. "Where are you going?"

"I'll explain later."

And with that I stormed out of the door, slamming it shut behind me. Just as I ran toward the car, black clouds had gathered above my head and it started to rain.

FORTY-NINE

RANDY

Randy stood in front of Joanne, his face a twisted mask of rage. The air around them seemed to be crackling with tension as he towered over her like a storm cloud, ready to unleash its fury at any second. They had been at it for hours. He had been yelling, and she had been begging him to stop. Joanne stared up at him, her eyes wide with fear and confusion. She had never seen him like this before, and it scared her.

"Why? Why would you do this to me?" His voice was thick with emotion and anger as he shouted at her. His fists were clenched and his body was trembling as he ranted and shouted.

"I... please don't hurt me anymore." Joanne touched her face where he had slapped her cheek. It was burning and painful. She wanted to plead her case, to explain herself to him, but the words would not come out. She just stared at him, unable to move or speak.

She knew it didn't matter what she said at this point.

"Have I not always been good to you, huh? Have I not given you everything you ever wanted?" Randy continued to scream at her, his words growing more and more venomous as he went on. He seemed to be barely holding back a primal urge to lash out at her, to do something momentous and irreversible. Joanne had never seen him so filled with hatred and contempt. And it scared her senseless.

Please dear God, please get him to stop. I can't take this anymore.

Randy's face was contorted with rage, and he began to pace around the room. He grabbed a framed photo of the two of them taken on their trip to Rome many years ago, then threw it against the wall. The glass shattered into small pieces and fell to the floor. Joanne clenched her ears and bent forward, while he picked up a lamp and it went the same way. Tears stung at Joanne's eyes as she watched him in stunned silence.

"You think I'm an idiot, don't you?!" he yelled, stopping mid-stride and turning to her. "You think I'm stupid enough to believe your lies?"

Joanne could only stare back at him in shock. His words felt like daggers piercing her heart as he continued his tirade.

"I trusted you!" he shouted, "I loved you. And this is how you repay me?" He thumped his fist against the wall and resumed pacing around the room.

"Please, Randy. Please stop."

Joanne watched him, trembling with fear and regret. She wanted desperately to apologize to him like she usually did, and then he would calm down. But in this moment she knew it would be pointless. He was too far gone to listen to reason now.

He grabbed a wineglass and lifted it with the intent to throw it.

"Just stop, Randy, stop it."

Randy suddenly stopped and turned to her again. He put the glass down. His voice softened slightly as he spoke, almost pleading with her for an explanation or apology that would never come.

"Why? Why would you do this?" he asked again, his voice barely above a whisper, his face streaked with tears of frustration. In them she saw so much pain and sadness. Desperation. Joanne shook her head sadly, unable to answer his question or make things right between them anymore. They stared at each other helplessly for a few moments before Randy finally slumped into a chair and put his head in his hands, overcome by exhaustion and emotion.

"R-Randy?"

Joanne was terrified. His sudden silence was even worse than the yelling and throwing of things. It was scarier. She had never seen her husband like this before; he was out of control and she was afraid for her safety.

What was he going to do?

She could see the gun on the table where it had been since he pulled it out of the safe after they came home. She wondered if she could make a run for it, grab it before he did, or if it would be better to go for the door, if she could get to it in time.

Or if it would be too late.

Randy looked up, and she saw something in his eyes that terrified her more than anything in this world. A darkness so deep it seemed endless. Joanne's heart pounded in her chest as Randy lunged for the gun on the table. He pointed it directly at her face, and she felt her breath catch in her throat as fear coursed through her veins. Time seemed to stand still as she stared into the barrel of the gun, not daring to move or even breathe.

Randy's finger curled around the trigger, and she braced herself for the deafening sound.

"Please, Randy, please don't do this." She begged him as tears streamed down her face.

The silence seemed to last forever as Randy closed his eyes as if he was trying to regain control of his breathing. He lowered the gun and swallowed hard, clearly trying to steady himself.

Joanne watched as Randy took a deep breath, like he was attempting to calm himself, as if he hoped to block out her pleading.

Then he lifted the gun and fired it.

FIFTY

BILLIE ANN

I stepped on the accelerator and the car leapt forward, barreling down A1A toward south Cocoa Beach. The sound of the engine roared in my ears as I weaved past other cars, pushing myself faster and faster. I had tried to call the hospital, but they said Joanne had been released the day before.

Her husband had taken her home.

The rain was pouring on my windshield, drumming loudly, intensifying the sense of urgency that lingered in the air. My heart beat at a rapid pace as thoughts raced through my mind; I slammed my hand on the steering wheel as if I believed it would help my car go faster or take me back in time so I could change my own stupidity. I couldn't believe I hadn't seen this before now. It was right there in front of me.

All this darn time.

The DNA found on Joanne was Rodriguez, but he didn't rape her. Rodriguez didn't rape her.

She'd gone willingly.

I drove up into a neighborhood called Snug Harbor, and rushed through the small streets toward the bigger houses located on the backside of the island. Inside of each of the houses people were getting ready to eat their turkey dinner, all gathered around the tables, mashed potatoes and gravy already on their plates. They would share what they were thankful for, while holding hands, and then eat themselves into oblivion, before passing out on the couch afterward, drunk on wine and turkey. Someone would bring up politics and then a heated discussion would break out between several of the family members, to the point where it almost destroyed everything, till someone said it was time for pie. In my family it had always been Joe and my dad who had the wild discussions. My mom would chime in, but mostly to support my dad's conservative views. One year we almost never made it to the pie before my dad proclaimed that it was time to leave. I had saved it by convincing them to at least stay till after pumpkin pie, and my dad said he preferred apple pie, but stayed and ate anyway. The worst Thanksgiving was the year my brother Andrew showed up. He was drunk and high on drugs, and began yelling at my mother. As a child Andrew had loved Thanksgiving. It was his favorite holiday, but as an adult he had missed most of them. I still wondered where he was. If he was okay.

Every year I both feared and hoped he would show up. Feared because if he was high then things would get out of hand with my mother. Hoped because I always thought there was a slight possibility that he could show up clean one day, and we could be a family again.

It was on Thanksgiving five years ago that we had seen him last. My mom had told him to never show his face here again.

That was Thanksgiving for you, and I was missing it again this year. To save someone's life. It wasn't the first time, though. I'd lost count of the amount of times my cases had taken precedence over my family life, but there were lives I could save here. I had just hoped that this year would be different, with all the issues we were going through as a family. I knew they needed me to be there for once. Yet I would have to let them down. Again.

I skidded sideways in a turn, then came to a halt in front of a three-story house with a huge pontoon boat strapped to the dock on the back of it, where the pool also was. I called Tom and Scott to let them know I was going to Joanne and Randy Edwards' house, and to bring backup ASAP, and then added a "sorry for ruining your Thanksgiving too."

I took in a deep breath, steadied myself, and felt my gun, just to be sure. I unstrapped it in my belt so it was easier to access, then got out. With quick steps I ran up toward the front door, using my jacket to cover myself from the pounding rain.

I reached the doorstep, just as I heard the gun go off.

I fumbled for the doorknob, praying it wasn't too late. The door was locked. I decided to kick it in. I burst through the door and found myself in a grand entrance hall. The walls were adorned with expensive paintings, and chandeliers hung from the ceiling, casting a warm glow in the otherwise dim room. There was a commotion coming from the back of the house, and I could hear someone shouting.

I hesitated for a moment, unsure of what to do next. Should I announce myself or sneak up on whoever was causing the disturbance? The decision was taken out of my hands as another gunshot rang out. I moved quickly, following the sounds of the chaos. I passed through a dining room that looked like a set from a movie, complete with a long mahogany table and crystal glasses, but I barely registered it.

Suddenly, I saw movement out of the corner of my eye. I turned and saw a figure dart into a nearby room. I ran toward it, my heart pounding in my chest. I burst into the room and saw her there, lying on the ground, blood pooling around her.

"Joanne!" I screamed, dropping to my knees beside her. "Oh my God, Joanne."

She tried to speak, but only gasped for breath. I could see the life draining out of her, her eyes losing focus.

"I'm here," I said, taking her hand and squeezing it tightly. "Just hold on, I'm going to get you help."

I stood up and looked around the room, scanning for any sign of the shooter. I saw movement out of the corner of my eye and turned to see a shadowy figure standing in the doorway.

It was Randy.

He raised the gun, taking aim at me. I dove for cover just as another shot was fired, the bullet whizzing past my ear. Without hesitation, I pulled out my own gun and aimed it at him.

"Drop the gun!" I shouted.

Randy hesitated for a moment before raising his gun again, staring down at me.

"Drop the gun," I yelled again. "Or I will shoot."

Randy shook his head, turned around, then stormed out of the door. I set off after him, but as I reached the back door, he was nowhere to be seen.

I let out a sigh and turned back to Joanne. She was still alive, but barely. I quickly called 911 and held her hand in mine as we waited anxiously for the ambulance to arrive.

FIFTY-ONE

Then

TRANSCRIPT OF INTERVIEW OF JOSEPHINE DURST
DEFENDANT'S EXHIBIT A
DURST PART I

APPEARANCES:
Detective Michael Smith
Detective Lenny Travis
Sergeant Joseph Mill

JOSEPHINE: I don't remember what happened next.
DET. SMITH: You don't remember or you don't want to remember?
JOSEPHINE: (*sighs*) I don't want to talk about.
DET. SMITH: I understand, Josephine. I totally do. Was it the first time George had come to your room?
JOSEPHINE: N-no.
DET. SMITH: So it happened sometimes? Often?
JOSEPHINE: (*nods*)

DET. SMITH: That's okay, sweetie. And so when your mom came in last night, was he on top of you?

JOSEPHINE: Y-yes.

DET. SMITH: And where was your brother?

JOSEPHINE: He was standing by the bed.

DET. SMITH: How long had he been there?

JOSEPHINE: I don't know.

DET. SMITH: Okay so just to get the story straight. You have Thanksgiving dinner, then you go watch a movie, but the movie is abruptly stopped when your mom realizes that George is... touching your brother. They then fight and you two both run into your room and hide. And then George comes in there and finds you?

JOSEPHINE: Yes. He grabbed my arm and pulled me out of the closet where we were hiding.

DET. SMITH: And then what did he do?

JOSEPHINE: Her threw me on the bed.

DET. SMITH: Did you scream?

JOSEPHINE: Yes.

DET. SMITH: Did your brother scream?

JOSEPHINE: Yes.

DET. SMITH: And then your mom came in and saw what was happening?

JOSEPHINE: Yes.

DET. SMITH: And then she shot him?

JOSEPHINE: (*sighs*) I don't know. I was fighting with him and suddenly he just... died. There was blood on me, and I cried. I pushed him off me.

DET. SMITH: That must have been scary, huh? Were you scared?

JOSEPHINE: Y-yes.

DET. SMITH: Did you see who held the gun when you looked at your brother and mother standing there?

JOSEPHINE: N-no. It was on the floor.

DET. SMITH: Okay. Thank you, sweetie. I want you to know none of this was your fault, okay? Your stepfather was a bad bad man.

JOSEPHINE: Can I have another soda now? And do you have any ice cream?

FIFTY-TWO

STAN

Stan liked his job as a mall cop. Actually, it was more than that. He loved it. He used to be a real cop, but he had never enjoyed it much, as he was too fearful especially when approaching vehicles he had stopped for speeding or other reasons. He was aways so afraid someone might have a gun in their glove compartment and that they would pull it on him. He had a colleague this happened to in Orlando, and he had been terrified of it ever since. But after twenty years on the force, he had been able to retire and now he made a little extra money as a mall cop. People respected him just the same, and he enjoyed their happy faces and all the smiles he got, especially from children he met.

It was Black Friday and probably the worst day of the year. At least according to everyone else. All the other mall cops never wanted to work on Black Fridays, but Stan enjoyed it. He was a lonely man, and he liked it when the mall was a hive of activity as shoppers browsed the multitude of stores and sought out the perfect item to take home for the best price. He knew that at the most he might have to separate two moms fighting over a dress or some lingerie, or maybe throw out some drunk who yelled at people walking by. The teenagers laughed at him behind his back, he knew it and heard it, but he prided himself at the fact that he was keeping them safe and if he caught them smoking in the restrooms, he would get his revenge by calling their parents to come get them.

It was all worth it in the end.

It was around noon when Stan did his rounds. He suddenly noticed a suitcase on one of the benches by Macy's. Alerted by this, he watched it for a few minutes to make sure no one was coming to claim it, and when no one did, he approached it cautiously, not wanting to startle anyone who might be nearby. There was no reason to scare people. There could be many reasons why a suitcase like this was left behind. Usually, it was just because some tourist forgot it, and they would come claim it soon after. He would have to take it to lost and found if no one came soon. Then he would have to file a report, and he really didn't want to have to do that. So he waited a little longer, and took a round inside of Macy's, greeting the pretty young girls behind the counters on his way.

When he came back, it was still there.

"Dang it." He cursed. He had really hoped it would be gone.

The place was still filled with people, hurrying in and out of stores, carrying bags of things they had found on sale, happy with the money they believed they had saved, but no one seemed to take any notice of the suitcase.

Stan took a few hesitant steps forward, feeling his chest tighten with each movement. He was sure that no one else was going to come and claim the mysterious suitcase, and now he couldn't stop himself from imagining the worst.

What if it's a bomb?

He had heard the stories and gone through the training. He knew this was not something you ignored. His pulse quickened as he heard an imaginary ticking sound in his head, and he reached for the gun tucked inside his belt.

He crouched down to get a closer look. He stared at the black suitcase, shaking his head in frustration. This could very well be one of those times when he couldn't afford to not react.

It was better to do it once too many than too few. His mom had always told him that.

Stan made the decision promptly. He called it over the radio, so they could sound the alarm from the security room, then blew his whistle to alert everyone and then yelled at people to make sure everyone heard him: "Everyone! Please leave the building! There is an unknown object that may be dangerous!"

The shoppers, startled by the sudden announcement, began to scurry in all directions, knocking over merchandise and trampling one another as they made their way to the nearest exit.

Some of the shoppers looked at Stan with confusion and fear, but they didn't hesitate to follow his orders. Stan felt a sense of pride as his training kicked in and he took control of the situation. He radioed for backup and waited for the police to arrive with their bomb squad, feeling good about himself.

He had done his job and done it well.

FIFTY-THREE

BILLIE ANN

Joanne stirred, slowly coming to consciousness. I watched her as she blinked her eyes open and tried to take in her surroundings. The beeping of machines had become a familiar sound, since I had been waiting for her to wake up for hours. I hadn't left her side since we got there the night before. She winced as she felt the tight bandages that had been wrapped around her chest and abdomen like a heavy suit of armor.

"What happened?" she whispered, her voice weak and strained. "What day is it?"

I moved to the side of her bed and took her hand. "It's Friday," I said, my voice heavy with grief. "Randy is on the run. He pulled his weapon at me and was about to kill you. He shot you in your chest. You were lucky, they said, that you made it."

Joanne looked out the window at the cruise ships in the distance. Tears welled up in her eyes as she turned back to me. I had rushed over to her home because I thought she had lied to me, but I hadn't expected to find Randy brandishing a weapon. I didn't trust him either, but it had been a surprise... I still didn't know what was going on, just that my instincts about this couple were off. And rightly so.

"Do you have any idea why?" I asked. "Why would Randy do something like that?"

She glared up at me, then shook her head slowly. "I don't know," she said. "He was so angry."

"What about?" I asked, frustrated. I felt like she was lying to me again. I wanted to be there for her, but I was rapidly losing my patience. "Do you remember?"

"No, not really."

I nodded and walked closer. "I'll tell you then."

"What do you mean?" she asked with a light gasp, looking at me with her big fearful eyes.

"I am just so mad at myself for not figuring it out sooner," I said. "I mean it was right there, in front of me."

"I don't know what you're talking about," she said and tried to sit up, but winced in pain.

I scoffed. "I think you do."

Joanne looked at me with fear and confusion in her eyes. "I don't know," she said, her voice quivering. "I don't remember anything."

I let out a heavy sigh and took a deep breath. "It was all fake, wasn't it?"

"What do you mean?"

"Don't give me that," I said. "I should have figured it out when we found Adam Rodriguez's DNA on you after you came back. We thought he had raped you, but he didn't, did he?"

Joanne's eyes widened in shock as she tried to process what I had just said. She shook her head, but I ignored it.

"You faked your own kidnapping, so you could go be with your ex-boyfriend, didn't you? You wanted out from your relationship with Randy, and you wanted to get back to your ex. To Adam. Don't bother denying it, I went through your Instagram feed this morning and found an old picture of you and him from three years ago. Didn't look like he had kidnapped you back then either. So what happened, why did you come back?"

Tears welled up in her eyes and started to run down her cheeks. She hid her face in her hands as she replied, "I'm so sorry. It wasn't supposed to go this far. All of a sudden it was all over the news, and Adam got scared, and he started to yell at me and tell me he was going to jail, that the police thought he had kidnapped me. I wanted to come home to Randy. I realized I didn't want to stay with Adam. I couldn't let Randy know I had run away to be with Adam. He would never forgive me. And so-so I came up with this story. That I had been kidnapped and got out."

I scoffed, angrily. "And you even went so far as to have him brand you with a hot metal object, didn't you? And beat you up, to make it look real? And cut your hair?"

She lifted her gaze and stared at me. "I'm so so sorry. I feel awful."

"Well you should. You've wasted our time. You do realize that, don't you? Someone dear to me might die because of you leading us in the wrong direction. It makes me so mad. So many people have been affected by this. By your actions. Randy found out and got mad too, right? He beat up Adam, who is still in a coma, and then he tried to kill you. We're still searching for him. He is out there somewhere, and I have placed a guard at your door, in case he tries to come for you again. I hardly think so since I believe it was an act of anger in the spur of the moment. I don't believe he wanted to kill you, just hurt you. Nevertheless, he will of course be prosecuted for it, when we find him. But to think that all this could have been avoided, had you just told the truth. It's unbelievable."

I looked down at her, shaking my head in disbelief. I couldn't stand looking at her. She made me so angry. Never had I met anyone more selfish.

"You'll be arrested, as soon as you're done with your treatment here. You can count on that."

I walked to the door and grabbed the handle, then stopped and turned to look at her.

"I hope it was worth it. I really hope it was."

I was fuming as I rushed back to my car and hit my hand in the steering wheel hard as I drove out of the hospital's parking lot. All this wasted time and resources. How was I going to find Danni now? Before it was too late?

FIFTY-FOUR

BILLIE ANN

I returned to headquarters and debriefed my team on Joanne Edwards' case and the new development. Tom told me Randy Edwards was still being searched for but they had found no sign of him yet. I told them to keep trying. He couldn't get away. But as I spoke my phone kept lighting up, and I realized it was Charlene, my oldest. She had called a handful of times, and I knew I had to go home and check on them.

My hand fumbled against the door handle, my fingertips barely managing to grasp it before I stumbled into the house. Exhaustion crept over me like a heavy blanket, and the oppressive stillness of the home weighed down on me as I trudged forward. I collapsed on the couch, and my eyes fluttered shut. All I wanted was a few moments of rest. Just a couple of minutes.

But I didn't even get that.

"Mommy!"

My youngest son, Zack, came running from the kitchen. He stormed toward me and jumped me on the couch, then hugged me tight.

"Where you been, Mommy?" he asked, his big eyes searching mine for answers. "You were gone for turkey day?"

I sighed. I couldn't really tell him what had happened. "I had to work," I said, my voice shaking with exhaustion. "I'm so sorry, sweetheart. I missed it."

"It's okay, Mommy," he said and gave me another squeeze before taking off, back to his PlayStation or Nintendo or whatever he was into these days. I could barely keep track of him anymore. "There will be another one next year."

I watched him take off up the stairs, with a chuckle, then noticed my oldest child, Charlene, was standing in the doorway of the living room, her arms crossed and her face etched with anger.

"I can't believe you. You weren't here for Thanksgiving?" she said, her voice tinged with accusation. "How could you do that? That's the worst thing ever! It's the one day we're supposed to be together, as a family. You made a big deal about how important it was that I stayed here?"

I exhaled. I was tired of having to explain myself constantly. "You know what, Charlene? I was working, okay? It was an emergency. Someone was in danger. Cut me some slack here. I'm doing my best."

She shook her head at me. "Someone is always in danger. Why can't they send someone else? Why does it always have to be you?"

"Because it's my job? And it pays the bills?" I said with a scoff. "I don't hear you complaining about it when I give you money to go to the mall, or when you got the truck."

"I thought Dad paid the bills," she said.

"In case you haven't noticed your dad doesn't exactly live here anymore," I said.

"And whose fault is that?" she almost screamed at me, then took off.

I exhaled deeply then lay my head back down on the

pillow. I was actually excited she was going to Orlando later today, so I didn't have to deal with her.

My soon-to-be ex-husband Joe stepped out from the kitchen, his expression dark.

But his look wasn't angry. It was worse. He was disappointed.

"You know I had really looked forward to this Thanksgiving?" he said. "It was our last chance to be a family. And you couldn't even give us that, could you?"

"So I guess I should just have let this guy kill his wife, then?" I said, feeling sick of all their reproaches. All I needed right now was a hug and understanding. Zack seemed to be the only one who understood that. I had almost been too late to save Joanne. It didn't exactly make me feel good. All I wanted to do was to crawl into the fetal position and cry. But there was no room for me to cry, or to be vulnerable. I had to do everything perfectly, and yet no one was ever happy.

That's what was exhausting.

"I don't even know who you are anymore," Joe said.

"Welcome to the club," I said, throwing out my arms. "I don't know who I am anymore either."

He nodded. "I guess not. Well I'm gonna go, there are leftovers in the fridge if you're hungry. I can't say the kids and I had a good time, since they missed you like crazy and no one really spoke during dinner, but Zack is right. There's always next year and by then we will do it differently. Christmas too. I can't do this with you anymore. We need to act like the separated couple that we are and start arranging our lives accordingly."

With that, he left, and I sat back on the couch feeling awful. I really couldn't make anyone happy anymore, could I? When the kids were younger it had been so easy. I missed those days, when my kids were cute. It was true what they said. Small kids meant small problems, big kids, big problems.

Speaking of. I got up from the couch, then walked up the

stairs to William's room. As I approached it, I could smell it right away, and my heart sank.

I opened the door, and was immediately hit with the pungent scent of marijuana. The room was filled with a heavy smoke, and William lay motionless in the middle of the bed, his eyes half-closed and his body slouched. It was clear he was high. Tears welled up in my eyes, and I noticed his bong on the side table and bags of weed scattered around. My heart ached as I gathered all of it into a garbage bag and stormed out of the room, hearing the door slam behind me. With shaking hands, I threw it all away in the dumpster outside.

Back inside, in my bedroom, I curled up on my bed, tears streaming down my cheeks, my whole body wracked with sobs.

I cried till I had no more tears in me, and then my phone rang. It was the Chief.

"We've got another body."

I immediately thought of Danni. I had lost all my leads with Joanne's deception. And my heart dropped in my chest.

FIFTY-FIVE

Then

TRANSCRIPT OF INTERVIEW OF CAROL DURST

DEFENDANT'S EXHIBIT A

DURST PART 3

APPEARANCES:
Detective Michael Smith
Detective Lenny Travis
Sergeant Joseph Mill

DET. SMITH: You gotta help me here, Carol, because there are things that are not quite adding up here.
CAROL DURST: (*clears throat*) And what is that?
DET. SMITH: Well, we just spoke to your daughter again, and she tells us that she was on the bed when George was shot. When we spoke to you, you said both kids were standing in the room, and the gun was on the floor.
CAROL DURST: On the bed? I don't understand.

DET. SMITH: Don't play stupid, Carol. You know what I am talking about.

CAROL DURST: I don't.

DET. SMITH: I'm getting a little tired of your lies. It's okay. The children have told us what he did to them.

CAROL DURST: Oh.

DET. SMITH: Yes, Josephine told us he pulled her onto the bed and crawled on top of her.

CAROL DURST: Okay, yes.

DET. SMITH: So she was on the bed when George was shot?

CAROL DURST: Yes, yes she was.

DET. SMITH: She couldn't have pulled the trigger then?

CAROL DURST: No of course not.

DET. SMITH: (*exhales*) So that leaves us with you and Bobby.

CAROL DURST: I guess so.

DET. SMITH: Can you see how this makes it hard for us to believe your innocence?

CAROL DURST: Bobby did it.

DET. SMITH: Your son? He went to the safe and got the gun out and shot your husband?

CAROL DURST: Yes, he must have.

DET. SMITH: So you didn't see it happening?

CAROL DURST: No, I was downstairs.

DET. SMITH: But you said both children were standing on the floor when you got up there. And now you're changing it to Josephine lying on the bed, with George on top of her?

CAROL DURST: Yes.

DET. SMITH: Were you lying?

CAROL DURST: No. No. I just... well a lot happened and I guess it can be hard to remember everything precisely.

DET. SMITH: Listen, Carol. I have children. If anyone hurt them, especially someone close to me, I would want to kill them too. You were just defending your daughter.

CAROL DURST: But I didn't do it.

DET. SMITH: I think you did.

CAROL DURST: No, no. I didn't. He was dead when I came up there.

DET. SMITH: So you're saying Bobby, who is ten years old, pulled the trigger on your husband?

CAROL DURST: It must have been him. Who else could it be?

DET. SMITH: And you're not just saying that because you fear going to jail, and maybe even get the chair, but if you blame the children, then the punishment won't be as hard?

CAROL DURST: N-no. Of course not. What kind of a mother would do that?

DET. SMITH: But your son says you fired the gun, and the gun was wiped clean of fingerprints afterward, and all your hands were washed so there remained no gun residue trace. I hardly think a young boy of only ten years would think about hiding the evidence like that. That's really clever. Don't you think?

CAROL DURST: It sure is.

DET. SMITH: Do you really want to ruin your son's life with this?

CAROL DURST: What do you mean?

DET. SMITH: If he goes to jail.

CAROL DURST: You just said he would get an easier punishment.

DET. SMITH: Maybe he won't. The DA is pushing for him to be tried as an adult.

CAROL DURST: Really?

DET. SMITH: Really. He might end up in a real prison. With adult murderers. He might end up spending his entire childhood there.

CAROL DURST: That's bad.

DET. SMITH: It's really bad.

CAROL DURST: I would like to change my statement. Can I do that?

FIFTY-SIX

BILLIE ANN

The mall's parking lot was nearly empty, save for a few police cars and an ambulance. As I approached the entrance, I noticed a yellow cordon stretching from one side of the building to the other.

Inside, the mall was deserted and eerily quiet. People had been evacuated and officers were scattered throughout the area, guns drawn and in defensive positions. In the center, near the food court, I spotted my Chief. She beckoned me over.

"They thought it was a bomb," she said, her voice low and solemn. "But when the bomb squad arrived, they quickly realized it wasn't."

She paused, then gestured toward the suspicious suitcase that had been quarantined in the corner of the mall.

Taking a deep breath, I stepped forward and looked inside of the unlocked case. I could feel my heart in my throat as my eyes fell on what was inside of it .

It was a head. The severed head of a male.

I felt my stomach churn and my knees buckle. I had never seen a severed head before, and the grisly sight was too much for me to bear. I stumbled backward, feeling a wave of nausea and revulsion wash over me.

I stumbled backward slightly. I heard the Chief call out to me, her voice a distant echo in my ears. I couldn't focus on her words, couldn't focus on anything except the sight that had just greeted me. I felt like I was going to be sick, and I wanted nothing more than to run out of there and never come back.

But I couldn't.

"What do we know so far?" I asked, trying to keep my voice steady. At least it wasn't Danni I was looking at.

The Chief looked at me with concern. "Look at the tag. On the bag."

I reached down and grabbed the tag, then stared at it for several seconds. It read:

BILLIE ANN WILDE

"What do you make of it?" she asked behind me. I stared at the tag, then realized I'd seen the luggage before. "This is mine. This is my suitcase."

"Are you okay?" the Chief asked placing a hand on my shoulder.

"I'm... I'm not sure," I said. " I didn't even know the suitcase was gone; it should be stored in my closet. I haven't used it in years."

I bent forward, holding my stomach, feeling a cold sweat starting to form on my forehead. Someone had been in my home. Near my children. If Danielle's name had been on the first suitcases and bags, and she had been kidnapped after, did that mean I was next?

I stood upright and turned to face the Chief. My mind raced, trying to piece all the clues together.

"What does this mean?" I muttered.

The Chief nodded, "We don't know but first we need to get you out of here. Get you to your children and ensure your house is safe."

FIFTY-SEVEN

BILLIE ANN

I moved aside so the forensic team could come into my house. I felt exhausted. I had barely slept all night, thinking about how there had been someone inside of my house, going through my things in my walk-in closet and taking my suitcase. I had been staring at it when I just came home, wondering how come I didn't notice it was gone. But it was hidden behind clothes that I never wear. It was eerie to realize that I didn't even know it was missing, and had no idea how long it had been gone.

I'd spent most of the night walking through my house, checking on the kids to make sure they were okay. I told them what was going on this morning, but I thought they'd need a good night's sleep.

I was hoping the team might find something, a fingerprint or maybe even DNA, but didn't get my hopes up, since they hadn't found anything when going through Danni's house. This killer knew how to be careful.

I didn't feel safe in my home anymore. I crumpled onto the couch, tears streaming down my face. The reality of the situation hit me hard. Someone had broken into my home. My safe haven. My sanctuary. And I had no idea who they were or why they had chosen me as a target. Was that why they had taken Danielle? Because they knew I loved her?

The thought made my heart race and my hands shake. I couldn't even fathom the idea that Danielle could be in danger because of me. I knew I had to find her, but I didn't have any clue where to start. I feared that we would find her body in the next suitcase that showed up.

I stood frozen in the doorway when the team arrived. Their hairnets and gloves a stark contrast to the casual disarray of our living room. The sound of footsteps echoed hollowly on hardwood floors as they moved about the space with methodical efficiency, documenting each speck of dust and splinter of wood. The crinkle of plastic bags filled my ears as possible evidence was bagged and labeled. Each step the men in blue bodysuits took was measured, each movement methodical. The sound of latex gloves snapping on and off filled the air more than the words spoken by the investigators. Everything was a dull blur of activity and noise.

Charlene came up to me and hugged me. I had told her there was no way she was going to Orlando now. I needed to be able to keep an eye on her. She had accepted, luckily.

"This is scary, Mom. I don't like it."

I hugged her back and kissed her forehead. "Me either. I want you to take your brothers and go to your dad's place. Spend the night there."

"But Mo-om, he lives in a tiny apartment and I have no privacy there. I don't have my own room, I share it with Zack and William. I hate it there."

"I know, sweetie, but right now it's for the best," I said, trying my hardest to sound like I was keeping it together. I had to force myself to stay strong and suppress the fear rising in my throat.

Charlene looked up at me and said, "But why can't we just stay here, Mom? With you? I'm scared."

I swallowed hard and hugged her tight again.

"I know, sweetie. But the police need to investigate everything thoroughly. I don't want you guys to be here while they do their work. It's just safer if you're somewhere else for now," I explained, my voice quivering slightly.

Charlene looked up at me with her big eyes full of fear and uncertainty. I wished I could make everything better for her, shield her from the horrors of the world. But I couldn't. All I could do was try to keep her safe.

"Okay, Mom," she said softly, nodding her head in understanding.

I kissed her forehead again and watched as she gathered her younger brothers and left with their overnight bags. I watched them go, feeling a pang of guilt in my chest. I knew how much Charlene hated going to her father's apartment, but I couldn't risk their safety. Once they were out of sight, I turned back to the investigators.

"Can you tell me anything yet?" I asked, hoping for some sort of answer.

The lead investigator shook his head. "Not yet, ma'am. But we'll let you know as soon as we find out anything."

They continued for several hours, dusting for fingerprints and taking pictures, then finally left. My house felt empty and cold all of a sudden. But I was more determined than ever to find Danni, even if it was the last thing I did.

FIFTY-EIGHT

BILLIE ANN

"Are you okay?"

Chief Harold had called me into her office. It was later in the afternoon and I had gone to the station even if it was Saturday and I had the day off. My house felt unsafe and empty without the children. I couldn't stand just staying there, while Danni was in trouble.

I exhaled and sat down. "To be honest, I'm barely keeping it together."

"I can understand that," she said. "You didn't have to come in today. In fact I didn't expect you to."

"I know. I just... I keep thinking about the victims, and my suitcase, and Danielle Simmons. I feel that we're back to square one. Now that everything we thought we knew turned out to be false."

"I can't believe Joanne made it all up," Chief Harold said. "The kidnapping, the detailed descriptions of the kidnappers."

"Which were kind of a stereotype, with the big earrings and all that. That was our first red flag. I should have seen it."

"But she was hurt? Beaten up and branded."

"All self-inflicted or done by Adam Rodriguez, her ex-boyfriend. But on her request, if you believe it."

"Geez. That's insane."

I nodded.

"You can say that again. She admitted to it all. But the worst part is that we wasted so much time and resources on her case. Meanwhile, the real kidnapper is still out there. And he has Danielle Simmons. Hopefully still alive."

Chief Harold sighed. "I know it's frustrating. But we can't dwell on the past. We need to focus on the present and the future. We can still catch this guy, but we need to start fresh."

I leaned forward. "What do you mean?"

"I mean, we need to retrace our steps and look for new leads. We need to work on the assumption that everything we thought we knew about this case might be wrong. We can't take anything for granted."

I nodded, feeling a glimmer of hope. "You're right. We need to start over. But where do we begin?"

I stared at the photograph Chief Harold handed me. It was of a man in his mid-thirties, with short brown hair and a closely cropped beard. He looked familiar, though I couldn't quite place where I knew him from.

"Who is he?" I asked.

Chief Harold sighed and folded her hands on the desk in front of her. The look in her eyes was serious. "His name is Michael Smith. He was a detective with the sheriff's office. The picture is about fifteen years old."

"Was?" I echoed faintly.

She nodded slowly. "It was his head we found in the suitcase. Your suitcase."

I could feel my stomach twisting into knots as the reality of what she was saying hit me. He was a colleague?

"He was getting ready to retire," she continued. "I spoke to his wife, and she hasn't seen him since he disappeared four days ago. She believed he went on a bender as he did from time to time. He would usually come back after a week or so, and tell her how sorry he was and promise it wouldn't happen again."

I rubbed my neck, unable to wrap my mind around this news. "You're saying that we need to find the link between him and Danielle Simmons?"

Chief Harold nodded again. "Yes, that's exactly what I'm saying. And also Carol Durst, the first victim we found." She opened up a folder and slid it across the desk toward me. "We've done some research into Michael's background."

Inside the folder were several documents detailing Michael Smith's life: birth certificate, job history, credit report, any other information that was needed to look closely into the guy.

I skimmed through the documents. He lived in the Orlando area. No known connections to either of the victims. It was as if he was a completely random victim himself.

"I don't get it," I said, looking up at Chief Harold. "Why would someone kill Michael Smith and then put his head in my suitcase? It doesn't make any sense."

"I know," Chief Harold said with a sigh. "But we can't ignore the fact that there's a connection here. We just need to keep digging until we find it."

I nodded, feeling a sense of determination wash over me. "I'll do whatever it takes to catch this guy. For Michael Smith, for Carol Durst, and for Danielle Simmons."

Chief Harold gave me a small smile. "I know you will. And I'll be here to support you every step of the way."

Feeling slightly better, I stood up. Chief Harold looked at me with a mix of concern and admiration.

"Just be careful, okay? I don't like the whole suitcase part, and the fact that he was in your house. It scares me. We don't know what we're dealing with here. And take some time off if you need it. Don't burn yourself out."

I nodded, feeling grateful for her concern. "I will. Thank you, Chief Harold."

"I mean it."

I smiled in agreement, knowing that I had already pushed myself to the brink. But I couldn't let that stop me. Not when there was a killer on the loose and Danni was in great danger.

If she was still alive.

You can't think like that.

I looked at the Chief, then realized I couldn't keep it a secret any longer. She trusted me and I had to come clean. It would come out anyway. At some point. With my name being on the tag, I was in too deep. It could be important for the case to know my connection with Danni.

"I-I need to tell you something," I said.

"Yes?"

"It's about Danielle Simmons, and the reason why my name was on the tag."

She folded her hands on the desk. "Go on."

I cleared my throat nervously. I felt awful. Like a kid being caught in a lie.

"I-I know her. She's a friend. A close friend."

She lifted both eyebrows and leaned back. "And you were afraid I would take you off the case if you told me, which I totally would have."

"Y-yes."

She scoffed. "That is very unprofessional of you. You should have told me."

"I know. I just... I really need to find her. Please don't take me off the case. I have to find her."

She paused and looked at me for what felt like an eternity while mulling it over in her head.

"Please," I said.

She leaned forward. "I told you I don't believe in second chances."

"I know."

She cleared her throat, then leaned back. "All right. It's too late to take you off it now, I guess. You're in too deep. But this can never happen again. From now on you're completely honest with me, do you understand?"

"Yes. Thank you so much, Chief."

"Don't make me regret it. Find Danielle Simmons and get this bastard locked up."

"Yes, ma'am."

As I left Chief Harold's office, I could breathe, relieved for the first time. My mind raced with the possibilities and connections that could lead us to the killer. But one thought kept creeping its way back to the forefront of my mind: why was Michael Smith killed? What was his connection to all of this? I thought this killer went for women, but it was becoming very apparent that I had gone about this case all wrong.

I knew that I needed to focus on the present and the future, but the past was still lurking in the shadows, waiting to be uncovered. And I couldn't shake the feeling that it held the key to everything.

FIFTY-NINE

Then

TRANSCRIPT OF INTERVIEW OF CAROL DURST
DEFENDANT'S EXHIBIT A
DURST PART 3

APPEARANCES:
Detective Michael Smith
Detective Lenny Travis
Sergeant Joseph Mill

DET. SMITH: What would you like to change your statement to?

CAROL DURST: I-I did it. I shot my husband. I shot George Andersson.

DET. SMITH: Okay. Can you tell us more? How did it happen?

CAROL DURST: Well he was doing things. To my children.

DET. SMITH: We know about the couch and your son, and what about your daughter?

CAROL DURST: Yes. Her too. He did stuff to her too.

DET. SMITH: How often?

CAROL DURST: I-I don't know. A lot.

DET. SMITH: Okay, so what happened on the night he was shot? You were watching a movie and then what happened?

CAROL DURST: (*clears throat*) I... walked up stairs and got the gun out of the safe, then walked into my daughter's room and shot him.

DET. SMITH: And where was he at the time of the shooting?

CAROL DURST: In her bed.

DET. SMITH: And she was in the bed as well?

CAROL DURST: Uh yes. Yes, she was.

DET. SMITH: And what were they doing? In the bed?

CAROL DURST: Do I have to talk about it?

DET. SMITH: It will strengthen your case.

CAROL DURST: (*clears throat*) Okay, well he was... um... touching her and stuff.

DET. SMITH: What do you mean by touching her and stuff?

CAROL DURST: You want me to give details?

DET. SMITH: If possible, yes.

CAROL DURST: I don't know... I... it all went really fast and I didn't really have time to think and I hardly remember much.

DET. SMITH: Just what you do remember.

CAROL DURST: Okay, he was in bed with her, and I shot him. I couldn't stand what he was doing to my children anymore.

DET. SMITH: Okay. Well, that makes sense.

CAROL DURST: I was just... so angry. I snapped.

DET. SMITH: Because of the abuse?

CAROL DURST: (*sniffles*) Yes. It had been going on for a very long time. I guess I just... finally lost it.

DET. SMITH: How long had it been going on?

CAROL DURST: How long? Uh... I don't know. Years, I think. Listen. I'm not a violent person. I just couldn't stand by and watch anymore. I had enough. You might not understand, but when someone hurts your children, it's just... I couldn't... (*cries*) I didn't mean to kill him, I just... wanted to stop him. Please know that I'm not a bad person.

DET. SMITH: It's okay, Carol. I have children myself and I understand. When was the first time you realized he was molesting your children?

CAROL DURST: (*sniffles*) When was the first time? Uh... Three years ago, I think.

DET. SMITH: And you didn't do anything then?

CAROL DURST: I thought it might stop. I hoped it would end. I guess I turned a blind eye.

DET. SMITH: Did you plan on shooting him? Had you thought about it?

CAROL DURST: No. It was a spontaneous decision. I just had enough, and couldn't control it. I snapped.

DET. SMITH: And you do realize what it is you're admitting to, right? You're admitting to murder of the first degree.

CAROL DURST: (*sobs*) Yes. I'm sorry. I really am. You must believe me when I say I didn't mean to kill him.

DET. SMITH: I believe you. Thank you for your honesty.

SIXTY

BILLIE ANN

I called the kids and told them to stay at their dad's again tonight since it still wasn't safe for them at the house. Charlene complained but I ignored her. This was for her own safety and I was her mother. Besides, I was working late and had no idea when I would be home.

Tom, Scott, and I sat in a cramped office with the overhead lights flickering. The walls were covered with evidence boards full of pictures and newspaper clippings. We silently pored through pages of documents, trying to make sense of the jumble of information before us. Then my phone buzzed with an incoming call. It was the lab technician—they'd found Mike Simmons' DNA on a sample from my house. We all exchanged grim looks.

I opened my laptop and found the surveillance video of Danielle again, and thought again about it being someone she knew.

"It's not a stranger," I said out loud.

Scott and Tom both looked up from their computer screens. "What's that?" Scott asked.

I stared at him, my mind racing. Mike was someone I had

trusted. But the more I thought about it, the more it made sense. He had always been very controlling about Danni, always texting her when we were together, doing lunches or going to the beach, asking about her constantly, wanting to know where she was at all times. And now, with the surveillance footage, it all clicked into place. And it all fit well with the fact that I had seen him at the motel with a girl. Had they planned it together? To get rid of her? He was there when I came over all flustered about the suitcase and the tag. He heard what I said about it.

I hurried into the Chief's office. Her door was open, so I walked in yet knocked lightly on the open door.

The Chief was sitting behind her desk, her eyes glued to the screen of her laptop. She didn't move or look up when I entered.

"Chief?" I said softly.

"Yes?" She finally looked up and noticed me standing there. "What is it, Billie? What can I do for you?" she asked.

"I want to book Mike Simmons."

She gave me a surprised look. "Arrest him? On what grounds?"

"Hair," I said. "They found a hair in my house, and paired the DNA with his that he gave us when Danielle went missing. It was a match."

The Chief's eyebrows shot up. "You're kidding me?" she said.

"No, dead serious."

I took a deep breath and tried to stay calm, although my heart was racing. I didn't tell her that Mike had been to my home before; I knew it would cause her to rationalize the scene. I wouldn't be able to bring him in, and I needed to. I thought perhaps he knew about me and Danni... if that was the reason I had been targeted too. But I couldn't tell the Chief that either. "The lab results just came in."

She pushed the laptop aside and leaned back in her chair, steepling her fingers in front of her face thoughtfully.

"Go on," she said quietly as she waited for me to continue.

"I don't have all the details yet, but I have a good feeling about this. I think he's our guy. I really do."

"And you are sure?" Her voice was stern now as she gazed at me intently for confirmation.

I nodded slowly, my stomach churning. "Yes, ma'am."

The Chief sighed heavily and stood up from her chair, pacing around the room thoughtfully for a few moments before speaking again.

"You're sure about this?" she asked, her voice wavering slightly. I nodded my head slowly, never breaking eye contact with her. She paused for a moment and looked away, taking a deep breath before finally speaking again.

"Hmm, I guess it makes sense. But wait, how exactly is he connected to Carol Durst and Michael Smith? I thought we worked on the theory that it's the same killer. And if he went to get your suitcase, then we must assume he killed at least Michael Smith, but probably also Durst, am I right?"

"That's what I am hoping to find out," I said. "We need to interview him at least. Put some pressure on, get him talking."

"Okay," she said. "Let's book him. We'll have a chat with him."

"This could be the break we're looking for," I said.

"You sound very certain. I don't think I have seen you this sure of anything before."

"I feel very confident," I said. "He has a tattoo on his shoulder very much like the one the guy who attacked me had."

She frowned. "And you know this how?"

My eyes grew wide. I still couldn't let her know I knew them both well. I didn't want to risk being taken off the case. Especially not now.

"Um he was wearing a T-shirt last time I spoke to him. I could see it poke out. It looked very similar."

She nodded. "Okay, if you are so sure of it, then let's do it. Go ahead and arrest him."

I gave her a small smile and nodded again. "Yes, ma'am," I replied.

I handed her the paperwork needed to book Mike Simmons, and she signed them, then gave them back.

"Be careful," she said as she met my gaze again, a serious look on her face. I could tell that this was important to her—more than just putting another criminal behind bars. This was one of the biggest cases she'd covered in her new role, and it was likely important everything went smoothly. I nodded in understanding.

"Of course."

SIXTY-ONE

BILLIE ANN

The tires of the police cruiser squealed as we came around the corner, headed toward Danielle's house. Adrenaline raced through my veins like a wild river. I felt like I was closer than ever to finding Danni.

It was just me and my team of officers. The engine of the squad car roared beneath me as we sped down Minutemen Causeway, red and blue lights flashing in the night. This was it —I was finally going to get justice for Danielle and hopefully find out what had happened to her. I was just praying that she was still alive and that she wouldn't turn up in a suitcase, nothing but body parts like the other victims. I just prayed that I wasn't too late.

Danielle's house was dark and quiet. The only sound was the wind rustling through the palm trees in front. I knew I had to keep my wits about me. I signaled to my team to proceed with caution, and we all silently slipped out of the car.

I gestured to my team to take their positions around the perimeter of the house, and I approached the front door alone, my hand on the grip of my gun. The door was ajar. Had he taken off? Was he trying to trap me? I pushed the door open slowly, careful to make as little noise as possible. It creaked as it opened and I held my breath, listening for any sounds of movement.

The house was eerily silent. I could see that the lights were off. I could hear my own heartbeat thumping in my ears as I stepped farther into the darkness.

With my gun drawn, I walked through the house. I could feel the sweat trickling down my back. I spotted a light on in the living room, and I proceeded, two officers coming up behind me. The closer we got, the more intense the feeling of unease grew within me. I could feel my breathing becoming more rapid as we approached the doorway leading to the living room.

I pushed it open and heard footsteps from inside. I saw Mike Simmons standing there. He was unshaven and unkempt, his eyes wild and angry.

"You can't just come in here," he said. "I know my rights."

My team of officers stepped up behind me, but he continued yelling at me.

"You have no right to come into my house!" he shouted, his face reddening with rage.

"I do," I said. "I have a warrant for your arrest."

I ignored his protests and stepped aside, letting the officers come closer. He stepped forward, then slammed the door shut in our faces. I heard him lock it from the inside and my heart dropped. The sound of the door slamming echoed through the empty house, and I could feel the tension rising as we stood in silence.

"Open the door!" I yelled.

I could hear him scrambling around inside, like a wounded animal backed into a corner. I edged closer to the door, my heart pounding in my chest.

"Mike, open the door," I said, trying to keep my voice calm.

"No! You can't come in here!" he shouted back.

I motioned for one of the officers to kick open the door, and they did so with a loud crash. Mike stumbled back, his eyes wide as he took in the sight of us pouring into his living room.

"What do you want?" he snarled, his fists clenched at his sides.

"We're here to arrest you on suspicion of kidnap and murder," I said, my voice cold and steady.

Mike's face contorted with fury, and he lunged at me. I sidestepped him easily, bringing my knee up and slamming it into his gut. He doubled over, gasping for air, and then he was on the ground, writhing in pain. I handcuffed him and read him his rights, while the other officers searched the house.

"The kids," he yelled from the ground. "They're all sleeping upstairs."

"I will make sure they're taken to their grandmother's," I said, knowing Mike's mother lived only two blocks away. I would take them there myself, to make sure they were safe.

SIXTY-TWO

BILLIE ANN

I leaned forward in my chair and locked eyes with Mike Simmons. I tried to remain composed. He made me so angry but I couldn't lose my cool. His face remained emotionless, and he didn't flinch under the harsh fluorescent lights. I felt a wave of determination wash over me as I asked my next question, determined to get answers about what had happened to Danielle. He had spent the night in the holding cell, cooling down, before I started my chat with him. We had been at it for an hour now and still he hadn't told me anything. I knew the Chief was listening in on the interview, on the other side of the mirror, so this was my chance to prove myself to her, to redeem myself for not telling her the truth about knowing Danielle.

"Where is she?" I asked, for the tenth time. "What did you do to her?"

Mike simply shook his head and looked away. I could feel his resistance, like a stone wall between us.

"I'm not telling you anything," he said in a low voice. It was the same answer over and over again. "You won't get anything out of me. I want to talk to my lawyer."

I leaned forward, trying to catch his gaze. "Your lawyer is on his way. But until then you and me can have a little chat."

He stared at me for a long moment, his eyes unreadable. Then he sighed and looked away.

"She's gone," he said finally. "And I can't bring her back."

The pain in his voice was palpable, and I could feel a wave of sadness wash over me. I had suspected it, feared it, but hearing the truth from his lips was almost too much to bear.

I closed my eyes, and we sat in silence for a few moments. Eventually, I opened my eyes and stood up.

"What do you mean by that? Did you kill her?" I asked, trying hard to keep my voice from shivering. Was this really true? Had he killed her?

He looked up, then shook his head. "No. But she isn't coming back."

I frowned. "How do you know? What did you do to her?"

"She said she wanted space, okay? She told me this just before she went on her run."

My heart pounded in my chest. What exactly was he saying?

"Was that why you killed her?" I asked. "Because she wanted a break?"

"What? No, you're not listening to me. She left me. She said she couldn't do this anymore. She needed time to think. And then she went for a run and never came back. I think she left me. At first I was all scared something had happened to her, but then I realized she had simply left me and the children. That's the only explanation."

"What do you mean she left you?" I asked. "And why didn't you tell us this before?"

He shrugged. "Does it matter?"

"Of course it matters." I groaned, annoyed, then looked at him again. "We have two dead bodies—two victims connected to her through her luggage. You know this. So you're saying she wasn't taken?"

He stared at me. "I don't think so. I think she just took off."

"But-but what about the video?"

"You showed me that video," he said. "All I see is her talking to someone in a car. Maybe she went with them willingly? Maybe she just left me?"

I looked at him, frustration and confusion rumbling inside of me. I didn't know what to think anymore.

I shook my head.

"And then you think she just threw her phone away? Just like that? Leaving her kids behind? No, not the Danielle I know. She would never leave her children. I don't believe that for a second."

"Yes. I have been thinking about it, maybe she just had enough."

I stared at him, unable to gather my thoughts properly. Then I shook my head. "No. No. I'm not buying that. You're trying to make it sound like there was no crime committed. We found your hair in my house. You took the suitcase. You took Danielle's suitcases and placed the body of Carol Durst in them. And you put the body of Michael Smith in mine. Maybe to frame me? I don't know. But it was you, and don't try and talk your way out of this one, Mike. You were in that car. That's why she walked up to the window, because it was someone she was familiar with. It was you, and then you had someone in the backseat come out and pull her into the car. Was it the woman from the motel? Did you two cook this up together?"

"What do you mean you found my hair at your house?" he asked, surprised.

"Just what I am saying. My suitcase was stolen from my house, and a severed head was put inside of it and placed at the mall. Your DNA was found there."

He shook his head. "I have been to your house a gazillion

times. I agree it has been some months since Danielle and I last hung out with you and Joe, but we have both been to your house a lot. It could have been there for a long time."

I gritted my teeth, feeling a surge of frustration with the way he kept denying everything. He was making a fair point though. He had been to my house many times before. It wouldn't hold up in court, I knew it wouldn't. I needed more.

"I swear, Billie Ann. I don't know what you want me to say. I didn't do anything. I love her."

I scoffed, feeling a twinge of anger. "You expect me to believe that? After everything you've done? After all the lies you've told?"

"What lies?" he asked, his voice rising in frustration. "I'm telling you the truth, Billie Ann. I didn't kill Danielle. I didn't kill anyone."

I stood up from my chair, feeling my heart hammering in my chest. "You're lying. I don't know how you did it, but you did. And I will prove it. Some way or another, I will. You wanted her out of your life so you could be with your new girl-friend, am I right? I saw you two together at the motel the other day."

"She's just an old friend. It's nothing. She visited for a day and then left. We went to school together. She's like a sister to me."

"I'm not quite buying that I'm afraid."

"I know you love her," he said.

"What's that?"

"I see it in your eyes. When you look at her, at Danielle, my wife."

"We're not talking about me now."

He narrowed his eyes, then scoffed. "She told me you two kissed. More than once. She told me she liked it, but that she wasn't a lesbian, and she loved her family."

I was beginning to feel uncomfortable now. The way he looked at me made me uneasy.

"Why did she tell you that?" I asked.

"Because I knew something was going on, so I kept pushing her till she admitted it. I see the way she looks at you too."

My heart dropped at his words. I glared toward the mirror, knowing the Chief would have heard that. It was too late to take it back.

"Was that why you killed her?" I asked. "Because she shared a kiss with me?"

He scoffed again and looked at his hands. "I need my lawyer now. I'm not saying a single word till he gets here."

SIXTY-THREE

Then

TRANSCRIPT OF INTERVIEW OF JOSEPHINE DURST
DEFENDANT'S EXHIBIT A
DURST PART I

APPEARANCES:
Detective Michael Smith
Detective Lenny Travis
Sergeant Joseph Mill

JOSEPHINE: Hello again, Detective.
DET. SMITH: How's that soda?
JOSEPHINE: It's good.
DET. SMITH: So, Josephine, we were just talking to your mother.
JOSEPHINE: Okay.
DET. SMITH: And she told us something very interesting. Do you want to know what it was?
JOSEPHINE: Sure.

DET. SMITH: She said that she shot George.

JOSEPHINE: Really?

DET. SMITH: Yes.

JOSEPHINE: Why?

DET. SMITH: What do you mean by why?

JOSEPHINE: Why did she say that?

DET. SMITH: Isn't it the truth?

JOSEPHINE: No.

DET. SMITH: What do you mean by *no*?

JOSEPHINE: She didn't shoot him.

DET. SMITH: (*sighs*) Listen, Josephine, you don't have to protect her anymore. She said that—

JOSEPHINE: She didn't shoot him.

DET. SMITH: What?

JOSEPHINE: She didn't kill George.

DET. SMITH: Josephine, she admitted to doing it. We have it all recorded. It's over. You're free to go. Your grandmother will come pick you up.

JOSEPHINE: No. It's not true.

DET. SMITH: But Josephine, don't you understand that—

JOSEPHINE: No. It's not the truth. She didn't do it.

DET. SMITH: Josephine, it's okay.

JOSEPHINE: (*cries*) It's not okay.

DET. SMITH: Yes it is, sweetie. We all understand that you have been protecting your mother, but now that she has told us the truth, you don't have to do that anymore.

JOSEPHINE: She didn't shoot George.

DET. SMITH: She told us she did.

JOSEPHINE: She's lying.

DET. SMITH: Okay if she didn't do it, then who did?

JOSEPHINE: I did. I shot him.

SIXTY-FOUR

BILLIE ANN

The Chief shot me a stern look, her eyes narrowed. She had called me into her office, and I could tell she wasn't happy. She had closed the door behind me, and asked me to sit down. She sighed. The sound of it made me feel awful. I could tell this wasn't good by the way she looked at me.

"So... here's the deal. Mike Simmons' lawyer let me know they're thinking of suing the department for harassment. I had no other choice but to let him go."

"You let him go?"

She lifted her eyebrows and gave me that look again. It made me feel like a child at the principal's office.

"Billie Ann," she said, putting weight on my name. "You never told me you two kissed." She exhaled deeply, and I shrank in my seat. I shifted uncomfortably in the Chief's office, feeling my stomach drop at her words. I had hoped she wouldn't find this out, but I had been fooling myself. Of course she'd find out at some point.

"And he has been coming in your house often? They both have?"

I bit my lip, realizing the implications of the Chief's questions. "Yes," I replied meekly. "They come over once in a while."

The Chief gave me a long, hard look before speaking again. "Danielle Simmons has been missing for a week now, and you never thought to tell me you knew her intimately?"

I shook my head, feeling my stomach lurch. "No," I said in a small voice. "We just kissed. No more than that. I knew you'd take me off the case. I didn't want that."

"You betcha I would," she said, sounding angry. "I can't have a detective on her case who is biased like that. Mike Simmons even told his lawyer that you are in love with her and that you and she have kissed several times, not just once? How could you keep something like that from me?"

I stared at her, mouth open. I couldn't believe he told them that. It was so private. I thought only me and Danni knew about it. But now he knew, surely she could see that this was motivation for him to murder her.

The Chief noticed the expression on my face and leaned forward. "Is there something you want to tell me?" she asked, her voice softer now.

I shook my head, feeling my eyes burn. "No, I don't know anything about what happened to Danni," I replied, my voice barely above a whisper. The fact that I was close to her, and even in love with her, made me look like a suspect. I realized that.

The Chief looked at me for a few more seconds before nodding and sitting back in her chair. "All right, I'll have to take you off this case," she said, her voice firm again. "I'll have somebody else, probably Big Tom, handle it from now on."

I nodded, feeling my heart sink. I had been so invested in this case, so determined to find out what had happened to Danni. I hadn't been thinking straight. I deserved this punishment. I stood up from my seat, ready to leave, but the Chief stopped me.

"I don't want to catch you anywhere near this case, do you hear me? I don't want to see you opening a file, or calling anyone, and you stay especially far away from Mike Simmons, do you hear what I am saying?"

"Y-yes. Okay."

"With that being said, I will keep this conversation between the two of us," she added. "I will hold on to your little secret till you're ready to tell people yourself, if you ever will be. That's up to you."

I nodded and smiled, gratefully. I hadn't come out to my colleagues yet and most certainly didn't want them to find out this way.

As I made my way out of the Chief's office, I couldn't shake off the feeling of guilt and sadness. I knew I had to stay away from the case, but how could I when the person I loved was gone? I thought back to the last time I saw Danni, her beautiful smile and piercing green eyes flashing through my mind. She was gone, and I felt like I had let her down.

I needed to clear my head, and the only way to do that was to be alone. I drove down to the beach, a place where I often went to escape the world. It was empty, a rare sight. The waves reached halfway up on the beach, whipping up white foam that skidded across the sand in the wind. The sand was being blown back toward the dunes, and it hit my pants and feet. It was rough to walk against the strong wind, but that was what I needed. I took off my shoes and walked to the edge of the water, breathing in the fresh air, letting the sound of the roaring waves calm me down. The horizon was pitch black and the winds howling, the ocean an angry mess as the storm was getting closer, inching toward us day by day. It had slowed down, they said, almost stalled, and that was when it became dangerous, because that's when you never knew what it might do next. If it might turn.

And the slower it moved, the stronger it grew, and right now it was a category four, but close to being a five.

As I sat on the sand, staring over the roaring steel gray Atlantic Ocean, letting the wind rip at my hair and skin, I sensed someone coming up behind me. I turned my head to see Mike Simmons standing there, his face twisted in anger.

"M-Mike?"

"Who the hell do you think you are?" he spat, yelling against the strong wind and loud waves, his fists clenched. "Arresting me for kidnapping and murdering my own wife? Don't you know I love her?"

I stood up, feeling my own anger rising. "You have a strange way of showing it," I yelled back firmly. "Running around with other women."

Mike took a step forward, getting into my personal space. The wind pulled at his T-shirt, and I could see his tattoo stick out on his left upper arm.

"Bullshit," he growled. "I haven't been with other women since the one time I cheated on her with my coworker. She forgave me for that and we moved on. Besides, I know that you and her have been a thing for years."

"We never did anything. Nothing ever happened. She respected her family and you too much for that. And so did I."

"I don't believe you. It was more than just a kiss."

"No. It wasn't. I promise."

His face became torn, and he looked like he was going to cry. "But you fell in love. With each other."

I backed away, feeling a knot form in my stomach. "I don't know what you're talking about," I said, my voice shaking slightly.

Mike's eyes narrowed, and suddenly he lunged at me. I stumbled backward, trying to get away from him, but he was too quick. He shoved me, and I tumbled backward, landing in the sand. He hovered above me.

"You think you can just go around kissing my wife?" he snarled. "You think you can just have her all to yourself?"

He placed a foot on my chest so I couldn't get back up. I struggled to breathe with the weight of him pressed on my chest, the pressure on my throat building. I felt my vision starting to blur. I feared I was going to pass out, but I refused to give up. I kicked him in the groin, and he stumbled back, lifting his foot from me. I gasped for air, trying to regain control of my breathing.

"Stay away from me and my wife," he spat, before turning and walking away.

I stayed there for a few minutes, lying in the sand, trying to catch my breath. I knew I had to tell the Chief about this encounter, but I also knew that I had to stay away from the case. She had told me to not come near Mike, and she might think I had gone to look for him, and not the other way around. I couldn't let my emotions get in the way of the investigation. I finally got up, walked back to my car, looking over my shoulder constantly expecting him to jump me from somewhere, or attack me in the parking lot. I drove home, speeding excessively and running a couple of very yellow lights, then rushed inside of my house and locked all the doors behind me. Heart pounding in my chest I collapsed onto the couch and buried my face in my hands. What had just happened? Mike had attacked me, and all because he thought Danni and I had something more going on between us. I couldn't believe it. I couldn't believe any of this was happening.

I sat there for what felt like hours, lost in thought. The guilt of not telling the Chief about my relationship with Danni was eating me alive. But now, it seemed like it had all blown up in my face. I couldn't be a part of the case anymore, but I couldn't just sit around and do nothing either. I had to do something, anything, to help find her.

My phone rang, and I jumped at the sudden noise. It was Danni's sister, Lily. I hesitated before answering it, unsure of what to say to her. I feared she was calling to ask for news about her sister. And I didn't have any.

"Hello?" I answered, my voice barely above a whisper.

"Hey, it's Lily," she said, her voice trembling. "I need to talk to you. Can we meet somewhere? It's really important."

I hesitated for a moment, wondering if it was a good idea to meet with her given what my boss had told me. But I knew I had to do something to help find Danni. I would have to deal with the consequences later.

"Sure, where do you want to meet?" I asked, trying to keep my voice steady.

"Can we meet at the big tree by the playground at Lori Wilson Park in Cocoa Beach? It's where Danni and I used to go when we were little. I feel like she's still there, waiting for us."

I nodded, despite knowing she couldn't see me. "I'll be there," I said, before hanging up.

I quickly got up from the couch. This was my last hope, and I knew it. I grabbed my jacket and headed out the door, feeling the humid air hit my face as I got into my car and drove with the windows down toward the park, praying that the Chief wouldn't find out what I was up to.

If she did, I would be facing suspension or, even worse, I would be fired.

SIXTY-FIVE

BILLIE ANN

As I approached the tree that looked like it had been around for centuries, in Lori Wilson Park, I could see Lily waiting for me underneath the dangling Spanish moss. She lifted her gaze as I approached, and I could see the tears in her eyes.

I walked up to her, gently placing a hand on her shoulder. "I'm so sorry we haven't found her yet," I said softly.

Lily nodded slowly, taking a deep breath before speaking. "I know you have your job and other cases and everything," she said quietly, her voice trembling as she spoke. "But I'm going crazy worrying about Danni—how close are you to finding her? Can you tell me anything? When I call for an update, no one is allowed to give me any information."

I hesitated. We stood there in silence for a few moments.

"We're following some leads, but I can't say more than that... Are you okay?" I asked softly, feeling a lump form in my throat.

Lily shook her head. "No, I'm not okay. My sister is missing, and nobody seems to care." Her voice was filled with anger and sadness, and I could feel her pain emanating from her.

"I care," I said firmly, looking her in the eye.

Lily took a deep breath before speaking. "There's something I haven't told you." She hesitated for a moment before speaking. "A few years ago I accidentally saw something in Mike's office at home, when visiting my sister. It looked like rental fees on an apartment at the Cape. At the time, I didn't think anything of it. Maybe he was planning a surprise for Danni? But last night I realized that it's never come up. No weekends away, no last-minute trips for celebrations. I don't think he's ever used it... with her anyway."

My stomach churned at the thought of Mike and a secret apartment. It was suspicious. And he had a motive to want to hurt Danni, since he believed Danni and I had been together. That we had shared more than kisses and stolen glances. "Where is it?" I asked, knowing that time was of the essence. If he was keeping Danni there, then she might still be alive. But for how long?

Lily handed me a piece of paper with an address written on it. "It's not too far from here. In Cape Canaveral. In one of those shady areas, where it's still cheap to rent a small place. Just be careful, okay? I don't trust him."

I nodded, pocketing the paper. "I'll be careful. Thank you, Lily. You have no idea how much it means to me that you've trusted me with this."

Lily gave me a small smile before walking away, and I watched her go, feeling a sense of determination wash over me. I had to find Danni, no matter the cost. Even if it would cost me everything, and not just for my own sake, but for her family as well. Her mom, her sister, her sweet daughters. They deserved to know the truth.

I got back into my car and drove desperately toward the address. What would I find there? Would I finally be able to uncover the truth about what happened to Danni? I knew I should tell the team what I'd found, but the Chief would be angry that I'd continued on this lead—she didn't see Mike as a suspect, it was only me who did.

I parked my car down the street, not wanting to alert Mike that someone was there. I walked up to the door, feeling my palms start to sweat. I took a deep breath before knocking on the door.

There was no answer, so I knocked again, harder this time. Still nothing. I then grabbed my lock pick gun and picked the lock, knowing I was well in over my head this time. If found out, I would be fired. But in this moment, I didn't care. I had to know if Danielle was in there, or if there was any trace of her at all.

I opened the door and stepped inside, the darkness swallowing me whole.

SIXTY-SIX

BILLIE ANN

I reached into my pocket, pulled out a flashlight and shone it around the dark space. The apartment was small, with only one room. There was a bed in one corner, and a table with a few chairs in another. There was a small kitchenette on the other side of the room. I could see various pictures on the walls, looking like they were just cheap generic ones you could buy in Walmart, but I couldn't make out what they were. Probably something beachy, like a conch shell.

I walked over to the bed, and as my flashlight shone over it, my heart skipped a beat. There was something tangled up in the sheets, a piece of fabric that looked all too familiar. I pulled it out. It was Danni's blouse. Her favorite one. What was it doing here? Did that mean she had been here? My stomach churned as I continued to look around the apartment, searching for any clues that could lead me to her whereabouts.

I walked over to the table and spotted an empty glass with a lipstick mark on the rim. But Danni didn't wear lipstick. It had to have come from someone else.

A noise from the bathroom caught my attention. I instinctively reached for my gun and approached the door, slowly pushing it open. The sound of running water filled my ears as I stepped inside the small bathroom. My eyes scanned the room, looking for any sign of Danni.

And then I saw her. She was standing in the shower, water cascading down her naked body. Her eyes were closed, and she had a look of pure pleasure on her face. I stood there, frozen, watching her as she ran her hands over her curves. It wasn't Danni. It was the woman from the motel. The one I had seen with Mike.

Suddenly, she opened her eyes and caught me staring at her. Then she screamed. Startled, I backed out of the room, and ran into the arms of someone who stopped me, grabbing me by the shoulders.

It was Mike.

"What the heck are you doing here?" he growled. "Are you stalking me now? This is bordering on harassment. And don't think I won't report you for this."

I pulled back, and walked around him, completely out of it. I knew he was right. I had nothing to do there. I had no right to be in his apartment, even if he was cheating on my best friend. Even if he was being a scumbag.

I lifted up the blouse. "This is Danielle's."

"Yeah I know."

"What's it doing here? Has she been here?" I asked.

He shook his head. "No. I had it in my car. My girlfriend borrowed it when I brought her here from the motel where she had been staying. She didn't know whose it was."

"So you lied to me about her being a friend and being gone? And she doesn't know about Danielle?" I asked. "She doesn't know you're married and have children? That's nice."

He grabbed my arm and pulled me closer. "It's none of your damn business."

I pulled my arm out of his grip. "What did you do to Danni? She found out you were having an affair, and then you decided to get rid of her? Am I wrong? What did you do? Take her to the swamps and feed her body to the gators?"

"You need get out of here, now," he said. "Before I call the cops on you. Then you can see what that is like. And to be honest, how do we really know that it wasn't you who hurt Danni? You have a pretty good motive. Because she didn't want you. Because she chose to stay with her family. Then you thought, if I can't have her, then no one can. How about that for a theory, huh?"

The woman came out of the bathroom, her body wrapped in a towel, and looked at us. Her long wet hair touched her shoulders.

"What's going on here? Mike, who is that woman?"

"She's nobody important, sweetie," Mike said. "She's about to leave."

He showed me toward the door like I was some stray cat or dog he wanted to get rid of. I began to move away, then stopped and looked at the girl.

"You know what? Before I go. You seem like a nice girl. You deserve to know the truth. Ask him about his wife and children. Bye."

"You bit—"

Mike reached out to grab me, but I was too fast. I hurried to the door, and was about to leave, when he yelled after me, his voice piercing through my bones.

"This is not over yet. You will hear from my lawyer."

SIXTY-SEVEN

Then

APPEARANCES:
Detective Michael Smith
Detective Lenny Travis
Sergeant Joseph Mill

DET. SMITH: You shot him?
JOSEPHINE: Yes. It was me.
DET. SMITH: (*sighs*) You expect us to believe that you shot your own stepdad? Really?
JOSEPHINE: Y-yes.
DET. SMITH: (*scoffs*) Listen, your mom already admitted to having killed him. There is no need to—
JOSEPHINE: But I did it. I got the gun in the safe and took it out and pulled the trigger.

DET. SMITH: You expect us to believe that you did that? When did you do that? While he was on top of you in your bedroom? Because that seems a little impossible.

JOSEPHINE: No.

DET. SMITH: No, it doesn't seem impossible?

JOSEPHINE: No, he wasn't on top of me when I did it.

DET. SMITH: Okay then where was he?

JOSEPHINE: Sitting on my bed.

DET. SMITH: He was just sitting there?

JOSEPHINE: Yes. They were fighting and then we hid in the closet and then he came to get us out. He sat on the bed.

DET. SMITH: And you already had the gun?

JOSEPHINE: Yes. I grabbed it when they started to fight. From the safe in my mom's bedroom.

DET. SMITH: And you took it with you inside of the closet?

JOSEPHINE: Yes.

DET. SMITH: Hmm. So why did you shoot him?

JOSEPHINE: Because I hate him.

DET. SMITH: Is that enough to kill someone?

JOSEPHINE: Because of what he did to my brother. And to me. But mostly to him. I wanted to protect him.

DET. SMITH: So you're saying it wasn't your mom?

JOSEPHINE: No. It wasn't.

DET. SMITH: And what happened to the gun after you had shot him?

JOSEPHINE: I dropped it on the floor. My mom didn't come up till after it happened.

DET. SMITH: (*sighs*) Do you want to go to jail?

JOSEPHINE: (*cries*) I don't want my mom to go to jail.

DET. SMITH: Is that why you're telling us you did it?

JOSEPHINE: Please don't put my mom in jail. Please.

DET. SMITH: I don't believe you did it, Josephine. I think you're just trying to keep your mom from going to jail.

JOSEPHINE: It wasn't her. I'm telling you.

DET. SMITH: It was you?

JOSEPHINE: She didn't do it.

DET. SMITH: Okay, let's say I buy your little change of heart here, and your little story. Then tell me one thing.

JOSEPHINE: What?

DET. SMITH: What's the code to the safe?

JOSEPHINE: (*cries*)

DET. SMITH: What's the code, Josephine? If you went to get the gun in your mother's safe, then you must have known the code, am I right?

JOSEPHINE: But...

DET. SMITH: What's the code, Josephine?

JOSEPHINE: I-I don't remember.

DET. SMITH: (*scoffs*) You don't remember? That's because you don't know it, Josephine. Because you didn't get the gun and you didn't shoot him. We have no further questions. You're free to go. Someone will call your grandmother and have her come pick up you and your brother.

SIXTY-EIGHT

BILLIE ANN

The night was dark and oppressive, and I felt like I was suffocating in my own home. With the kids still away, the house felt empty and lifeless. I moved around in a daze, my thoughts swirling around in my head like a cyclone.

Every little noise made me jump. A creak of the floorboard, a swish of the curtains, a gust of wind outside. I was on edge, my senses heightened. It felt like I was being watched, or that someone else was in the room with me. I tried to tell myself it was just my imagination, but I could not shake the feeling.

It's late, Billie. You need sleep.

My heavy feet trudged up the stairs and down the hallway, finally stopping in front of my bedroom door. I pushed it open and sank into bed, exhausted from the day's events. My eyes closed; visions of Danni danced around in my mind as I drifted off to sleep. She was surrounded by birds, big flapping birds that were diving at her and grabbing her hair with their talons.

Suddenly, I jerked awake and for a moment confusion reigned, unable to remember where I was.

Danni!

My mind drifted back to the soft voice of Danni's mother,

her words tinged with sorrow, when she spoke about her daughter and the loss of her father. I had barely paid attention at the time; my thoughts consumed by grief. But now, it was like a lightbulb illuminated in my brain.

My eyes felt heavy and I groggily dragged myself out of bed. I shuffled over to my desk and opened my laptop, the soft hum of the fan coming to life as I flipped open the lid. I yawned as I began scrolling through pages of information, my eyes burning from the blue light. My fingers flew across the keyboard as I plunged into a sea of online resources, skimming articles and piecing together facts. My heart raced as I parsed through documents, each thread weaving together to form a clearer picture. After hours of searching, something inside me clicked as I realized what it was that I had found—it seemed almost impossible but undeniable. I grabbed the phone and called Danni's mom.

"What was the name of Danielle's father?" I asked, speaking so fast, my tongue could barely keep up.

She sounded tired on the other end. "Why?"

"It's important," I said. "Please just indulge me. I can explain later."

"Of course," she said.

Then she told me the name, and I wrote it down, my hands shaking heavily. I then went into the police database and made a search.

There it was, all in black and white:

The transcripts of the interviews made in connection with the murder of George Andersson. Married to Carol Durst. And the stepfather of Josephine and Robert Durst. I printed out the transcripts of the interviews and I spread the papers across my desk and began to read through them. As I read, I pulled out photos of Carol Durst, Josephine and Robert Durst. I looked closely at each one, making sure I could remember their faces and distinguish between them. My eyes gleamed as I read through it all, taking note of every little detail.

With every new discovery my heart rate increased while the wind howled outside my windows. The answers had been right in front of me all along, and I finally realized it. Goosebumps tickled my skin as my mind reeled with the realization.

I had found the connection, finally, there it was in black and white in front of me.

I grabbed my phone and called Big Tom. He was barely awake when he picked up.

"H-hello? Billie Ann?"

"It's not an eagle," I almost yelled. "It's a swallow."

"W-what? What on earth are you talking about, Billie Ann? It's three o'clock in the morning."

"The tattoo. The one on the shoulder of the person who attacked me at the house, and the one in the footage from the motel of the person with the suitcase and the bags carrying the remains of Carol Durst out. Using Danni's bags. I knew I had seen it before, but just couldn't place it."

He moaned at the other end. "And this couldn't wait till the morning, because—?"

"Because I know who has Danni, and we need to get to her before she is killed. We need to get to Jolene Pena's house, aka Josephine Durst, ASAP. I will pick you up on the way."

SIXTY-NINE

BILLIE ANN

As soon as we rounded the bend on West Point Drive, I noticed the roaring fire. It was like a giant torch above us against the night sky, fed by the strong gusts of wind. My heart dropped as I sped up the car, Big Tom sitting next to me.

"Alert the fire department," I yelled at him, and he pulled out the radio and told dispatch.

I threw the car at the curb, then stormed out, Big Tom right behind me.

We raced up the small hill toward the house, our breaths matching the rhythm of our feet. My heart pounding, I pushed my feet ever faster up the incline that led to the house. My sneakers thudded on the pathway in unison with Big Tom's. When we reached the steps, I kicked the door so it flew open, and a wall of heat crashed into us. Fire engulfed the entryway, orange and purple flames licked the walls and arched toward the ceiling. Ash rained from above as if the heavens were weeping. We had to hunch our heads and cover our mouths against the smell of charred wood and smoke. Tongues of orange flames licked at the walls, blackening the ceiling with soot and smoke.

Big Tom grabbed my arm and pulled me back before I could take a breath of burning air. Everywhere there were signs of destruction—furniture overturned, windows shattered, artwork reduced to ash.

"We need to wait," Big Tom yelled. "For the fire department."

I stared into the raging inferno, knowing he was right. This was too dangerous. I had to make a decision and it had to be quick. And that's when I heard it. The sound of someone screaming, and it came from inside of the house. I stared up at Tom, and he heard it too. I didn't have to say more.

As we burst inside, a scene of chaos and destruction greeted us. The once ornate entryway was in flames, the walls now punctured with gaping holes. Big Tom and I shielded our faces from the heat, trying not to draw too deep a breath as the smoke and ash clouded our vision. We pushed forward, the heat from the fire burning our cheeks and stinging our eyes.

Big Tom was right behind me when a large chunk of crumbling concrete fell. I heard it happen and then I heard the scream. Gasping I turned around and saw him. He had been struck in the shoulder. He screamed out in pain, toppling to the ground and clutching his arm as he let out deep, guttural moans. Blood seeped from the jagged wound and pooled around him.

"Tom!" I screamed. All I could think about was Gale and Elliott in this instant. They needed him. I needed him. I had to help him.

"Leave me," he said. "Go get whoever is in there!"

For a second I hesitated. I knew he was right, but I couldn't just leave him. I had to get help.

"Billie Ann, please," he panted through clenched teeth. "Go."

He stared back at me, full of pain and fear. I nodded and raced toward the source of the screams. Someone was in there, and in serious trouble. I pushed onward, running past flaming debris and leaping over smoldering ash. The heat was unbearable, the flames growing larger, and the smoke thicker the farther I went. I coughed, my whole body shaking. I had to do what I could to save whoever was in there. I ran through the flames, jumping over furniture and dodging falling debris as I went. It was too hot. I squeezed my eyes shut as I ran, the heat searing my eyelids and making them water and sting. Bits of ash fell into my hair, clinging to my forehead, burning my scalp. The smoke made it hard to breathe. I coughed and choked, but I forced myself forward, around the corner, and down the hall.

I heard a loud crack and I stopped in my tracks. The roof was caving in. I couldn't stop. I had to keep going. I had to find the person I had heard scream. I had to save whoever was still in there. I searched frantically, calling out, but there was no answer. Then, in a far corner of the hallway, I saw her. She was slumped against the wall, motionless, her eyes closed. Only a weak moaning coming from her lips.

"DANNI!"

I cried tears of joy and pain. She was covered in soot and ash, her once pristine white running shirt now torn and dirty. I rushed over to her, and what I saw shook me. She had been shot. A bullet wound leaked blood from her shoulder, soaking her shirt.

Without a moment of hesitation, I wrapped my arms around her and lifted her upper body from the ground and pulled.

My eyes stung from the smoke and my throat tightened with panic as I raced through the roaring flames. Grasping her limp body tightly in my arms, I stumbled over burning debris. With each step, I thought for sure this would be my last.

I could feel the heat radiating off the walls in waves and see sparks of orange and red reflecting on them. Windows popped around me. My feet couldn't find a grip, and I was slipping periodically.

Eventually we made it to the entrance of the burning building, and just as we arrived an explosion ripped through the ceiling, sending chunks of debris raining down all around us. And that's when I realized that we were trapped. Flames were all around us.

She coughed, her body squirming in my arms. Her eyes fluttered open and she looked at me, tears in her eyes. I knew she was ready to give up, but I wouldn't let her.

"I won't let you," I told her.

"You know I love you," she whispered, and her eyes fluttered shut again.

"Danni!"

"No," I shook her. "Danni, no."

She coughed and her body shook. I had to do something. I had to get us out of here. "Think," I muttered. "Think."

I looked up and saw the hole in the window. It was big enough to fit through. I had an idea.

I placed Danni against the wall and climbed through the hole in the window, kicking pieces of glass out so they wouldn't cut us. With the flames licking at my heels, I grabbed onto the edge of the window and pulled myself up. I reached my hand down to Danni and pulled her body up with me. The fire roared around us as we dangled from the window, but I held on tight, knowing we had to make it out alive.

As we clung to the edge of the window, I looked down and saw the ground below. It was a risky move, but I had no other option. I had to jump. I knew I could survive the fall, but I wasn't sure about Danni. She looked at me, groggy. I stared deeply into her eyes and saw the fear and uncertainty there, but she trusted me.

"You can do it, Danni. I know you can."

She nodded weakly.

"Jump now," I yelled over the roar of the flames.

Danni nodded again and let go of the windowsill. We plummeted toward the ground, the heat of the fire fading as we fell. My heart pounded in my chest as we hit the ground, our bodies tumbling forward.

As soon as we were out of the house, I saw Big Tom, bleeding and weak, being held up by two firefighters.

"Tom!" I screamed and ran toward him, dropping to my knees beside him.

He looked up at me and smiled weakly. "I told you to go," he said. "Don't feel guilty."

"You're gonna be okay," I assured him, holding his hand as the firefighters put him on the stretcher.

As the ambulance drove away with Tom inside, I looked at Danni. Her eyes were glazed over, and her breathing was shallow. I knew that the wounds were too severe. She didn't have much time.

"I'm sorry," I whispered, tears streaming down my face. "I'm so sorry."

But she smiled at me, and it was the most beautiful smile.

"I love you," she whispered, reaching up and resting her fingers on my face.

"No." I shook my head. "Don't say that. Don't say goodbye. Don't you dare say that."

She smiled at me and her eyes closed for the last time. Her fingers fell from my face and I swore I could still feel her touch.

"Danni," I whispered, tears streaming down my face, then screamed while looking desperately around me.

"HELP? SOMEONE HELP ME?"

The paramedics came running. Someone was yelling at me, but I couldn't hear him. I couldn't hear anything but the pounding in my head, thumping against my skull. I felt empty, like something vital had been ripped from me. I was staring at her still form, her body covered in blood.

"She's gone," I said, choking back tears. "She's gone."

I felt lightheaded and couldn't breathe properly. As I stared at the paramedics taking Danni from my arms, the world began to spin, and I tried to stand to my feet. But it wouldn't stop turning, and soon I fell face-first into the grass.

SEVENTY

BILLIE ANN

I awoke with a start, feeling as if I had been sleeping for days. My mind felt foggy and my vision was blurred when I opened my eyes, only to discover I was in a speeding ambulance. I could hear the shrill siren of an ambulance and feel movement beneath me—we were speeding toward somewhere. The sirens were blaring and the bright lights of other cars it was whizzing by nothing but a blur. My limbs felt heavy, my head cloudy, and my heart raced—but I was certain of one thing: I wasn't going to the hospital. Not now. I had to stop them.

"Lie still," a deep voice commanded. "You're hurt. We're almost at the hospital. We have to take you to Holmes Regional on the mainland. We just got news that the hurricane has turned and is coming toward us. They say it will make landfall tonight as a category five. They're evacuating everyone from the island including the hospital."

"My kids!"

They're with Joe. He will make sure they're evacuated. Easy now. Zelda too. He wouldn't leave her here.

"Please try and lie still," the voice said again.

"No," I shouted, feeling a sudden surge of adrenaline. "I can't go to the hospital. I need to get them. I need to stop them."

The paramedics in the back exchanged confused looks and one of them spoke up.

"Who are you talking about?"

"I need to get off."

"Are you crazy? Didn't you listen to what I said? There's a hurricane coming. No, no, we're taking you to the ER. You've been in a fire."

"No, I have to get back."

"What on earth are you talking about?"

I didn't answer. I didn't have the time. They had killed Danni and I wasn't going to let them get away with it. I knew they would if I didn't act fast. There was no time to waste. There was a reason they had set the house on fire with Danni inside of it. Because they were getting out of here. To erase evidence. Nothing was more efficient at erasing evidence than a fire. I couldn't go to no darn hospital. I couldn't waste all that time.

Instead, I quickly yanked out my IV drip and scrambled up inside of the ambulance. The paramedics screamed at me to stop, and tried to grab me, but I ignored them and threw open the door. As the ambulance slowed down, I leapt out, determined to finish what I had started.

I ran as fast as my legs could carry me, turning onto side streets and cutting through alleys. Thunder was rumbling in the distance, and the winds seemed impossibly strong to run against. Still, I did it. I wasn't going to give up. With each step, the memory of what had happened slowly trickled back into my mind. The fire, Danni in the grass, taking her last breath. Tears began streaming down my cheeks, and I ran faster and faster as rain began to whip at my face. My phone alerted me that there was a tornado warning in my area, and to take shelter immediately.

I didn't stop till I reached the house I was looking for at the end of the cul-de-sac. I breathed heavily as I watched it while standing in the street, letting the rain soak me. The lights were on, and a lot of turmoil going on inside. Suitcases were being packed and closed, while they were yelling at one another. Seconds later the front door flew open, and they came out with bags and suitcases rolling after them. They threw them in the back of the pickup truck, then got in.

As the engine roared to life, they were about to start driving out of the driveway, when they spotted me in the headlights, standing right in front of them, drenched, holding my gun, pointing it at them.

SEVENTY-ONE

BILLIE ANN

"STOP! Get out of the car with hands where I can see them at all times."

I kept the gun aimed at the driver's face behind the windshield. He stared at me, eyes wide. For a few seconds I could tell he was contemplating what to do. A loud thunderclap hit close by, but I didn't budge an inch.

The driver slowly opened the car door and stepped out, hands raised in the air. He was dressed in an old T-shirt and jeans. He had a scared but determined expression on his face. I kept my gun trained on him as I cautiously approached.

"Keep your hands where I can see them," I said again as a reminder.

The driver lifted them up higher, his movements cautious. He stood by the truck, his eyes still fixed on the barrel of my gun. I motioned for him to back up, and he complied, taking small steps away from the truck.

I approached him, my gun still trained on his chest. I could see fear in his eyes, and I knew he was afraid. But I had to remain in control, or else things could quickly spiral out of hand.

"Turn around and put your hands on the truck," I said.

He did as he was told, his breaths coming out in short gasps. I patted him down, feeling for any weapons. When I found none, I stepped back. His passenger, a small blonde woman with a tattoo on her hand, stared at me.

"What's going on, Detective?" she said, her voice shivering.

I pointed my gun at her. "I need you to come here and stand next to your brother and put your hands on the car."

"You know who we are?" Randy Edwards said.

"Oh I know more than that, Robert. I know what you have done."

"W-what do you mean?" Josephine said, approaching me.

I kept my gun on her at all times.

"You are Robert and Josephine Durst. The two youngest to ever to have been tried as adults and sentenced for the murder of your stepdad, George Andersson, on Thanksgiving night thirty years ago."

They both looked at me with surprise. "I figured it out when I realized you both had the same tattoo. The swallow. You Robert, or Randy Edwards, as you changed your name to when released, so no one would know who you were. You got yours on the shoulder, whereas your sister who now goes by Jolene Pena, got hers on the wrist, a smaller version of it, but still the same. You both got it in prison. It's symbolic. If you look it up, it will say that people get that very tattoo to symbolize they have done their time, which you both have. You did fifteen years for the murder of Danielle Simmons' father. And she's the reason you went to jail in the first place, isn't she? Because you almost got away with it, and almost had your own mother admit to murder, just to protect you. And you made up some lie about him abusing you so it would look like self-defense."

I moved toward them, closer, my gun still lifted. "And you almost got away with it, till suddenly his daughter, Danielle, at the age of just fourteen, entered and gave her testimony."

SEVENTY-TWO

Then

TRANSCRIPT OF INTERVIEW OF DANIELLE CARSON

DEFENDANT'S EXHIBIT A

DURST PART 2

APPEARANCES:

Detective Michael Smith

DET. SMITH: First of all, thank you for coming in, Danielle. Can you state your full name, age, and address?

DANIELLE: It's... um... Danielle Carson, 135 Hickory Avenue, Palm Bay, Florida. And I'm fourteen years old.

DET. SMITH: Okay, Danielle. I want to express my condolences for the loss of your father.

DANIELLE: (*sniffles*) Thank you.

DET. SMITH: I understand that your parents were divorced?

DANIELLE: Yes, they have been for years.

DET. SMITH: How was your relationship with your father?

DANIELLE: It was good. I have always been Daddy's girl, at least that's what my mom says.

DET. SMITH: I bet you missed him after they got divorced, then?

DANIELLE: Yeah I did. A lot.

DET. SMITH: Did you go visit him often?

DANIELLE: In the beginning yes.

DET. SMITH: But then what happened?

DANIELLE: (*sighs*) He got married. To a new woman.

DET. SMITH: Carol Durst?

DANIELLE: Yes.

DET. SMITH: Did you like her?

DANIELLE: Not really.

DET. SMITH: And why is that?

DANIELLE: It was like he got a whole new family and he'd forget about us. And she didn't like me. I don't think so.

DET. SMITH: How did you know that she didn't like you?

DANIELLE: She would never let me see him. There was always something that came up or some reason why I couldn't come over and visit. So I never saw him, only a few times.

DET. SMITH: That sounds like it was hard for you?

DANIELLE: It was.

DET. SMITH: And what about holidays? Christmas and Thanksgiving?

DANIELLE: We were supposed to go there this year for Thanksgiving, me and my sister.

DET. SMITH: But you didn't? Why not?

DANIELLE: He called that same morning and said to my mom that we couldn't come. There wasn't enough room, since his new wife had started renovations in the kitchen.

DET. SMITH: How did that make you feel?

DANIELLE: Angry. I had been looking forward to it. I hadn't seen my dad in months. I missed him.

DET. SMITH: So what did you do?

DANIELLE: I had dinner with my mom and sister, and my grandparents, and then I left the house.

DET. SMITH: To go see your dad?

DANIELLE: Yes. I just wanted to see him and say happy Thanksgiving and maybe give him a hug.

DET. SMITH: Because you missed him?

DANIELLE: Yes.

DET. SMITH: Okay and how did you get there?

DANIELLE: (*starts crying*) I-I stole my mom's car. I know I wasn't supposed to, but I was so angry. I didn't care. (*cries harder*)

DET. SMITH: It's okay, Danielle. Take your time.

DANIELLE: I-I parked it in the driveway. I walked up to the front of the house, when I heard a strange noise.

DET. SMITH: What kind of noise?

DANIELLE: Like someone was struggling, and then pleading.

DET. SMITH: What kind of pleading?

DANIELLE: Just this... (*cries*) voice going "no please don't. Be careful with that thing. Put the gun down."

DET. SMITH: And did you recognize that voice?

DANIELLE: Y-yes.

DET. SMITH: Whose was it?

DANIELLE: (*sniffles*) It was my dad's.

DET. SMITH: And then what did you do?

DANIELLE: I walked to the window and peeked inside of the bedroom, where the noises were coming from. The window was left ajar so I could hear everything.

DET. SMITH: And what did you see?

DANIELLE: (*sobs*)

DET. SMITH: Take your time.

DANIELLE: I-I saw my dad.

DET. SMITH: What was he doing?

DANIELLE: He-he was standing in there, pleading with them.

DET. SMITH: Why was he pleading with them? And who else was in there?

DANIELLE: Those two... the children. Her children.

DET. SMITH: Josephine and Robert Durst? Both of them?

DANIELLE: Yes.

DET. SMITH: Was it just them?

DANIELLE: Yes, just those three in the room.

DET. SMITH: And what were they doing?

DANIELLE: They... they had a gun. It was pointed at my dad.

DET. SMITH: Who was holding the gun?

DANIELLE: The-the little boy was.

DET. SMITH: The boy huh? And what happened next?

DANIELLE: My dad kept telling him to put the gun down, but he didn't want to.

DET. SMITH: What do you mean he didn't want to?

DANIELLE: The boy just looked at my dad, then said out loud, that he didn't want him here anymore. That he wasn't his dad. That he hated him, and to stay away from his mother.

DET. SMITH: Was your father threatening to any of them at this point?

DANIELLE: No. He seemed desperate and scared.

DET. SMITH: And then what happened?

DANIELLE: Then he fired the gun. And my dad he-he...(*cries*)

DET. SMITH: The boy fired the gun?

DANIELLE: Y-yes.

DET. SMITH: Then what happened?

DANIELLE: The mom came running in. She started to scream.

DET. SMITH: Did she say anything?

DANIELLE: She yelled at the children, "what have you done?" and then she calmed down.

DET. SMITH: And what did she do next?

DANIELLE: She took the gun and cleaned it, then told the kids to tell the police that he touched them, that he did things to them. Sexual things, touching and stuff. That way they would get a smaller punishment. Because it was self-defense. Those were her words.

DET. SMITH: What did you do?

DANIELLE: I ran. I ran as fast as I could to my mom's car and drove home to my mom. Then I cried all night, but I still couldn't tell anyone. My mom would be mad because I took her car. But I couldn't stop crying. And then after two days my mom asked me what was going on, and I finally did tell her. She told me to talk to you.

DET. SMITH: And we are very grateful you decided to do that. Thank you, Danielle. I know it doesn't bring your dad back, but hopefully it will give you and your family justice.

SEVENTY-THREE

BILLIE ANN

"I read Danielle's statement last night. I had never thought of that connection between her and her kidnappers. But it dawned on me, all of a sudden last night, to call her mom and ask for the father's name. Then it didn't take long before it all came up as I searched the case archives. I read through all the transcripts of your testimonies back then. But what I can't figure out is why you killed your mother. She did nothing but try and protect you."

I stared at the two of them. They exchanged a look, before returning to look at me. "Because once Danielle's testimony came out, she backed up and admitted that she had lied for our sake. And then she told them how she knew we had planned to kill him, and she had a feeling that we might try something like it. Putting the last nail in our coffin. She told them she was scared of us, of her own darn children. Who does something like that? She and Danielle and Detective Smith are the reason why we had to spend fifteen years in jail, why me and Josephine had to grow up inside of a freaking prison."

"You did kill her husband in cold blood," I said. "You planned it, and followed through with that plan. That's cold."

He shrugged and I kept my gun trained on him. "So now thirty years later you kidnapped Danielle and tried to kill her. But you had to hurry up because you sensed we were getting closer to the truth. So you shot her and set the house on fire. It wasn't supposed to be done that way. She was supposed to end up in my suitcases, because you stole more than one. I realized this yesterday when going through my closet. There were two suitcases missing. You were going to put her in that one, and somehow put her in a place where I would find her, right? To torture me. Once I knew who you were, Josephine, and I recognized your picture as the same person I spoke to at Danielle's workplace, I went to your house, and that's when I saw the fire. The whole motel appearance was just a decoy; you were trying to lead us to think it was some tourist who had planted the bags, not someone local. This is the end of the line for you. I'm taking you both in."

As I said the words, something happened to me that I wasn't in control over. My lungs felt like they were about to burst all of a sudden, and I started to cough, hard. As I bent over, desperate for air, struggling to get a breath, Josephine and Robert made their move. Taking advantage of my vulnerable position, they sprinted back to their truck. I quickly recovered and lunged forward, hoping to catch them before they could get away. But they were too fast.

Reaching for my gun, I yelled, "Stop!" as the truck's motor roared to life. But it was too late. With a jerk, they threw the truck into reverse and hit me with the bumper, hard. I flew backward, slamming into the ground. The last thing I saw through the rear window was Robert's face, a satisfied smirk on his lips. Then, they were gone.

In the aftermath of the attack, my senses slowly returned. I was lying on the pavement, my head spinning. I felt something warm and wet on my face. I wiped at the substance and was shocked to see my hand covered in blood.

My throat tightened and my stomach lurched. I had been so close. But now they were gone, and all that remained was the sound of the engine fading into the night.

I dragged myself to my feet, my head throbbing with each movement. The blood gushed from my nose as I stumbled toward Robert's garage that they had left open. Inside was an old Toyota Previa, and the keys were on the hooks on the wall beside it. Almost too easy.

I fumbled with the keys, the metallic clang reverberating in the garage.

With a shaky hand, I inserted the key into the ignition and started the car. My mind was filled with thoughts of revenge. They had killed my Danielle. I knew I couldn't let them get away with it.

I drove down the dark road, my eyes scanning the surroundings for any sign of their truck. The adrenaline coursing through my veins blocked out the pain, and I pushed the car to its limit.

Finally, I saw the truck up ahead, parked outside an abandoned warehouse. I pulled up alongside it.

Without a word, I got out of the car, my gun already in my hand. Seeing me approach, Robert reached into his glove compartment and grabbed something. It was a gun.

"Put your weapon down," I yelled, approaching him, my gun pointed at him.

Robert's fingers twitched on the black handle of his gun, a sinister smile on his face. I felt my heart start to beat faster and understood there was no time to waste; I had to act before he had the chance to fire.

But before I could make a move, something unexpected happened.

Josephine stepped out of the truck, her own gun aimed at

Robert. "That's enough, Robert. I'm done with this life," she said, her voice filled with resolve.

Robert's smirk faded as he stared at Josephine, shock etched on his face. "What the hell are you doing?" he spat, his hand still holding his gun.

"I'm ending this. Now," Josephine said, her finger tightening on the trigger. She was shaking, and sobbing, but kept the finger on the trigger, the gun pointed at her brother.

In that moment, time seemed to slow down. I watched in shock as Josephine fired, the sound of the gunshot echoing through the night. Robert fell to the ground with a thud, blood pooling around him.

I stared at Josephine, my mind reeling. I had thought she was just as cruel and heartless as Robert, but now I realized I had been wrong. Josephine let out a piercing scream. "I'm sorry, I'm so so sorry."

She turned to me, her eyes filled with a mix of fear and determination. I stared at the gun in her hand.

"He was all I had. He was my everything, my family. I wanted to plead guilty, I tried to. My brother shot him, he hated George. He said he was going to kill him and wanted me to help. When they said my mom was going to jail for it, I broke down and told them I did it."

"But they didn't believe you. I read that in the statements too. You were the one who had a conscience. Not your brother."

"And then he came up with the revenge, and I pleaded him not to. But it was too late, he had it all planned out. First our mother, then the detective, and finally Danielle Simmons. So much... there was so much hatred."

I listened as Josephine spoke, standing there in the pouring rain, her story unraveling before me. I could see the pain in her eyes, the weight of her guilt and regret. She lowered the gun, her hand shaking as she looked at me.

"I didn't know what else to do. I thought it was the only way to protect my family. But now, I see that it was all wrong. I want to turn myself in. I want to make things right. Help me."

I watched as Josephine's eyes filled with tears and I could see the sincerity in her expression.

"I believe you," I said, holding out my hand. "Let me help you."

She hesitated for a moment before placing her gun in my hand. I could sense her trust in me and the weight of responsibility that came with it.

SEVENTY-FOUR

BILLIE ANN

I took her to the police station, where we rode the storm out all night. They had closed the bridges and it was too late to get over to the mainland. Oscar made landfall around three a.m., as a powerful category five storm. Luckily our building was brand new and built to sustain storms like this. We found shelter in one of the back rooms, where a few officers who were on duty had gathered. We waited, watching the storm from the window as the night wore on. The wind was howling, sounding like a freight train, and the sky was a deep shade of black.

Around four a.m. a loud crack of thunder shook the building. The power went out and the room became dark. We all held our breath as the AC stopped and we felt the heat envelop us, and sweat began to tickle on our foreheads.

The rain kept pounding against the windows, and the wind kept blowing in gusts. We stayed up all night, talking in hushed voices, until finally, the rain stopped and the sky lightened. The power finally turned back on, and everything went quiet.

As I left the precinct, my mind was numb, and my heart was heavy. Josephine Durst and her brother Robert were monsters; and she had been under the heavy influence of her narcissistic brother her entire life. That was the picture she had painted for me while we rode out the storm and talked. She had told me how they had gotten into my house, using the sliding door in the back that wasn't locked and how they had done exactly the same getting into Danielle's house, stealing the suitcases. I was glad that Josephine was finally going back behind bars, wanting to make things right. But at what cost? So many lives were lost, and worst of them all: the love of my life was gone.

My beloved Danni.

As I walked down the empty streets, looking at the damage the storm had caused, downed trees and powerlines, fences ripped apart, and ripped off roofs. It was going to take a while for the town to look like itself again. Tears streamed down my face. Everyone had left town, and the only sound was my sobs. I missed my children, and I wished I could be with them, but work had consumed my life, and I had neglected them. Joe had texted me and said that he had evacuated with the children and Zelda, and boarded up the house before they left. They were staying at a shelter on the mainland, while the storm raged.

Just then, my phone rang, and I saw that it was Big Tom. I answered.

"How are you feeling?"

He coughed and said, "I'll be okay. A couple of broken ribs and burns, some smoke in my lungs, but nothing major."

"That's good to hear. That's really good."

"But that's not why I am calling," he added. "I wanted to tell you that Danielle is alive and will be okay. I just spoke to the doctor and he told me that they were able to bring her back to life in the ambulance. She's still in ICU but stable now."

I could barely breathe. Was this really true? My beloved Danni was alive? I almost didn't dare to believe it. I cried tears of joy and relief, feeling as if a heavy weight had been lifted off my chest.

"Thank God," I whispered.

Big Tom's voice was soft and gentle. "I know you've been through a lot. I'm here for you, and I always will be."

I wiped away my tears, feeling slightly embarrassed for crying so hard when he could hear me. "Thank you," I said. "I appreciate it."

"Anytime," he replied. "You need to get some rest. You've been through a lot today."

I nodded, even though he couldn't see me. "I will. Take care of yourself too."

"I will," he promised.

As I hung up the phone, I felt a sense of hope and joy that I hadn't felt in a long time. Danni was alive, and I knew that I needed to see her. I rushed back to my house, and saw that a tree was down in the back, but other than that we seemed to have fared pretty well. Lots of water in the street, but it wasn't completely flooded. I got into my car and headed straight to the hospital, my heart racing with anticipation. The sun was rising over the Atlantic Ocean as a new day began, and maybe one with more promise.

The bridges had been reopened, and I rushed to the mainland, and Holmes Regional Medical Center, the streets eerily empty, driving through flooded areas and escaping downed trees, and branches that had fallen. When I arrived, I rushed to the ICU and saw her lying there, hooked up to machines and wires. She looked so fragile, yet so beautiful. I took her hand in mine, feeling the warmth and life flowing through her again.

I thought I lost you.

"Danni," I whispered, tears streaming down my face. "I'm so sorry. I should have been there, I should have found you. I was so close all this time; if only I had been faster, smarter, something. I love you so much."

As I spoke, she stirred, her eyes slowly opening. She saw me and smiled weakly, her lips barely moving as she whispered, "I love you too."

We stayed like that for hours, holding each other's hands and talking about everything and nothing. We laughed and cried and shared our hopes and fears for the future.

But as the night fell once again, our conversation took a turn. Danni's eyes became darker, and she started recounting her experience of being kidnapped by Josephine and Robert. I listened in horror as she described how they had kept her captive, in the back of Josephine's house, torturing her in unspeakable ways.

"They were insane," she muttered. "They enjoyed hurting me."

I felt a surge of anger at the thought of those monsters enjoying someone else's pain. I wanted to kill them, to make them pay for what they had done to Danni and so many others.

But as I looked at her, seeing the pain etched on her face, I knew that my priority was to take care of her. To make sure that she was safe and loved, and that nothing like this would ever happen again.

So I held her hand tighter and whispered, "I won't let anyone hurt you again. I'll protect you, no matter what."

She looked at me with tear-filled eyes, gratitude and love shining through.

"I know you will," she replied softly. "And I'll always be here for you too."

In that moment, I knew that nothing could tear us apart. We had been through the worst, and we had come out stronger together.

As the night passed, we fell asleep, our hands still intertwined. And for the first time in a long time, I slept soundly, knowing that the woman I loved was safe by my side.

EPILOGUE

Two weeks had passed since Danni was hospitalized. Her condition had improved significantly, and the doctors were optimistic that she would be able to go home by the end of the week. The hospital room was now starting to feel like a second home. I only went home to sleep at night. The kids were going to come home today, and as I drove up into the driveway, they were already there. Zelda too, and she ran to me, tail wagging, and whimpered slightly with joy. I hugged my children tight, then realized Joe was there too. He had brought them home, and apparently was waiting for me.

I was surprised to see him. He looked different, like he was wearing a mask of some kind. His presence made me uneasy, and I felt my heart racing.

"Joe, what are you doing here?" I asked, trying to keep my voice steady.

"I need to talk to you about something important," he replied with a serious expression on his face.

I watched him as he sat down on the couch opposite me.

"What is it?" I asked, feeling a sense of dread in the pit of my stomach.

"You're not gonna like this, but here it goes. I want full custody of the children," he said, his voice firm and resolute.

My heart stopped for a moment, and I felt a surge of anger rising within me. Then I panicked.

"What? You can't do that, Joe, they need me!" I yelled at him. "First you want the house and now the children? What's going on here?"

"You're not enough, Billie Ann. They need their father," Joe said calmly. "You're never home. You're always working, and there is no one to take care of them, or keep an eye on them. Did you know that William has been experimenting with prescription drugs?"

I sighed. "Yes, I took it from him. He said he tried it once but that was it. He said it won't happen again."

"Oh and that of course makes it all go away," he said. "Not even you can be that stupid. You're so oblivious. So naïve. These kids need more."

I couldn't believe what I was hearing. Joe had always been a good father, but he was never interested in full custody before. It felt like he was using Danni's hospitalization as an excuse to take the kids away from me.

"I'm their mother. I love them and I take care of them. They need me," I said, tears filling my eyes.

"I'm not saying you don't love them, Billie Ann. But I can give them the stability and attention they need. I have a stable job, a home, and a family that can support them. You're always running around, trying to solve some case. It's not fair to them," Joe replied, his voice still calm.

Trying to solve some case. The way he said it, made it sound like I was doing it for fun. Like it was some silly hobby, and not my job.

I felt like I was losing control. I couldn't bear the thought of losing my children, but at the same time, I knew that Joe had a point. I had been struggling to keep everything together, and I was always tired and stressed out.

"I'll do better," I said, my voice shaking. "I'll try to be there for them more. But Joe, please, don't take them away from me."

"I'm not trying to take them away from you," he said, his tone softening slightly. "I just want what's best for them."

I looked at him, tears welling up in my eyes. "I love them, Joe. I love them more than anything in this world. Please, just give me a chance to prove it to you."

He sighed and rubbed his forehead.

"I'll think about it, Billie Ann. But you need to understand that this isn't just about you and me. It's about the kids and their future. We both need to do what's best for them."

I nodded, feeling a sense of relief wash over me. At least he wasn't making any immediate decisions. I knew that I had to step up and be more present for my children, but the thought of losing them was still too much to bear.

"I'll try harder," I said finally. "For their sake."

Joe stood up and gave me a small smile. "We'll see about that."

As he left, I sat on the couch, feeling drained and emotional. It was like everything was falling apart around me, and I didn't know how to stop it. But one thing was for sure, I wasn't going to give up my children without a fight.

I can do better. I know I can.

I sat there for a long time, feeling lost and alone. I didn't know what to do, or where to turn. The thought of losing my children was too much to bear.

Then, the phone rang. I picked it up, hoping it was good news about Danni. It wasn't. It was Chief Becky Harold.

"There's something I need to talk to you about, can you come down to the station?"

. . .

I walked into the police station, my heart racing with anxiety and anticipation. Chief Harold reeled me in as I walked into her office, my pulse quickening. I had been taking some time off to heal and take care of Danni so I hadn't been at the station for a little while. I was greeted with a warm smile and a firm handshake.

"How are you holding up, Billie Ann?" she said, motioning for me to take a seat.

"I'm okay. A little nervous as to what this is about? I thought I had till the end of the week before I returned?"

She gave me a serious look.

"I did say that. But I need to show you something."

I couldn't help but notice the pile of papers on her desk. My eyes darted to the computer screen, where she had pulled up a folder filled with emails. She turned the screen so I could see.

"This is the stuff that was found on Robert Durst's computer," she said, pointing to the screen. "Take a look at this,"

"What am I looking at?"

"A bunch of emails, they're all about Danielle Simmons. As we go back through them, this person is basically telling him about Danielle and where she is now. Her address, her name after she married. All that is needed to find her. Then there are transcripts of her testimony back in the day when she told the police about what happened to her father. And this person is sort of urging Robert on, telling him he should get back at her. Giving him the idea to revenge the time he and his sister spent in jail."

I leaned in close to the monitor, trying to read the words on the screen. It was a series of emails between Robert Durst and some other person, all talking about Danielle. They were discussing her whereabouts and how to find her. And then they were fantasizing about how to hurt her. It made me feel sick.

"Someone told them about Danielle and how to find her?" I said. "Why?"

"Well, I asked that too, but look at the sender. It was actually Big Tom who recognized the name. He said he was your former partner? Travis something?"

I stared at the name on top of the email, my heart pounding against my ribcage. Travis Walker, my former partner who raped me and wanted me to retract my statement and clean his name. Travis who ended up in a wheelchair after Joe hit him using Charlene's truck. Travis who left town with his wife Betty earlier in the year, when we found out that he was covering up an old kidnapping of a little girl, because the man who did it was his friend, and police officer.

That Travis.

I felt a cold sweat break out on my forehead. What the hell was Travis doing being involved in this? Why was he helping Robert Durst? And how did he even know about Danielle in the first place?

Did he know I was in love with her? Was that why he had led Robert Durst to find her?

"Does anyone know where Travis is now?" I asked, my voice shaking.

"No one's seen him or Betty since they left town. We think they might have fled the state."

I felt a sense of panic rising in my chest. If Travis was involved in this, then there was no way he was stopping now.

This was just the beginning.

A LETTER FROM WILLOW

Dear reader,

I want to say a huge thank you for choosing to read *Then She's Gone*. If you did enjoy it, and want to keep up to date with all my latest releases, just sign up at the following link. Your email address will never be shared, and you can unsubscribe at any time.

www.bookouture.com/willow-rose

I hope you loved *Then She's Gone* and if you did I would be very grateful if you could write a review. I'd love to hear what you think, and it makes such a difference helping new readers to discover one of my books for the first time. The inspiration for this book came from a real story that recently took place here in Florida where I live. Three suitcases showed up in the Intracoastal Waterway in Delray Beach, all containing a woman's body parts. A man was later arrested for having murdered her, and she was his wife. You can read more here:

www.nbcnews.com/news/us-news/womans-remains-found-floating-3-separate-suitcases-florida-waterway-rcna96060

Also, the story of the siblings getting punished as adults for the murder of their stepparent, was also taken from a real story. They were twelve and thirteen years old when they killed their stepmother. They became one of the youngest in US history to be sentenced to adult prison.

https://www.wesh.com/article/florida-catherine-jones-juvenile-justice/43995154#

And let's not forget the story of a woman faking her own kidnapping. It has actually happened several times, but especially this story from California had my attention. The woman got eighteen months in prison for it. She even got her ex-boyfriend to hurt her and brand her with a tool, to make it look like she was tortured. Just like Joanne in this book. For years authorities were searching for two Hispanic looking women, till they finally found out the truth. It was all fake. It's quite the story. You can read about her here:

www.cnn.com/2022/09/19/us/sherri-papini-fake-kidnapping-sentence/index.html

As always I want to thank you for your support. As long as readers like you keep reading, I will keep writing. Also, I want to thank my editor Jennifer Hunt for all her hard work helping this book come to life.

Take care,

Willow

KEEP IN TOUCH WITH WILLOW

www.willow-rose.net

facebook.com/authoroleary

x.com/madamwillowrose

instagram.com/willowroseauthor

bookbub.com/authors/willow-rose

PUBLISHING TEAM

Turning a manuscript into a book requires the efforts of many people. The publishing team at Bookouture would like to acknowledge everyone who contributed to this publication.

Audio
Alba Proko
Sinead O'Connor
Melissa Tran

Commercial
Lauren Morrissette
Jil Thielen
Imogen Allport

Cover design
The Brewster Project

Data and analysis
Mark Alder
Mohamed Bussuri

Editorial
Jennifer Hunt
Sinead O'Connor

Made in the USA
Monee, IL
27 March 2024

55714018R00184